Whatever Is True

by

Pamela S. Meyers

Bling!
Romance
Lighthouse Publishing of the Carolinas

WHATEVER IS TRUE BY PAMELA S. MEYERS
Published by Bling!
an imprint of Lighthouse Publishing of the Carolinas
2333 Barton Oaks Dr., Raleigh, NC 27614

ISBN: 978-1-946016-83-6
Copyright © 2019 by Pamela S. Meyers
Cover design by Elaina Lee
Interior design by Karthick Srinivasan

Available in print from your local bookstore, online, or from the publisher at:
ShopLPC.com

For more information on this book and the author, visit: www.pamelasmeyers.com

Brought to you by the creative team at Lighthouse Publishing of the Carolinas (ShopLPC.com):
Jessica Nelson, Managing Editor
Connie Troyer, General Editor

Library of Congress Cataloging-in-Publication Data
Meyers, Pamela S.
Whatever Is True / Pamela S. Meyers 1st ed.

Printed in the United States of America

Praise for *Whatever Is True*

Hunky cowboys and sigh-worthy romance. What more could you want? *Whatever is True* has it all.

~Ane Mulligan
Author of bestselling *Chapel Springs Revival*

Pamela S. Meyers is at it again, writing the best in Cowboy Romance with her signature slash of realism. A great read!

~Linda W. Yezak
Award-winning author of the *Circle Bar Ranch series*

ACKNOWLEDGEMENTS/AUTHOR NOTE

By the time I finished writing *Second Chance Love*, I sensed that Clint Palmer and Lacy Roberts, supporting cast in the story, had a story of their own to tell. Even so, when I started to write the story, I couldn't get Lacy to "talk" to me. Then I realized that although it was truly both their story, it was Clint's to tell. Thus, I began it from his point of view and suddenly the story began to flow.

Although I do not consider myself to be a seat-of-the-pants writer, there was much about Clint that I didn't know until I began writing and he revealed it to me. If you are not a novelist, you are probably thinking I must be losing my marbles. But that is how it sometimes happens when one begins to write a story.

Aside from that, I needed a lot of help from others to put this story together. The setting for *Second Chance Love* was a familiar place—on a Texas ranch near San Antonio. I needed to know about ranch life, raising cattle, and Texas in general.

I owe much gratitude to fellow Penwrights member and good friend Linda Yezak, who pointed me in the right direction through referring me to resources she has counted on for similar settings. It was also she who set me straight on the issue of basements. Most Texas homes, particularly around San Antonio, do not have basements because of the earth's composition. It took a while for this born-and-bred Midwestern gal to wrap my head around that fact.

I also must thank my friend Ed Crowder for his willingness to answer about a zillion questions I had on horsemanship, ranching, and all things Texas. He's hung in there with me from the beginning of *Second Chance Love* until the end of *Whatever Is True*.

Thanks also to fellow Penwrights and Sharpened Pencil members (including a special thanks to Yvonne Anderson) for critiquing this story from start to finish.

Thank you to my dear friend Ane Mulligan for her impromptu consultations and encouragement. More than once she has talked me "off the ledge" when I've felt overwhelmed.

Thanks also to the Bling team at LPC Books, headed up by its new managing editor, Jessica Nelson. It's been a great pleasure to once again work with my wonderful editor, Connie Troyer, on making this story look like I know what I'm doing. This is the third book she's edited for me, and I hope it won't be the last.

To my readers, thank you for trusting me enough to purchase this book. The sense of abandonment is a serious issue many people face, and it can affect us for many years in the choices we make and the relationships we endeavor to have. I hope that in some small way this story has helped those who are struggling with it. It is also my prayer that you are blessed by spending a few hours of time with Clint and Lacy and you grow to love them as much as I do.

Last of all, but certainly not least, I thank my Lord and Savior Jesus Christ for calling me to this fun gig of writing novels. As in all things in my life, I needed His strength and patience to get through this project.

Until next time, God bless!

Pam

Chapter 1

"Clint Palmer, if you don't say something soon, I have a question for you." Lacy Roberts was staring at him across the corral with those gorgeous eyes of hers, and here he was acting like a stupid kid with a crush instead of a thirty-one-year-old man. But the words he'd rehearsed in front of his bathroom mirror for a half hour that morning remained stuck in his throat. Whatever made him think he was good enough for her to date?

Before he could force out his words, she dropped the currycomb she'd been using and said, "Well, I have a favor to ask. Are you up for it?"

Now was not the time to ask his own question unless he wanted to make it look like he was asking for a date in return for doing a favor. Hopefully he would get another chance. He smiled tightly. "Depends on what the favor is."

"Have I ever asked you to do something you haven't liked in the end?"

He shook his head. "Not that I recall—unless it was when you asked me to fill in for you that time you were to babysit the Beckner twins and they almost burned the house down."

Lacy snorted and rolled her eyes. "That was years ago. And you still remember it?"

He chortled. "Yeah. It cured me of babysitting for anyone ever again."

She picked up a brush and held it while she spoke. "Well, I need your help tonight. My parents are coming, and neither Jace and Syd nor Aunt Carolyn are available...." She cleared her throat. "You know I don't get along well with them. If someone else is there, I won't have to listen to my father carry on about how being a ranch cook is no career for a college-educated business major." She flashed him her killer smile. "What do you say? I'm trying out a new recipe for chicken Marsala."

Ever since Lacy had become what she called a "foodie," the meals on the ranch had morphed into something usually found in a five-star restaurant. Some of it didn't taste half bad, but the name of this meal sounded too foo-foo for his taste.

Clint stepped closer, and Lacy's mare bobbed her head and nuzzled her nose against his shirt pocket. He chuckled. "Shiloh, do you think I always carry around treats for you?" He rubbed the horse's nose and then held out a snack in his open palm. "Change the menu to steak on the grill and I'm in, Lacy. It's way too hot for an oven meal."

She pressed her lips together as if thinking about his request. "September is always hot in Texas. Besides, I'm not using the oven, and the house is air-conditioned. It's important that I show my cooking chops to my father. I'll make steaks for all of us soon. Please?"

"Chops would be good too." Clint grinned at his joke.

A puzzled expression marred her face. "What? Oh, I get it. Cute, Palmer, but no dice. Are you coming?"

As if he could say no to the most beautiful gal in all of Texas. Just to spend a couple of hours in her company—even enduring a fancy meal he'd probably hate and spending time with her less-than-enjoyable father—was a good enough reason to accept.

"You know, Clint, a question does require an answer." She gripped the brush in her hand, turned toward Shiloh, and began whisking away the dust that the comb had brought to the surface.

Again he'd stood staring for too long without answering—according to her. Did it matter if he was slow to answer? "Sure, I'll be there. Do I have to dress up?"

"As long as you put on a clean shirt and jeans, you'll be fine."

He laughed. "Don't I always wear clean clothes to dinner at the house?"

She turned and poked him in the ribs with the brush. "My aunt wouldn't allow you in if you didn't."

"I think not. What time?"

"Instead of the usual five p.m., let's make it six. That's more their normal dinnertime." She resumed brushing her horse. "So, what's on your schedule for today?"

"Same as always. I'm about to feed the bulls, and then someone's coming this afternoon to see the Brangus Jace has up for sale. The guy is looking for a good stud bull to keep his ladies happy. The bull didn't turn out to be a bucker, but he won't be disappointed in his life's new direction." He caught the smirk on Lacy's face as he turned toward the pen on the other side of the barn. "See you at six."

"Come a little earlier than that if you'd like."

He waved his acknowledgment as he walked around the large horse barn that also contained his private living quarters up on the second floor. The building was new as of five years ago. Before that, they'd been using a small barn that had to be at least seventy-five years old and Clint had lived in a bunkhouse that looked to be the first structure built on the property a century ago.

Lacy may want him to come early to dinner, but he'd pass. Having Fred Roberts interrogate him about bullfighting with rapid-fire questions the way he had last time? No thanks. Feeling belittled once by the older man was enough. Not that his feelings about her father would ever stop him from wanting to date her. But he could count his blessings that the man lived in California. As large as Texas was, even being in the same state was too close to suit Clint.

Lacy glanced at the clock on the kitchen wall. Fifteen minutes ago, her parents had called to say they were in San Antonio. She inhaled and held her breath. They'd be arriving any moment. Time to cowgirl up and build her defenses against her dad, who was hardly a paragon of fatherhood. She exhaled and gave the chicken breast in front of her a strong wallop with the meat mallet and then laid it next to the ones she'd already prepared. She picked up another breast and pounded it into submission too, as what felt like a ten-pound lump of guilt grew in her throat. Her father's ways and comments weren't nice, but he wasn't *evil*. She supposed he meant well, but he was clueless about how arrogant and controlling he sounded. Or was he that unaware? She never could tell.

She stepped over to the sink and looked out the window, across the white rock-covered yard stretching between the ranch house and the horse barn. She was about to turn back to her meal prep when Clint stepped out of the shadows near the outdoor stalls at the barn's west side. She caught a glimpse of the pail in his hand and smiled. Even from a distance, his broad shoulders and muscular arms were evident. But if he was just finishing up feeding the horses that boarded at the ranch, he wouldn't be arriving early for dinner as she'd hoped. Hopefully, Dad would be in a good mood.

She returned to the counter, picked up the last chicken breast, and gave it a whack with the mallet. She'd much rather be cooking for two, with only Clint as her dinner guest and not as a buffer between her and Dad. But if she and Clint were the only ones at the table, knowing him, they'd keep the conversation in the "friend zone" as always. She'd hoped that when her cousin Jace married Sydney last spring after a rather rocky start to their dating relationship, Clint would see how happy they were and want the same thing. But apparently he hadn't noticed.

When she and Clint shared a couple of kisses at the wedding, Lacy's hopes had soared, thinking that their solid friendship had moved to the next level.

With kisses tender and strong enough to cause her to almost go limp in his arms, who wouldn't have assumed they were now a couple? But instead of wanting to spend more time with her, the cowboy seemed to go out of his way to avoid her. Sydney suggested that it meant he was interested. But this wasn't middle school.

Lacy had since resigned herself to the notion that the kisses meant nothing more to Clint than being caught up in the moment. Maybe that's all it was. After all, with his new close-cropped haircut and western-style wedding attire, his magnetic appeal had ramped up big-time that day. Months after the kisses, he still had the haircut, but even with him back in his old Wranglers and scruffy boots, he still got her heart beating overtime.

Trouble was, she'd never get over him while they lived and worked on the ranch together. That—coupled with a dark shadow suddenly overhanging her rodeo competitions—had made it clear to her: it was time to move on.

The sound of car tires crunching over the gravel in front of the house broke into Lacy's thoughts. She crossed from the counter to the window over the sink and peered out a second time.

Dad stood next to his metallic-gold Escalade, tall and erect, before lifting a suitcase from the back. The passenger door opened and Mom climbed out, wearing cream-colored slacks and a black-and-cream tunic. Lacy shook her head. Her mother had been raised on this ranch, but you'd never know it by her attire. Those light-colored pants wouldn't stay pristine unless she hunkered down in the house the entire time they were here. But knowing Mom, that was probably what she intended. She hated the ranch and only endured it when she had no choice—the last time being two years ago when she'd attended her brother's funeral. Uncle Ted was the patriarch of the family, and her mother wouldn't have missed his service for anything.

Lacy washed her hands and went to the front door. She said a quick prayer for the Lord's help to get through the next twenty-four hours and forced a smile as she stepped outside. Her father came up the flagstone walk with a suitcase in each hand. He'd gained at least ten pounds since she last saw him—and all in his belly. Eating too many high-fat meals during business meetings was taking a toll. As a younger man he could burn it off, but not now.

She approached him and reached for one of the cases. "Hi, Dad. Let me help."

He held his grip. "I've got this. Just take us inside and show us which room is ours."

She stepped back and let him pass. *Well, hello to you too.*

Mom came up, arms open. "Don't mind your father. It's been a long day of travel."

That was Mom, always making excuses for her father's lack of kindness. Lacy stepped into her mother's embrace. "Nice to see you, Mom. I've learned to not let him bother me … much."

"I know, dear. But today he's grumpier than usual. We had to take a detour in New Mexico, and you know how he gets when that happens."

"Well, let me show you to your room, and you can relax until dinner. I'm getting the meal ready now. We'll be eating at six."

Her father had set his load on the wide-planked front porch. He checked what appeared to be a new Apple watch on his wrist. "That's over two hours away."

Lacy frowned. "It's five fifteen now."

"Dear, you're still on San Diego time." Mom joined him on the porch.

He waved a hand and picked up the suitcases. "You know I stay on Pacific time for working with the home office. Whatever. Take us to our room."

By the time Clint arrived shortly before six, Lacy had the floured chicken breasts simmering in a large skillet with prosciutto and cremini mushrooms. A tossed salad and jasmine rice sat in bowls on the island.

With his hair still damp from a shower and wearing a plaid shirt, Wranglers, and polished boots, Clint gave off a most appealing vibe. He glanced into the family room that also served as the main dining room on the other side of the island. "I saw your parents arrive. They still in their room?"

"Yes. They'll be out soon. Want to put the rice and salad on the table while I take care of the chicken?"

He agreed and had just finished when Mom stepped into the family room from the hall that served all the home's bedrooms except for the master. "My, something smells delicious." She glanced at the farmhouse table sitting a few feet from the island. "Everything looks so nice. Can I help with anything?"

Lacy shook her head. "It's all done. Once Dad gets here, we can sit."

Clint turned from filling a glass pitcher with water. "Nice to see you again, Mrs. Roberts."

Mom returned his smile as she came into the kitchen. "I remember meeting you at the funeral, but I'm sorry, I've forgotten your name."

"This is Clint Palmer, Mom. He's Jace's right-hand guy and a bullfighter in the rodeos."

Mom nodded. "Now I remember. The one who got hurt last year."

Clint turned his head, but Lacy hadn't missed the grimace on his face. He hated being reminded of that dark time back in Illinois.

He looked at her mother, nodded, and held out his hand. "That would be me."

A minute later, her father joined them, and they all settled at one end of the long table—Clint and Lacy on one side and her parents facing them. Lacy asked Dad to pray, and he spoke his usual formal blessing. Just the beginning of a normal family meal, like those families she'd watched on the old 1950s sitcoms. She was almost tempted not to tell her news and spoil the ambiance.

But she had no choice if she wanted to explain things in person.

Chapter 2

Lacy waited until her father took the last chicken cutlet from the serving platter and scooped up the remainder of the Marsala sauce to drizzle over the meat. "Dad, you must really like this recipe for you to go back for a third serving."

"It's the best Marsala chicken I've tasted in a long while. Can't let it go to waste." He cut off a bite-sized piece and dragged it through the sauce before putting it in his mouth.

Her breath hitched. He hadn't paid her a compliment since she was little and learned to walk sooner than most kids. The only reason she knew about it was from watching the video of her toddler self unsteadily walking across the kitchen floor toward Mom's outstretched arms.

She shot a smile at Clint. "For a man who thought he'd only enjoy a steak, it appears the meal agreed with you. Your plate looks pretty clean."

He grinned. "Yeah. I think you could even serve it to the ranch hands during calving season and get no complaints."

She laughed and held back from thrusting a fist in the air in celebration. "I doubt it. Those guys are hard workers and deserve a hearty meal of steak and potatoes." She drew in a breath. She'd set the stage perfectly. If she didn't speak soon, the opportunity would pass. "I have an announcement."

Dad continued to eat, but Mom put down her fork and watched her. Next to her, Clint twisted in his chair and stared at her, his eyes wide. It was him she'd miss the most, but life had to move on. She cleared her throat and lifted her chin. "Ever since I turned thirty last June, I've yearned to make a change. These past years of cooking for the ranch have sparked a love of developing recipes and preparing food. After much prayer and thought, I've decided to become a chef, and I'm planning on attending a culinary school in the East."

Clint sat as if frozen in place, the proverbial deer-in-the-headlights look on his face. Mom gaped at her. Lacy had been sure she'd get a rise out of her father with her plans, but, as usual, he remained self-absorbed, calmly cutting his meat. She wanted to knock that fork out of his hand. Had he even heard her?

What did it take to crack that veneer? "I realize I've shocked—"

"I'm glad to see that you've come to your senses regarding rodeos and horses, but a chef is still nothing more than a glorified cook." Without expression, Dad set down his fork and sipped his water.

Lacy glanced at Mom, who then stared at her lap. Did Dad realize how he'd emotionally beaten her down? Did Mom? Her mother used to have no problem stating her position on something, even if her opinion was unpopular. And now look at her.

Lacy flipped her hair over her shoulder and worked to channel her anger into strength to remain calm. "*Chef* is not a fancy name for *cook*. A trained chef is highly regarded and very well paid. I could end up as an executive chef in a large five-star restaurant or possibly owning my own business. In fact, that's my goal."

"Restaurant work is hard, Lacy."

She looked at her mother. "Not any more than ranch work. You should know that, Mom."

"I do, which is why I smartened up and got off this ranch as fast as I could."

She toyed with a snarky response about staying on the ranch being far better than marrying her father, but she pressed her lips together instead. The remark would only hurt her mother.

"How expensive is culinary school?" Dad asked.

"No more than college in most cases, and it doesn't have to take four years to complete the program." She drummed her fingers on the wood table, her nails clacking. "I have some money saved and plan to apply for a partial scholarship."

"Dear, maybe we could help her with tuition."

Dad shoved the last piece of his chicken into his mouth and chewed.

Of course, Lacy already knew her father's answer to her mother's suggestion. The only time he'd said yes was when she agreed to major in business instead of animal husbandry. She never heard the end of how she had betrayed him when she didn't go for an MBA, instead continuing to rodeo and work on the ranch. She was glad the idea of becoming a vet never grew legs. Who knew the biz degree would pay off the way it was about to?

Dad set his glass firmly on the table and tea splashed out, covering the wood surface with tiny droplets. "I've already paid for a business degree that is getting no use at all. Why should I pay for cooking school? I'd rather see you earn an MBA. That, I would pay for."

Lacy swallowed hard against the lump in her throat. "But I don't want business to be the main thing. I like preparing food and enjoying the pleasure of feeding others. What I learned in college will help with running a restaurant."

"I'll think about it." He stacked his plates and utensils. "Now, what's for dessert?"

She gave him a tight smile. "Pie made with peaches from the ranch's own trees." She doubted she'd ever see a dime from him. But it didn't matter. If God wanted her in culinary school, He'd open the door.

Clint tucked the last glass into the dishwasher and closed the machine. "Guess that's it. But before I leave, can we step outside for a couple of minutes? There's something I want to ask you."

Lacy frowned. "Why can't you ask me right here?"

He lowered his voice. "Because I don't feel comfortable. How do we know someone won't overhear?"

She hung a dishcloth on a nearby rack. "You're right. Let's go."

They exited the house through the mudroom to the wooden deck, then down the steps and across the lawn to a firepit. He brushed off the top of a long rectangular rock with his hand and waited for her to sit.

She did so and then stretched out her legs. "I suppose you have questions about my decision. It's something I really want, Clint."

He picked up a forgotten marshmallow roasting stick from the last weenie roast they'd had and poked it into the dirt. "Where did this culinary school idea come from?"

"I've been mulling it over and praying about it for a while."

"And in all the times we've talked, you never said anything."

"I wanted to, but by keeping it to myself, I wouldn't have to do a lot of backtracking if I changed my mind. And now it seems I've hurt your feelings. I'm sorry."

"No problem. But I thought you loved barrel racing and the ranch." He sensed Lacy tensing up with his question.

"I like competing, and you know I love being on the ranch and helping with the chores when I'm not cooking. I've been waffling over what to do. A few weeks ago, a person I used to know started competing in our circuit. He's not a nice guy, and his presence has affected my times. I haven't placed once since he showed up."

"Who is it?"

"I'd rather not say. It was a personal situation that didn't involve anyone else. I'd already been leaning toward culinary school, but that sealed it."

"So it wasn't because of something I did?"

She rested her hand on his forearm, sending tingles through him. "Oh, Clint, no. Not ever. You and Jace—and now Sydney—have always made the rodeos fun."

He felt his shoulders relax, thankful it wasn't his kissing her at the wedding that did it. He hadn't intended for the kisses to happen that night, but those slow songs and dancing with Lacy in his arms made her too hard to resist. The way she'd kissed him back, it seemed at the time that she felt the same about him, but by the next morning he'd come to his senses. She was far too good for him, so he kept his distance. He was glad they were moving back to the friendly banter and close talks they'd always had. But this dude she'd just mentioned was news to him. Already, he didn't like him.

Clint faced her. "Have you thought about competing in a different way? Like entering barrel-racing competitions that aren't in a rodeo?"

"I'll think about it if this school thing doesn't work out. But I really do want to be a chef. I can't be a barrel racer forever."

He didn't miss the catch in Lacy's voice, and he longed to gather her in his arms and tell her that he'd be happy to take care of her for the rest of her life. But a ranch hand and bullfighter whose rodeo days were numbered didn't add up to a secure livelihood. He couldn't expect her to move into his quarters on the barn's second floor. It was a nice enough apartment, but during calving and the other times when they needed extra help, he wasn't the only one living there.

"None of this is happening soon," Lacy said. "It's already September, and the fall semester began last month. I'm still praying about it."

He tensed. There she went again, talking as if God was going to speak directly to her. "Do you think God is going to text you, saying 'Go to school' or 'Don't go'?"

"Of course not. I pray for wisdom and then trust Him to direct my thoughts and lead me to Bible passages that will help me decide."

Clint stood. "If it makes you feel better to make decisions that way, good for you. I prefer to skip that step. See you tomorrow."

He trekked across the grass, then crunched his way over the crushed white rock that separated the house from the barn. Inside the barn, he crossed to the stairs leading to his apartment.

The oak door slammed behind him, and he tossed his Stetson toward a wall of hooks. It dropped to the wood-planked floor. He heaved a sigh and hung the hat the conventional way instead, then walked to the kitchen attached to one wall of the open-concept room. He flung the refrigerator door open and stared at the contents. Why did he have to get so terse with Lacy about her praying? Her faith wasn't a secret. She'd always talked about church and her Bible study group, and he was usually able to give it no mind. But tonight, her daddy's negative attitude put him on edge. He reached for the jug of OJ, then pulled back his hand and closed the fridge. What was he doing? After that great meal, he wouldn't be hungry *or* thirsty until morning. He wandered to the living space and plopped onto the leather couch.

Finding out that some creep from Lacy's past had been giving her a hard time troubled him. He had no idea who it was, but he must have hurt her badly. Good thing she hadn't said his name, because if he knew, he would find it difficult to keep his fists to himself.

What he really needed was to step up his game and get into a better job situation, earning more money, before he woke up some morning and found Lacy gone.

Chapter 3

Lacy carried what was left of the beef bourguignonne to the kitchen and grabbed a container for the leftovers.

"Lacy, if you keep making these fancy meals, I'm going to have to buy bigger jeans." Carolyn McGowan set several water glasses on the counter.

Lacy laughed. "I'm sorry. Maybe tomorrow's meal should be salad."

Her aunt waved a hand. "That wouldn't go over very well with the men." Her eyes misted over. "I love having a full dinner table. With the twins at college and Jace and Sydney in their own house, if it weren't for your delicious meals to tempt them, we'd hardly require the big table. It was nice having your parents here last weekend. I wish your mother didn't dislike the ranch the way she does. After all, she's a McGowan and part of its legacy."

"I don't know why she never liked it much," Lacy said. "She does have other interests."

Aunt Carolyn came closer and gave Lacy a hug. "Well, I'm so glad you're here. Otherwise, I would just be rattling around in this big house by myself. Sometimes I think I should have had Jace build a smaller home for me so he and Sydney could live here. I'm sure it won't be long before they'll start growing a family."

Lacy cast about for something to say that would break the melancholy mood her aunt had shown the past couple of weeks. Not nearly as talkative as normal, today she'd not bothered with makeup either, and her usually styled salt-and-pepper hair was twisted into a messy bun—a favored hairdo of younger girls, but not Carolyn McGowan. Something wasn't right. Lacy yearned to share her decision about culinary school but had been delaying the announcement until her aunt was in better spirits. "I'm sure it's not my cooking that draws them here. They're family, and there's nothing like the dinner table to bring kin together."

Aunt Carolyn tossed the dish towel she was holding onto the counter beside the water glasses. "You are right, of course. But good food doesn't hurt."

Lacy laughed. "I'll cook for as long as they come." She opened the dishwasher and loaded the glasses onto the top rack, but her chest tightened, and she bit on her lower lip to stop its quivering. She wasn't being honest with the woman who was more of a mom to her than her own mother. And even more, Aunt Carolyn was her employer. Lacy owed her enough time to find a replacement, although she likely wouldn't be leaving until next summer or fall. It wasn't fair that Mom knew of her plans and—

"Well, it's apparent that the Lord has gifted you with more than horsemanship. If you ever decide to stop barrel racing, you'll have no trouble finding a new direction to take." Aunt Carolyn walked toward the hall that would take her to her master suite.

Lacy's pulse escalated. Talk about the right opening. She forced a smile. "Actually, there is something you should know."

Her aunt turned and stared at her. "Oh? You're not thinking of giving up barrel racing, are you?"

Lacy shook her head. "No … I mean, I don't know. It depends." She drew in a breath and exhaled. "You have a few minutes?"

Her aunt raised her hands, palms out. "All the time you need." She settled on a stool at the island and patted the seat next to her.

Lacy slid onto the next stool. "First, I want to say how much I love you— and all the McGowans. You've been like a mom to me."

Aunt Carolyn's brows rose. "Don't tell me you're moving back to San Diego to be near your parents."

Lacy frowned. "That's never going to happen. Ever since I started taking my cooking seriously and trying out new things, I've sensed a pull to learn as much as I can. I've decided to look at culinary schools, and the three I'm most interested in are all near the East Coast."

The corners of her aunt's mouth turned down, and silence settled between them. Aunt Carolyn picked up a paper napkin that had been left on the counter and began unfolding and refolding it.

Lacy's heart sank. The last thing she wanted was to disappoint her aunt. "It probably won't be until next year sometime, and I'll help you find a replacement."

"I'm not concerned about that. What troubles me most is that I went shooting off my mouth, talking about how without you living here, I'd be alone in this big house. That must have made you feel uncomfortable." She took the napkin she was holding and dabbed her eyes. "You've been the daughter I never had. When Sydney married Jace, I was thrilled to have a second daughter to enjoy, but she has her work, and newlyweds need time to themselves."

"Maybe I could look at a school in San Antonio."

"You'll do no such thing. If the school you want is in another state, then that's where you should go. Don't pay me any mind. You're young, and you need to find your way in life." She took Lacy's hand and squeezed it. "But I sense there's more to your wanting to go to a school so far away and leaving Shiloh behind. I doubt you'd be able to afford boarding her. What are you running from, Lacy?"

As usual, Carolyn McGowan cut right to the chase. Lacy looked to a picture on a shelf in the family room of her and Shiloh, after she'd won first place in a barrel race. That was only her second race, and Shiloh had been with her through her whole rodeo career. "I'd like to think I'm running to the next season of my life. Nothing is carved in stone. I'll know more after this weekend's rodeo."

Her aunt leaned back and stared at her. "Does it depend on how you do in the races?"

"Not entirely. Just pray for me."

She pulled Lacy into an embrace. "I already do, every day. Care to talk about the other things?"

Lacy sat back. "What other things?"

"You said your decision wasn't entirely about how you do in this weekend's races."

"Oh." As tempting as the invitation was, Aunt Carolyn wasn't the right person for pouring out her frustration over her love life, or lack thereof. "There's nothing more. Thanks for understanding about culinary school. I'll give you plenty of notice once I know when it will all happen."

Aunt Carolyn stood. "No worries. I'm sure we'll do fine. You just focus on your races next weekend and take one thing at a time."

Did she dare ask her the question that hadn't left her mind for the past several days? "Wait. I have something to ask."

Her aunt retook her seat. "Okay."

Now she had to either ask what she intended or find something else plausible.... "I've been concerned. Lately you don't seem yourself—like wearing Uncle Ted's old T-shirts and not bothering with makeup. For some that would be normal, but..."

"But it's not my usual way." Aunt Carolyn stared off a moment before bringing her gaze back to Lacy. "You're right. I've also been holding back on you. I found out the other day that I have breast cancer."

A sinking feeling came over Lacy, and her hand flew to her mouth to cover her gasp. "And here I am going on about my future plans that include leaving you at the worst possible moment."

Her aunt patted her hand. "I never want to stand in the way of your hopes and dreams. Besides, by the time you are ready to leave, the treatment will be over and I'll be good as new. Please don't say anything to the others, because I want all the puzzle pieces put together before I do. The oncologist told me I can have a lumpectomy and hope that they get it all out, or I can opt for a mastectomy, which gives me a stronger chance of the cancer not returning. That is, if the disease hasn't already moved into the lymph nodes. We won't know until I have a sentinel node test. That's next week."

Lacy stared at her. "Next week? Don't they want to test for it right away and get the cancer out of you?"

Her aunt heaved a sigh. "You would think, but both the oncologist and the surgeon assure me that waiting a week is not going to change anything. My surgeon's daughter is getting married this coming weekend, and he won't be available to do the test until next week."

Lacy crossed her arms. "I don't see why another doctor can't do the test."

"I was tempted to suggest that, but then I realized that I need to trust these doctors. They have been dealing with this type of cancer for a long time. As the saying goes, this isn't their first rodeo."

"When is it scheduled?"

She dropped her gaze to her lap. "I'd rather not tell you. You'll only worry. I'll let you know when I find out the results."

Lacy searched her aunt's face with her eyes. "No. I want to go with you when you have the test."

"It's already arranged. One of my friends from church is going to take me. You've got a lot on your plate right now with the ranch work and barrel racing and finding the right culinary school."

Lacy slammed her palm onto the counter. "Forget culinary school. This is way more important."

Aunt Carolyn stood and started toward her room. "That's exactly why I'm not telling you any more than I have. Remember, I've not told the boys or Sydney about it, and I don't plan to until I know all the details."

Aunt Carolyn's back blurred as she walked away, and Lacy swiped at a tear as it trailed down her cheek. She had half a mind to cancel everything. But she would try to take one day at a time. She could always change direction if necessary.

Lacy spotted his trailer the moment she drove into the grassy pasture next to the rodeo arena reserved for competitors. She glanced around. About a half dozen horse trailers already occupied the area. She picked out a spot for her trailer, next to Darcy Blount's two-horse trailer—the farthest place from him—and maneuvered it into position.

She braked and let out a sigh. The man she least wanted to see ever again hadn't been at the last two rodeos, but now he was back. In his absence she'd managed two placements—one second and one first. What more proof did she need? A stressed rider made for a bad race, and Austin Jennings had taken all the fun out of barrel racing.

She glanced over at Darcy's trailer for any signs of her presence and found none. Darcy had been "chasing cans" for almost two decades, had gone to the National Finals Rodeo in Vegas three times, and was still pulling wins when most others would be slowing down.

Darcy was living what had once been Lacy's dream. If someone had told her a few years ago that she'd want to leave barrel racing, Shiloh, and the ranch behind, she'd have told them they were crazy. And sometimes she herself wondered if she were a bit bonkers. Was this chef dream more a self-devised escape from the past or something the Lord had laid on her heart?

She spotted Jace's rig parked on the far side of the meadow. His quarter horse, Charley, stood tethered to the trailer, but neither Jace nor Clint were anywhere in sight. Sydney usually came with them to the rodeos, and she and Lacy hung out together. But Syd had drawn a weekend shift at the therapeutic horse center. Most times Lacy didn't mind being on her own, but this weekend she'd miss her friend's company more than ever. But maybe it was better Syd wasn't there, because Lacy couldn't talk about the other thing keeping her awake at night: Aunt Carolyn's cancer.

She opened the trailer door and stepped inside to unhook Shiloh. The seasoned horse nickered as she backed out of the enclosure without prompting. Lacy came up next to her and spoke softly as she rubbed a circle under her forelock. "Good girl. Two hours wasn't a long ride, was it?" She reached into her back pocket and tugged out a couple of carrot-and-oatmeal-flavored horse treats. While Shiloh finished her snack, Lacy checked the halter and flicked a piece of hay off her hindquarters. "Let's head over and see your buddy."

After situating Shiloh next to Charley, Lacy went in search of her cousin. She found him next to the chutes, talking to one of the men in charge of the rodeo.

Jace offered his usual crooked grin as she approached. "Hey, cuz, glad to see you made it okay." Then his smile dissolved. "Someone was looking for you earlier."

She tensed. "Who?"

He excused himself from the others and led her away until they were out of earshot. "He wasn't anyone you'd want to talk to."

Her whisper matched his. "That's what I was afraid of. I saw his trailer."

He raised a brow. "You know the trailer he's using these days?"

She nodded. "I should have told you before. He showed up at a couple of rodeos when you were at those futurity events. I'd hoped he'd move on. I'll hide out until race time. No need to be accessible until intermission."

Jace winced. "I hate to see you have to do that. It's been a long while…"

She let out a sigh. "Maybe for you, but for me, thirteen years seems like a month. The way he hit on me last time was enough to make me want to throw up, acting as if what we'd had was only a youthful fling. I'd hardly call …" She bit her lower lip and looked away.

He frowned and pulled her into a side hug. "Want me to tell him to knock it off?"

She shook her head. "I think if I ignore him and keep a distance, he'll get the message. What I ever saw in him, I'll never know." She turned and headed toward the trailers.

"Keep me on speed dial!"

Jace's shouted comment comforted her, but she doubted she'd need his assistance.

She returned to where Shiloh was tied and led her to their trailer, where she slipped on the horse's bridle. Deciding to not bother saddling her until later, she mounted the horse bareback, then reached down and stroked her withers. "Let's loosen up, girl." She held the reins in both hands and leaned forward. Shiloh began to trot, and they circled the small pasture. Tension flowed out of Lacy's shoulders. Loving the feel of the wind in her hair, she made a clicking sound and Shiloh sped up as Lacy's body moved in unison with her gallop. Riding bareback was the best. Countless times, a ride like this had relaxed her when she couldn't deal with stress. Going to school in the East would be a difficult adjustment. Would she be able to handle being apart from Shiloh? Maybe Aunt Carolyn was right about finding a culinary school in Texas.

As Lacy rode back to her trailer, the rodeo announcer's voice drifted over from the arena, advising that the competition was about to begin. She had a bit of time before she needed to saddle Shiloh. She dismounted and gave the mare a pat. "Be ready to race, girl. We're gonna smoke the competition; I feel it in my bones. I'll be back soon." She headed for the door to the trailer's sleeping quarters for a little time of solitude. A horse ride and prayer: the perfect combination for race prep.

An hour and a half later, Lacy mounted Shiloh and headed for the arena by circling around the back of the chutes and holding pens. Hopefully the ropers had already scattered after their event and her nemesis was on his way to another rodeo. With his trailer out of sight from where she'd parked, she couldn't tell.

She rode up next to Darcy and stopped. "Hey, Darcy. Long time no see."

The pretty brunette turned, and a grin took over her face. "Hey, yourself. You and Shiloh going to give me and Donner here a good race tonight?" She patted her paint gelding.

Lacy sat up and ran her fingers through Shiloh's mane. "You bet we will."

The announcer's voice interrupted them. Intermission was over, and Lacy lined up behind the first four racers. She liked being in the middle of the group. The dirt may be torn up some, but knowing the fastest run so far and aiming for that helped her to do her best. This arena was a bit smaller than most, but she and Shiloh had worked all week on hitting the pocket at the first barrel to set up the next two and then speed for the finish. Tight turns and speed always made for a good race. She could easily beat Darcy tonight.

She directed Shiloh toward the passageway that led to the bigger alley they would take into the arena.

"Have a good race, Lacy Lynn."

Only one person ever called her by both names. Her shoulders tightened, and she forced herself to look straight ahead. She had to focus. *One, two, three, breathe. Relax.* A vision of her race played like a video in her mind: Shiloh hitting the pocket around the first barrel, then racing to the second in the familiar cloverleaf pattern, with a tight turn around the barrel before heading for the third.

Shiloh flipped her ears back and forth and stomped her front foot.

Lacy patted the horse, then sat back and gripped the saddle. "It's okay, girl. We're going to do this." They walked ahead into the large alleyway. She kept her focus on the pocket of the third barrel ahead of them, then made a clicking sound with her tongue and nudged Shiloh with her heels. They tore into the arena, and Lacy leaned forward as they sped toward the first barrel on their right. She straightened as they approached and Shiloh slowed in response, keeping tight in the pocket around the barrel.

"Have a good race, Lacy Lynn."

She leaned forward as the mare sped for the next barrel but didn't straighten soon enough. To keep from falling, the horse took the barrel wide. They headed for the third and last barrel. Lacy got Shiloh slowed enough to round the barrel. They'd lost several seconds back there—could they make it up on the run for the finish? She leaned forward and yelled, "Go, girl!" Shiloh picked up speed and galloped past the infrared signal that would register their time. Lacy shouted, "Whoa!" and Shiloh halted just short of the fence rail.

As they trotted toward the arena gate, the announcer shouted into the microphone, "Fifteen point five! Not enough to overtake Darcy Blount's twelve even. That problem on the second barrel did Lacy Roberts in."

Not waiting to see where she ended up in the standings, Lacy took the horse the same route they'd traveled earlier, stopping long enough to watch the bull riding. Clint mastered the art of bullfighting like he always did. She then headed for her trailer and ruffled Shiloh's mane as they trotted along. "You did good, girl. It was me who messed up. We'll do better tomorrow night."

At the trailer, she dismounted and began to loosen the cinch on the saddle.

"Figured I'd find you back here. Tough race."

She straightened and turned.

Austin Jennings raised his Stetson, revealing dark blond curls she didn't know he had. Back when she had dated him, he'd sported a buzz cut. He was good-looking when he was a rookie bronc rider, but now, with those curls, he probably had the buckle bunnies swooning. Broad-shouldered and lean, he sat tall on his sorrel horse and, to her relief, made no move to dismount.

She wanted to avoid his steely gaze but managed to stand her ground. "I thought you'd be on your way out by now."

"I do have a rodeo I need to get to up north, but I wanted to talk to you first."

She lifted the saddle off Shiloh's back and started toward the side door of the trailer. "We've nothing to talk about, Austin."

"When you hear me out, I don't think you'll want to give me that cold shoulder. It's about our daughter."

<h1 style="text-align:center">Chapter 4</h1>

Clint couldn't take his eyes off the scene across the meadow. Was it two old friends exchanging greetings or a stranger bothering her? By Lacy's body language, he guessed it was not the first. She stood as straight as a pole, her arms crossed.

He narrowed his eyes and studied the guy on the horse. An insanely high-pitched laugh came from the pair's direction, and suddenly realization hit him. He'd never met Austin Jennings in person, but he'd heard plenty about his less-than-stellar reputation. Clint wanted to walk over, but what would he say when he got there? He turned away. Lacy was a big girl and could handle herself. Then a thought slammed into his head, and he whirled around. Was Jennings the dude she'd mentioned the other night?

Jace walked up and gave Clint a friendly punch on the arm. "Nice job tonight with that rank bull Peters drew."

Clint answered without taking his eyes off Lacy. "Thanks. I got lucky."

"I wouldn't call it luck." Jace looked across the way. "I was hoping Jennings would be out of here as soon as the rodeo ended. You know him?"

He gave Jace a sideways glance. "She mentioned that a guy she used to know had started competing in the circuit and was giving her a hard time. I was just wondering—"

"If Jennings was the one?"

"Yeah. He doesn't have the best reputation." He needed to look away but couldn't. The pair had continued to talk, while Lacy's expression became grimmer by the moment. Couldn't Jennings take a hint that she wasn't interested and move on? He had half a mind to go over there and tell the guy to lay off his girl. But she wasn't his girl.

Lacy stepped around the saddle she'd set on the ground earlier and moved closer to Jennings, her shoulders squared. Her voice had risen, but she was too far away for them to hear her words. Clint fisted his right hand and pounded it against his left palm. "I think we ought to go over there."

"I can't, since she told me not to interfere. But she didn't say that to you,"

Jace said. "I suggest you dial down that anger and go tell her we're going to Burger Junction for lunch tomorrow and want her to join us. I'm heading for the shower."

Jace's words were all the encouragement Clint needed. He'd only stay long enough to show Jennings that Lacy had people watching out for her. He marched across the grass, mentally repeating the mantra "Keep your cool" with each step.

Lacy's gaze shifted to him as he approached. She smiled. "Hey, Clint. Good bullfighting tonight."

Unable to hide his smile at her comment, he stopped several feet away from them. "Thanks."

Jennings turned and peered at Clint from beneath the brim of his Stetson. A sneer filled his grizzled face. "Well, look who's here. Heard you got too banged up to fight bulls anymore." His annoying laugh pierced the air. "I thought you were smarter, Palmer. Time to find a new line of work before you get killed out there."

Clint fisted his right hand. "I could say the same about you. I'm healed up now." He relaxed his fingers and shifted his focus to Lacy. "Jace and I plan to grab some lunch tomorrow at Burger Junction, so don't make other plans if you want to join us."

She offered a tight smile. "Sure. Love that restaurant. Sounds great."

Silence fell over them and Clint waited for Jennings to take his leave, but he didn't move.

Lacy narrowed her eyes as the skin around her mouth tightened. "See you later, Clint. Okay?"

She wanted to continue the conversation with the jerk? What was she thinking?

"The lady said she'd see you later, Palmer. You're interrupting a private conversation."

Forget Jace's advice. He wanted to send a right hook into the guy's jaw and wipe that evil grin off his face. She might think she could hold her own with him, but could she? Clint turned and scuffed across the grass instead. Jace had probably used up all the trailer's hot water by now. Maybe a cold shower would be better anyway.

Lacy waited until Clint was out of earshot and then returned her attention to Austin. A smile had replaced the sneer he'd projected on Clint. He was the epitome of those Jekyll and Hyde characters she'd read about in literature class.

She drew in a breath and let it out. "You didn't have to be so hard on him. He didn't do anything to you."

Austin shifted his weight, causing the saddle to creak. "He interrupted us when it was obvious that we were in the middle of a serious discussion. It was rude. But no matter. He's gone. Back to discussing our daughter."

She harrumphed. "You make it sound like my giving birth to her was a mutual experience. You have no right to call her your daughter. As soon as you heard I was pregnant, you disappeared from my life. Were you there during my morning sickness or enduring the pain of being rejected by my parents and sent off to go through those nine months without their support? Were you around when I felt as big as an elephant and had only my aunt and uncle for comfort? Were you in the delivery room while I endured hours of labor, only to have to give the baby to her adoptive parents, never to see her again? You gave up all your rights when my lawyer chased you down after she was born and had you sign the release form to allow her to be adopted. There is nothing to discuss."

He pressed his lips together and shook his head. "All of that could have been avoided if you'd done what I asked you to do."

"Abortion was out of the question. I could never do that."

He leaned back, a pensive expression on his face. "It was your choice to have her. But all that aside, I admit I acted like a jerk. Truth was, I was scared. And I'm sorry. Now I'm glad you had her. I love the idea of having a daughter even though I've never laid eyes on her. It kills me that our love produced such a beautiful child and I missed seeing her."

She'd had enough. "There was never love between us. Only your pushing me to do what I knew was wrong produced the baby. I was nothing more than another conquest to you. There was no love involved, Austin."

He leaned forward, resting his forearm on the saddle horn. "Would you like to know where our girl is living now and how she's doing?"

Her breath hitched. In the thirteen years since she'd handed her precious baby to the adoptive parents, not a day went by that she didn't wonder about her. Was she happy and healthy? What was her name? Did she like horses? Did she make good grades in school? Where did she live? Countless times Lacy had looked at every young girl who appeared to be the same age and wondered whether she was her child.

"You haven't answered my question, Lacy Lynn."

She snapped out of her thoughts and glared at him. "Don't you ever call me that again."

"You're cute when you get riled up. Answer my question. I need to blow out of here soon."

She tilted her head back and blinked away unwanted tears. "To answer your question, of course I would like to know every detail about her. I think about her all the time. But it was a closed adoption. There's no way we can find out that information until she turns eighteen, and then only if she wants her biological parents to find her."

"There's always a work-around. I mentioned our daughter to a PI. He says he can nail down where she's living and even get a picture or two without anyone knowing."

She picked up the saddle and turned toward the trailer. How did he expect her to believe him? And why the sudden interest after so many years?

"Don't you want to see what the PI can find out?"

"I don't believe you. I gave up my right to take pictures of her the day I signed her over to her new parents."

She tensed and glared at him. "You wanted nothing to do with her. You ordered me to leave your name off her birth certificate. No one knows you're the father. What if the PI is caught and arrested for stalking? Or worse yet, accused of being a predator? I don't want anything to do with it." She stepped inside the trailer and placed the saddle on its rack as a cocktail of regret, sadness, and a sense of missing out on being part of her little girl's life grew in her chest.

She tugged her purse out of her duffle and found her wallet. Sliding her finger into a pocket designed to hold a credit card, she tugged out the picture, now creased from being folded for so many years. She opened the photo one fold at a time, fearing it would tear at the creases, and stared at it. She'd begun thinking of her daughter as *Alicia* the moment she found out during an ultrasound that she was carrying a girl, but she'd never told anyone. Alicia was only a couple of hours old when she'd slipped into the nursery and snapped the photo. The baby was still a bit red from the difficult delivery but so beautiful with peach-fuzz blond hair and a dimple in her chin, Austin's only contribution to her looks. Lacy palmed a tear off her cheek before tucking the photo back into her wallet.

It would be wonderful to see a current picture, but what he was suggesting couldn't be okay. Something didn't add up. He obviously didn't care that he'd stirred up all kinds of emotions in her—feelings she'd managed to tuck away except during those lonely hours in the middle of the night when she'd wake up and find her pillow damp from her tears.

She stepped outside the trailer, hoping Austin had left. But he hadn't. She rested her fists on her hips and stared at him. "What's behind all this? Why now?"

He dismounted and came closer. "Like I said, I want to make up for the years I've neglected my own flesh and blood and make sure our daughter is doing okay. I've changed, Lacy."

She took a step back. "I don't buy it."

"It's true. I told the PI to do some quick research to see what he could find. He thinks she's living in New York or Jersey."

"Even so, what you're suggesting could be breaking the law."

"I'm not suggesting we make contact with her."

She rested her fists on her hips and glowered at him. "Then what's the point?"

He reached out with both hands as if he were going to place them on her shoulders. She stepped out of his reach, and he dropped his arms to his sides. "Aren't you at all curious to know what she looks like? I am. The PI said he'll make sure he's shielded from view and take the picture with a long lens. I checked his references. He knows what he can do and what he can't."

"Where did you find this guy?"

"He's a friend of a friend."

Austin made it sound like taking her picture would be nothing at all. The child probably had her picture taken a lot. Maybe it was already on Facebook or one of the other social media sites. Was taking a photo really all that wrong? Seeing a recent snapshot of her daughter would be almost like seeing her in person. "How much is he charging?"

"Haven't discussed the fee yet. I'm hoping to get a deal in exchange for my doing him a favor."

"Which is?"

"You don't need to know right now."

She stared at the ground. Nothing about this sounded right, but what if he was telling the truth? "I need time to think."

"Okay. How can I reach you?" He pulled out his phone.

She recited her phone number, and he typed it into the device. Jace's words about Austin's reputation rang in her head. But Jace had changed a lot in the past couple of years. Austin could have changed too.

He mounted his horse and turned the sorrel toward the other side of the field. "I'll call you tomorrow."

Lacy entered her trailer and went to the sleeping quarters. Jace knew about her past with Austin, but Clint didn't. Maybe she should cancel the lunch plans. If they asked why Austin was there, how could she explain without divulging to Clint the biggest mistake of her life? Not the best way to tell him. Besides, if Jace learned she was even considering Austin's plan, she'd never hear the end of it. The idea was wrong on so many levels, but if she could see a picture of her girl, maybe the middle-of-the-night crying spells would stop once and for all.

Chapter 5

Clint breathed in the aroma of frying burgers as he followed Jace into Burger Junction the next day. His stomach growled. With his insides churning half the night and into the morning, he hadn't been hungry until now. They left their orders at the counter, then filled the tall paper cups the counterman had provided with Dr Pepper and sat at a booth.

Jace took a swig of his drink. "I'm surprised you ordered the cheeseburger special, the way you moaned about your stomach the whole way over here."

Clint removed the wrapper from his straw. "Ever since last night, I can't shake the sinister feeling I had when I was talking with Lacy and Jennings. He couldn't get rid of me fast enough, and she seemed to want me gone too. I hope I did the right thing by walking away. I looked for her this morning, but she wasn't around. I wish she hadn't canceled lunch with us."

A teenage boy with a hint of a mustache arrived with their meals. Clint unwrapped his cheeseburger and waited while Jace unwrapped his burger, shook his fries onto the wrapper, then bowed his head for a quick prayer. Relieved that Jace didn't say the prayer aloud like he did when others were around, Clint snagged a fry from his own meal. Jace raised his head, and Clint popped the fry into his mouth.

Jace squirted ketchup next to his potatoes. "I wish Lacy had joined us too, but she's off with Darcy. They've been friendly competitors for a long time. Lacy assured me she could handle the situation with Austin and said not to worry. Guys have come onto her at rodeos before. She can take care of herself."

"Yeah, but this situation seemed different. I sensed it was more serious than flirtation."

Jace visibly stiffened. "Like what?"

"I can't put my finger on it. They definitely wanted me gone. The guy gave me a bad vibe with his snarky attitude."

"You sure that vibe isn't more to do with you wanting a different relationship with Lacy?"

Clint frowned. "What do you mean?"

Jace's upper lip lifted in the beginnings of a smirk. "It's been clear to me that your feelings for her didn't lessen after you were hurt last year."

Clint stared at him. "Clear how? We haven't talked about it since then—when you brought it up."

"You didn't have to talk. I see your face when you're watching her and think no one is noticing or when she walks into a room."

Pushing away the uneasy feeling that had come over him, Clint shrugged. "Maybe." He picked up his burger and bit into it. The mingled flavors of beef, bacon, and cheddar cheese that usually tasted like an explosion of goodness instead tasted like a lump of nothing. He swallowed and looked around the eatery. "Whatever it was with them, I didn't like it. She loves this place. She could have invited Darcy to join us."

Jace swirled a French fry in the puddle of ketchup and put it into his mouth. "At least we saw Jennings's truck and trailer pull out of the grounds before we hit the sack. Hopefully that will be the last of him."

Clint nodded. Seeing Jennings leave last night was a great sight. He'd let the guy get under his skin and lose all sense of reason. Lacy was planning to leave the ranch by sometime next year, and he needed to make his own plans. He took another bite of his burger and realized that his taste buds had come awake.

They ate in silence until Clint shoved the last fry in his mouth and gulped down several swallows of his Dr Pepper. He looked at Jace. "There's something I need to talk to you about before we head to the arena."

Jace leaned against the back of the booth. "Can't we talk on the way?"

Clint shook his head. "We could, but I'd like to be able to look you in the eyes."

"I hope you're not giving notice that you've got a new job."

"Not a chance." Clint paused and focused on a clock on the wall. The words he'd written out—to make sure he said it right—had left his brain. He brought his gaze back to Jace's puzzled expression. "I love the ranch. It's home to me, and it has been for a long time. I want to be more than an employee. I want to buy in—to be a partner in the business—if you'll have me."

Jace stared at him as if he'd announced that he was running for governor of Texas. Was the idea too outlandish? Clint picked up his drink but then set it down without taking a sip. "I said it too fast and didn't say all I wanted to. What I mean is, the ranch has been in your family for a long time, and with you and your brothers around to give him a hand, most of the time your dad was able to keep it going without extra help. But now Cory has his medical practice in Colorado, and Cole is planning to go into computer work. That only leaves Tanner. The ranch is huge, and there's also the bull business—"

"I love the idea."

Clint stared at his friend. "Wait, did you say you like it?"

Jace laughed. "I didn't say *like*; I said *love*. But I can't agree until I talk to Tanner and Mom. He's always planned to be a part of the operation after he graduates from college, much like I did. That doesn't mean there isn't room for you. We just need to work out the details."

Clint grinned, his energy level suddenly soaring. "I didn't expect you to seal the deal right here. I've saved some money but not as much as I know a partnership would require. You could deduct some out of my pay, and I'm willing to put in extra time to go as credit toward my share."

Jace chuckled. "Here I thought you were all tensed up from thinking about Jennings coming on to Lacy, and it was just from talking to me about a partnership. You sure look relaxed now. You've never mentioned anything like it. What brought this on?"

Clint scrubbed his cheeks with his palms. "My leg has never been the same since I broke it last year. It aches like crazy after every rodeo, and it takes a day or two for the pain to go away. My days of bullfighting are numbered, and I can't be a ranch hand all my life. Not if I want to have a family someday."

"I was right. It's Lacy."

Clint blinked. "What?"

"You've got ideas of settling down because of Lacy."

He made a face. "I do like her that way, but it's clear she's not feeling the same."

Jace flashed him a wicked grin. "I know otherwise. So what's holding you up? If she goes through with those plans to attend culinary school, you'll lose your chance with her. You know the old saying, 'Strike while the iron is hot.' "

Clint frowned. "I think the iron might have already cooled. I overheard her talking to Syd the other day, saying that maybe if she moved away, she'd find a nice guy who made God a major part of his life. That's not me."

"Maybe it's time you stop turning your back on God. Not so you can get the girl, but so you can get your life headed in a better direction."

He shook his head. "God doesn't want the likes of me. Seriously, though, Lacy and I are a lot different from each other. I'm more down-home, and she wants to go off to some fancy cooking school in the East—maybe even own a high-class restaurant someday."

A grin split Jace's face. "When love works its magic, all bets are off. Look at Sydney. She thought she'd be a Chicago lawyer for life, and here she is married to me, a Texas rancher and bull rider, and she's not even lawyering anymore. Doing what she'd always wanted to do, instead." Jace gathered up the used napkins and paper cups and nested their empty trays. "We can talk more about your partnership idea over the next couple of days."

Back in Jace's truck, Jace started the motor and pulled out onto the road. Clint took out his phone and clicked on an e-mail from his doctor's office. He groaned. "Can anything else go wrong?"

"What?"

"At my doctor's appointment last week, I got a chest X-ray to follow up on last year's lung injury. The doc thinks I may have a heart issue now. Wants to know if there's a family history of heart disease."

"What kind of issue?"

"Something about an enlarged heart."

"Lots of athletes have those."

"I know, but he wants to make sure it's not a sign of some other problem."

"Your mom can tell you your family medical history, can't she?"

He slumped his shoulders. He hadn't been to Mom's trailer for several months. Half the time when he stopped by, she was so drunk that she didn't even remember the last time he was there. Since he'd started living with the McGowans in high school, Carolyn had been more of a mother to him than his own. "If Mom is sober enough to remember the facts about her family. But what about my father's side? She claims she doesn't know who he is."

Jace pulled off the road and cut the motor, then faced Clint with a serious expression. "I know she's rarely been without male companionship...."

"That's putting it mildly. I don't think a night went by that she didn't have someone coming home with her after the bar closed."

"I was going to say that despite her social habits, she must have a good idea of who your father is."

"She claims it could have been one of three guys, but she won't tell me their names. We go round and round and get nowhere. I think she's afraid."

"I'm sorry, Clint. I can't imagine not knowing my parents and grandparents. I hope you can get her to tell you. I have another thought on what we were discussing earlier, though, which might lift your spirits."

Clint stared at his friend. "What's that?"

Chapter 6

Wearing a denim jacket against the chill of the predawn darkness, Lacy scurried to the barn. She flicked on the overhead lights, and Shiloh whinnied and bobbed her head as Lacy approached her stall. She rubbed under the horse's forelock. "Good morning, sweet girl. Have a good sleep? I'll get your breakfast ready; then you'll head out to the pasture and I'll get your stall clean."

At the feed station, she mixed Shiloh's favorite breakfast of honey and oats and then added a supplement. She could buy the oats and honey already mixed, but she liked preparing it herself.

As she stirred the mixture, she stared up at the ceiling. Clint's bedroom was right overhead, and without the sounds of running water or creaking floors, she knew he was likely still asleep. It wasn't entirely by design that she hadn't seen him since he'd interrupted her upsetting conversation with Austin, but spending Saturday afternoon with Darcy had given her a good excuse not to have lunch with him and Jace. Yesterday she'd left for home early from the rodeo, and the guys hadn't gotten back until late evening.

She pressed her lips together, puffed out her cheeks, and then blew out the air. The time had come to do what she'd intended many times. Because of fear of rejection, she hadn't been able to get out the words about her past. Now, with Austin back in the rodeo circuit, she didn't want Clint hearing about the baby from someone else if Austin got to shooting off his mouth. But those words sure weren't going to be the first ones she'd say when she saw him this morning.

A short time later, with Shiloh in the pasture behind the barn they used for the horses, Lacy grabbed a shaving fork and sifted the straw in her horse's stall, dumping the droppings in a nearby bucket. Not her favorite barn chore, but it came with the territory when one owned a horse. As the ranch hand, Clint mucked the stalls for the horses they boarded along with his horse and Jace's. He would have for Shiloh too, but she liked caring for all of Shiloh's needs.

She'd known some owners, especially at the high-end stables, who left all care of their horses to the stable's employees and only showed up when they wanted to ride. They never developed a connection with their animals and often had difficulty teaching them new things. One thing about chores—they gave her time to think. But she'd soon have to head back to the house to get breakfast started.

Pleased with her showing at Saturday night's rodeo, after Austin was no longer around, she planned to make as many events as possible for the rest of the season. It could be her last year competing, if she moved on to culinary school next year.

As always, the hated sensation of being pulled in different directions came over her. She loved rodeo, and she loved cooking. Until now, she'd been content to do both, but cooking pulled harder than rodeo these days. She'd even confided her plans for culinary school to Darcy on Saturday. Darcy was surprised and asked whether the reason for the change was more to get away from something or someone. Lacy had told her that she felt in her gut it was time to switch gears. But was it?

She loved all things about ranch life and barrel racing, and she loved the McGowans to death. In terms of experiencing family life as a unit, they were more a family to her than her own parents. When she was still living in San Diego and Dad wasn't traveling for work, it hadn't been unusual to go days without a full conversation with her parents. Texas was home now.

After weeks of wondering whether being weary of loving someone who showed no romantic interest in her was reason enough to look for a school out of state, she now had an even more viable reason: to get as far away from Austin Jennings as possible. Even if it meant leaving rodeo and the ranch for good.

With Austin's cockamamy story about a private investigator being able to locate Alicia and get a picture of her, a new wrinkle had been added to her dilemma. Hearing that a lot of adoptees and their biological parents were connecting even though their files had at one time been sealed, she'd already tried to locate Alicia. But the adoption records were on lockdown until Alicia turned eighteen, as had been agreed to at the time.

She'd been hesitant to agree to the stipulation, but knowing the kind of person Austin was, it seemed best to protect her child. She'd already gone thirteen years without immediate knowledge of her daughter's whereabouts; she could make it five more. But who was to stop Austin from going through with the scheme if she backed out? She was compelled to agree to his offer if only to make sure he didn't do something stupid.

The boards above her head creaked. Clint was up. She imagined him standing at the bathroom sink, shaving his handsome face and making sure the cowlick he'd discovered when he started wearing his hair shorter behaved itself. She liked the longer style he'd worn for as long as she'd known him, but when he went shorter a few months ago, she found she loved how ruggedly handsome and mature he looked. No more like a kid.

The loud footfalls above told her he'd put on his boots. They became louder and closer as he descended the stairs around the corner from the stall. She jammed the fork into the straw, lifted it, and gave it a shake—

"Good morning."

She dumped the droppings into the bucket and turned, relieved at the smile on his face. She answered with one of her own. "Good morning to you."

"I usually hear you down here sweet-talking Shiloh. Didn't today and figured you'd already been and gone."

"I've had a lot on my mind and got started earlier than normal. I didn't hear sounds upstairs, so you were probably still sleeping. What's your schedule for today?"

"Feeding the bulls and horses first, then breakfast, if the cook plans on fixing one." He winked. "What's occupying your thoughts?"

Trying to ignore her flip-flopping stomach, which happened whenever he winked at her, she sighed. "I'm about to go in and start cooking. It's cold enough for oatmeal and bacon and eggs. As for what's occupying my thoughts, it's just my future plans and wondering how they'll play out. I know I shouldn't borrow trouble, but sometimes it's hard not to fret a little bit."

A *V* formed between his eyes. "I thought your plans were set in place. Your parents sounded like they would help with the tuition."

"The plans are loosely set, but there are still a lot of questions in the air. I'm not yet sure which of the three schools I'll attend. Or if I'll be accepted by my first choice."

He took a step closer, the lines on his brow deepening. "I've had you on my mind ever since I interrupted your conversation the other day. I have no idea what's going on between you and Jennings, but be careful. I don't know him that well, but I've heard talk, and none of it is good."

She stiffened and slid the fork into the already-sifted straw. "There's nothing between us. He hit on me, and I sent him away. But thanks for the warning."

"Good to know."

"I wanted to thank you for coming over, though. I don't know if Jace sent you or if you did it on your own, but I appreciated your concern."

"It was a little of both. I told Jace I was going over there to make sure you were okay, and he agreed. You didn't look like you were enjoying yourself much."

"I wasn't." Lacy turned her back to him and slid the fork through the straw once more. Silence settled over them. Had he left? She turned, and their eyes met.

He dropped his gaze to the floor. "I was wondering if, sometime, when you have nothing going on, you might like to go to dinner. Maybe we could talk about things easier away from here."

Was he asking because he wanted to spend time with her, or was it just to offer his ear? "You mean like on a date?"

"Yeah." He looked up.

Her heart squeezed at the expectant expression on his face. Where had he been four months ago when all she'd had on her mind was the feel of dancing in his arms and his lips touching hers? She wanted to say yes, but he'd have to convince her that he cared for her the same way she did him and it wasn't just casual dating he was looking for. "With me planning on moving east soon, it's better if we don't start dating."

The smile on his face faded. "You already got accepted?"

"No. But I should hear any time now. I'll apply to other places if I'm not accepted at the three I chose. I'm determined to make my dream happen."

He lifted his Stetson and ran his hand over his hair, then replaced the hat. "It doesn't have to be a date. Just a couple of friends getting together for a meal."

She allowed a smile. "Friends sounds good. Let's talk about it next week. This one is pretty full."

"Just let me know." He turned and walked away, his boot heels dragging across the barn floor.

An ache filled her throat. Now that he'd put it that way, why put him off? She dashed out of the stall. "Clint, wait!"

He paused at the open barn door and turned, the same expectant expression on his face.

"You didn't say whether you were working next weekend's rodeo."

He grimaced and stared at the ground. "I don't know. My doc saw something he didn't like on my last chest X-ray and strongly suggested I not do any more bullfighting until he clarifies what's going on. I've never paid much attention to doctor's orders before, but after my last stint in the hospital, I'm thinking I should listen to him."

Memories of the night Clint almost died from a goring to the chest flashed in her mind. "What did he see?"

He crouched down and picked up a scrap of paper from the floor. "I have an enlarged heart. He wants to make sure that's all it is and not a sign of something more serious. He'll know more next week after the test results come back. Are you racing next weekend?"

"I plan to. It's too late to make enough points for the NFR, but that's not the only reason I race."

He grinned. "Sometimes it's good to just make ourselves the competition and work on besting our own last run."

Lacy laughed. "I agree. See you later." She returned the shavings fork to where it was kept and started for the house. Her phone rang and she pulled it from her pocket, then checked the device and grimaced. She swiped the screen and put the phone to her ear. "I told you before, Austin, I'm not interested, so please stop calling."

"He's found her. You still not interested?"

Chapter 7

Clint twisted the last string of wire around itself until he was satisfied that the barbed wire would stay in place for years. He stood and removed his Stetson to wipe his brow. "Sure is hot today."

Jace pushed to his feet from where he had been mending another breach in the fence a few yards down. "You can say that again. Let's dig into those sandwiches Lacy sent before we tackle the other side of the pasture." He gathered up the fencing pliers and wire puller. "Can you grab the come-along?"

Clint picked up the tool that assisted in stretching the wire and walked beside Jace to the four-wheeler. He much preferred using his horse to get to the multiple pastures on the ranch, but when the horses would be standing around in the Texas heat for hours, the four-wheeler was the way to go. They deposited the tools, and then Jace grabbed the cooler and a jug of ice water.

After they plopped in the shade of an old oak tree, Clint filled a paper cup with the water. He chugged the cold liquid in three swallows, then refilled the cup and took off his hat. Holding the cup over his head, he tipped it. The icy water drizzled over his head and face and down his back. "Not as good as a dip in the river, but it does the trick."

Jace laughed and poured his water over his own head. "When I was a kid and my brothers and I would head over to the river after helping with the herds, we'd strip down and dive in. Dad warned us not to let Mom know he was allowing us to skinny dip. It wasn't like we were on public land, but she still insisted we wear swim trunks."

Clint chuckled. "Don't you think she knew?"

"Dunno. Maybe. But it was more fun keeping it a secret."

Clint pushed away the threat of self-pity that usually showed up when hearing the McGowans talk about family memories. He'd learned to compartmentalize his life, and he had to do it here. No matter how involved he might become in the ranch, he doubted he'd ever lose the feeling of being slighted when it came to his early years. Nothing could take away the joy he'd had working with Jace. Funny how Jace's liking the idea to partner in the ranch business gave him a boost in self-confidence he'd not had in a while.

He removed the foil wrapper from his sandwich and took a bite, savoring the unique flavor. He had no idea what Lacy did to raise the bar on her meals, but whatever it was, she had a way of putting her special touch on ordinary food. "Sounds like I came to live on the ranch too late to enjoy those high jinks."

"Yeah. It all ended by the time I got to high school. And, of course, after Lacy moved in, her presence brought a feminine vibe to the house, one I'm sure Mom welcomed."

Clint took another bite of his sandwich. "And now she's planning to leave. I'm going to miss her cooking. She even makes ham taste better."

Jace took a gulp of water. "She knows her way around a stove better than anyone else in my family—a far cry from how she cooked when she first came to the ranch." He chuckled. "I remember the first meal she made over Christmas break when I was home from college. The fried potatoes were burnt to a crisp, and the steak was well done. You lucked out, being up in Wyoming and not living here that year."

Clint chuckled. "She must have improved quickly, because by the time I got back that summer, her cooking wasn't bad. But I don't know about lucking out. That winter I spent up there was brutal. It cured me of thinking I wanted to settle there for good."

"I tried to warn you." Jace munched on a carrot stick. "The way you're talking, it sounds like she's nailed down a school and been accepted. Did I miss something?"

"No. I'm just thinking ahead."

"You know there's still time to turn your status with her around."

Clint frowned. "Meaning?"

"Time to make a move, bro. She likes you."

"Likes as a friend. I did ask her to go to dinner one night, and she turned me down. Said it's no use taking our friendship to the next level since she's moving. I took the word *date* off the table and she agreed to set a time after next week. She'll likely end up marrying a chef."

Jace laughed and shook his head. "You two need to stop dancing around the obvious and admit your feelings." He crumpled the foil sandwich wrapper and tossed it into the cooler. Then he leaned back, using his arms as a prop. "Before we start the next job, there's something I want to discuss."

Happy to move the conversation away from Lacy, Clint leaned against the tree trunk and took a swig of water. "Okay."

"I spoke with Tanner and the rest of the family about your buying into the ranch operation, and we're kind of split down the middle. We all agree that you're like family to us, and if we wanted to bring someone in, you'd be our first choice. But Tanner is still interested in being involved with the ranch after graduation, and we're not sure how adding a third person to the mix would work."

Poof. In a nanosecond Clint's dream crumbled. He stared at the ground and swallowed hard. Now what would he do? He couldn't move ahead in life on a ranch hand's salary or the little income he made bullfighting. He worked to keep his disappointment from showing. "I understand. I'll have to figure out something else." He looked up expecting to see Jace's pained expression from letting him down.

Clint frowned. "What's with the grin?"

"How does partnering with me in the bull-stock operation sound? That's where I really need help. Running it alone is taking up more and more of my time, and if I'm to get my bulls to PBR standards, other things will have to be neglected. I can't think of a better person to grow the business with than you. When it comes to bulls, you're like a walking encyclopedia of knowledge."

Clint straightened. His grin had to be as cheesy as Jace's. "Are you serious? I'd love it."

Jace chuckled. "I figured you would. You can start almost immediately. You know that old saying, 'Happy wife, happy life?' "

He nodded, unsure whether he really had heard it before, but it sounded reasonable.

"Syd mentioned wanting to take a vacation up to Banff next winter for some skiing, and then there are her quarterly trips back to Chicago for board meetings at the nonprofit her dad started. She wants me to tag along sometime and take a couple of days to visit her family. I told her I didn't see how soon we could make that happen, what with running both the ranch and the bull business. I said I was going to approach you about coming in on the bull business with me and, if you agreed, I'd hire a part-time ranch hand to pick up the slack. Now that you've agreed to come on board, I'll call a guy someone mentioned to me who might take the other job. Hiring extra help will give us some flexibility to take time off once in a while."

Clint wanted to jump to his feet and dance a jig, regardless of the heat. Working with the bulls was his first love, but he'd never considered asking about joining the stock-contracting business. "Can I start this afternoon?"

Jace threw back his head and laughed. "Let's wait until we get a guy on board and the paperwork done. This is going to be great, because the next step is to get into the genetic area in a big way—start breeding with lines belonging to top-scoring bulls."

They both stood, and Jace raised his hand, palm out.

Clint high-fived him. "I guess we shouldn't announce it until the papers are signed and it's official, but I'm pumped."

"Me too," Jace said. "I'll let you know if I get an interview set up with the guy. He's a college student, so if he's a good fit, we'll have to work around his class schedule." He bent to pick up the cooler.

"Wait, I have something else we need to discuss. Here's as good a place as any."

Deep lines appeared on Jace's forehead. "Should we sit again?"

"That's not necessary." Clint pulled from his pocket the belt buckle he'd been carrying all day. He ran his thumb over the raised form of a bull below the words, *Bullfighter of the Year*. "This may have belonged to my dad. Mom gave it to me the last time I hassled her for his name—I think it's under all those scratches. She did a good job of making sure it would be unreadable. I need more information, like where the rodeo took place and who worked there as a bullfighter. I've tried searching for it on the computer, but nothing has shown up."

Jace took the buckle and ran his thumb over the surface. "How long ago did she give this to you?"

"After I told her about the doctor wanting to know my family medical history. She said I'd never get the name of that 'sorry loser' out of her and I'd have to find him a different way. She gave me the buckle and said that if I find him, return it because it belongs to him."

Jace studied the buckle's front, then flipped it over and studied the back. "If this belongs to your daddy, we now know where your bullfighting ability comes from. Shouldn't be too hard to search for names of the bullfighters who won this award thirty or so years ago."

"I thought so too."

"I bet there's someone out there who can tell us what rodeo this came from and maybe even who it belongs to. Mind if I keep this and do some digging?"

Clint let out a huge breath. "That's why I'm giving it to you. As a guy who lives on the edge every time I step into the arena, it's not like me to sit out rodeos. The possibility of something heart-related happening seems less likely than being mauled. Still, I'd like to know for sure that I don't have heart disease."

Jace chuckled. "The likes of us drive the medical profession crazy. Mom was all upset last night after Corey told her on the phone that he was treating a bull rider over the weekend who had a fractured neck."

"He should know better than to tell her that stuff. He used to ride bulls."

"Back in high school. But since he went into medicine, he's gotten all reasonable about such things. Hey, we need to get going. Plan on sitting in on that interview when I set it up."

Clint came alongside Jace, who was already walking toward the four-wheeler. "I'm happy to sit in on the interview, but I thought I wouldn't be a part of running the ranch too."

"Not as an owner, but you're still my right-hand guy. You've always acted more as a ranch foreman than a hand. You never know—we may need to use the new guy with J and C."

Clint frowned. "J and C?"

Jace slid behind the controls of the four-wheeler and grinned. "J and C Cattle Company. Has a nice ring, doesn't it?"

Chapter 8

Despite getting up earlier than his customary five a.m., when Clint ambled into the ranch-house kitchen, Jace was already there making coffee.

"Morning." Clint rested his hat on a hook near the mudroom door and grabbed a thick white coffee mug from a cabinet. "You couldn't sleep either?"

Jace stepped aside to allow Clint to slide his mug under the Keurig's spout and drop in a coffee pod. "Sort of. Sydney has to be at the therapeutic center extra early to work with a kid before school. Once she was up and moving around, I couldn't sleep for thinking over the conversation we had yesterday about you partnering with me in the bull business."

Clint grinned and lowered the machine handle over the pod, then pressed a button. He breathed in the rich aroma of the extra-strong coffee. Already his brain cells were waking up, and he hadn't yet had a taste. "I had trouble falling asleep and then woke up before the alarm, thinking about it too. I've got ideas swirling in my head. Do you have a five-year plan on how to grow the business?"

Jace poured Raisin Bran into a bowl. "You know about those kinds of things?"

"Never done one, but I've been researching how a successful ranch runs. I assume there are some similarities to a stock business. I'm willing to give developing a business plan a shot if you don't have one."

Jace sloshed milk over his cereal and then returned the gallon jug to the refrigerator. "One in my head is all. Why don't I jot down what I'm thinking and then you can try to work things into a spreadsheet?"

Clint slid a bowl of oatmeal into the microwave and started the machine. With a whirring sound filling the room, he faced his friend and new business partner. "Sounds like a plan."

"One more thing. The guy I want to interview about the ranch-hand job called me back late last night, and he is interested. Grew up on a ranch and has experience. He's free this morning, so we set a time for ten o'clock. We'll use the barn office."

Clint grinned and shook his head. "Things are happening fast. Faster than

I'm used to, but I want this guy before someone else grabs him."

"My goodness, what are you two doing up so early?" Carolyn stood in the kitchen doorway, tying her pink robe closed around her waist, then finger-combing her thinning hair. "If I knew people were already up, I'd have made myself more presentable."

Startled at how small she appeared, Clint diverted his attention to his hot cereal. He'd learned long ago to never mention a woman's weight, even in a flattering way, unless he knew why it had changed. "Too many exciting things going on to sleep."

She padded across the room to the coffeemaker and then stared at it. "My stomach feels a little unsettled this morning. I think I'll just have tea."

Jace pulled his mom into a side hug. "You look fine. We love you just the way you are. You okay?"

She selected a box of tea from a cupboard, then placed a tea bag in a cup and set the cup under the spout of the Keurig. She waited as hot water streamed over the tea bag. "I love you both as well. You can be honest; I look awful. Nothing a shower won't take care of, though. And I'll be okay. What are you boys working on today?"

"Interviewing a possible part-time ranch hand and working up a five-year plan for the bull business. Clint's agreed to join me as a business partner."

A soft smile emerged on her lined face as she looked at Clint. "Oh, I'm so happy to hear that you agreed to it, Clint. I felt terrible having to say no to your request."

"Me too. I'm excited." Clint poured milk over his oatmeal and carried it to the table. "If the man coming to interview later is as good as he sounds, he'll be able to pick up the slack on the ranch work, and I'll be able to work more with the bulls."

"Yes." Carolyn brought her cup of tea to the table and sat with them. "Then we'll need to work out how we cover for Lacy when she leaves. I'm happy that she seems to have found the right direction for the next stage of her life. I can manage cooking for the family, of course, but during those times when we have to hire extra help, we'll need a cook. Lacy is good at preparing sizable meals to feed a crowd. Me, not so much." She stood and picked up her tea. "I think I'll take this back to my room. You boys be sure to leave a note for Lacy that she doesn't need to fix your breakfasts this morning."

A heavy ache filled Clint's chest. He didn't want to think about Lacy's plans—plans that didn't include him. She may as well have put it on a billboard that her feelings for him were more sisterly than romantic. Her going to a school several states away would likely put an end to Jennings harassing her and give

Clint's heart time to heal. So good on her for following that dream of hers.

Later that morning, Clint stepped into the tack room and breathed in its earthy aroma. There was nothing like it, except maybe that of a good steak sizzling on the grill. He grabbed a ladder and positioned it under the overhead florescent light, then went about removing a spent tube. His phone rang, and he tugged it out of his pocket and answered. "Hey, Jace."

"The applicant is here. Are you nearby?"

"In the tack room. Be right there."

A dark-haired man sat in front of Jace's desk when Clint stepped into the office.

Jace stood. "Here he is now. Clint Palmer, this is Luke Barnes."

Luke stood and faced Clint, dwarfing both men by several inches. He had to be at least six feet four. Add to that his tanned face and killer smile, and he looked more like a male model than a college student in need of a ranch-hand job.

He stuck out his hand. "Nice to meet you."

Luke firmly shook it. "Likewise."

Clint rolled over a chair from the other side of the room, and the three men took their seats.

"Luke grew up on a ranch in Wyoming and is attending UT San Antonio with the hopes of getting into vet school after that," Jace said.

Clint's eyes widened. "I worked a ranch up there for a year. One winter was enough for me to hightail it back here. Were you anywhere near Sheridan?"

Luke shook his head. "No. We're close to Laramie. Our winters can be pretty brutal. Why do you think I came down here to school?" He chortled. "I'm no fool."

Clint liked the man's laugh and easygoing manner.

Jace rested his elbows on the desk and looked at Luke. "Mind if I ask why you aspire to be a vet?"

"I've always wanted to be a veterinarian. When I was a kid, I followed the vet around when he came to our ranch. I loved watching him work. When I entered high school, he hired me as an assistant at his clinic, and that sealed it for me. I'll be going on to vet school after I get my bachelor's two years from now."

Clint tried to follow the conversation as the two men continued to discuss their college experiences, but it was evident that he was out of their league when it came to education. Heaviness filled his chest. He didn't even have a high-school degree since he'd dropped out just before Jace convinced his parents to take him in. Carolyn had offered to homeschool him, but he'd declined. Who needed an education to work the rodeo circuit? He was just getting into bullfighting and needed skill and courage for that, not math and chemistry. What a fool he'd been.

How did he think he could hold his own when running a business? Best friends or not, was it fair to Jace to partner with him when he couldn't handle a simple job interview? The conversation faded as thoughts about getting that high-school degree whirled in his mind. He'd check out what he needed to do to get a GED as soon as the interview was over.

"Clint, why don't you fill Luke in on the chores you do on the ranch and what should be done on a daily basis?"

Feeling as if he were back in school and had just been called on by the teacher, Clint forced a smile. "I'm sure it must be similar to what you grew up doing—feeding, mucking, maintaining the tack room, running errands…. And then there are the periodic chores such as dehorning, doctoring, chasing down lost cows, moving herds…. I'm sure I'm leaving something out."

Luke nodded and laughed. "Been there, done that."

"Yesterday Clint and I spent the morning repairing fences, and he had to push through the afternoon to get all the chores done." Jace picked up a pen and tapped it on the desk. "There might be times when you'll be asked to help Clint with the bull stock—feeding, mostly. But it may include working with the young ones and getting them ready to be buckers. Would that appeal to you?"

Luke nodded. "I'd love to learn that side. Never rodeoed myself but have always loved attending them and even worked part-time for one when they were in town. All this experience can't hurt for later when I'm in vet school."

"Good. Do you have any questions?"

"Only, if I'm hired, when would I start?"

Jace looked at Clint with a questioning look in his eyes that Clint understood to mean Jace wanted his approval. He gave a slight nod.

"I'll check out your references this afternoon, but I don't expect to learn anything that would stop us from hiring you." Jace tossed the pen onto the desk and held out his hand. "Welcome. As soon as you can, please email me your class times so I can work up a schedule. We're thinking twenty to twenty-five hours a week."

Luke grinned and shook his hand. "Thanks. I'm excited to be here." He picked up a leather case from where it sat on a corner of Jace's desk and pulled out a paper. "Here's my class schedule for this semester."

Jace scanned the paper. "Looks like you don't have a class on Mondays until three. Your first day can be Monday at nine o'clock. Sound good?"

"Sure, but I know you must start much earlier."

Jace grinned. "You bet we do. We usually begin the day here in the barn no later than seven o'clock and sometimes sooner."

"Then that's when I'll arrive."

The rancher nodded. "We'll have you fill out paperwork, and if the starting wage we discussed last night is okay with you, that's what it will be."

"Works for me. See you Monday morning."

Clint and Jace sat without speaking until Luke exited the barn. Clint smiled. "Well, looks like Lady Luck was in our corner today."

"More like God's blessing, I'd say. Syd and I prayed last night that he would be a good fit. Looks like our prayers were answered."

Clint stood. "Hey, if that's what you believe in your world, cool." *Not so much in mine.* He headed for the tack room, ignoring Jace's comment about how someday he'd change his mind. He doubted that. As for now, he needed to get his work done so he could look into signing up to get his GED.

One week later, Clint waved Jace and Lacy off to a rodeo, then stood next to the bull pen jotting notes on a new arrival and trying not to feel sorry for himself. He'd almost gone with Jace but decided it would be too hard to be at the rodeo watching the bullfighter that had been hired in his place. Besides, he already had homework from his first meeting with the GED tutor assigned to help him prepare for the test.

"Clint, I'm glad I found you."

He looked up as Luke approached with a concerned expression on his face. "Do you know where Jace is? I need to ask him something."

Was he already going to quit? The guy had been doing great so far. "He already left for the rodeo he's competing in, and he took several of our bulls and Lacy with him. It's a three-day event, and he went a day early to meet with other stock contractors."

"I thought Lacy was here. Her horse is in her stall."

"She decided to leave Shiloh home this weekend and use a friend's horse. Shiloh picked up a rock in her shoe and needs to rest her foot. Is there something I can help you with?"

"I don't know. A buddy of mine needs a place to board his horse for the weekend while he's out of town. I wanted to ask Jace about keeping him here.

My friend is willing to pay the going rate. He's leaving the day after tomorrow, so I need the answer ASAP."

Clint frowned. "I can tell you that he won't agree without assurance of the horse being healthy. Our standard practice is that any horse must be checked out by our vet before it can mix with the other horses. As it is, we don't have stall space right now. Even if Jace would agree, the horse would have to stay in one of the outdoor stalls or be pastured by himself and away from the others until he's been cleared healthwise."

"Even if he's already been vet-checked, he'd still have to wait for your veterinarian to check him out?"

"That's been our practice. I can call Jace to confirm. Provided the owner produces papers certifying that the horse is healthy and because it's only for a weekend, maybe something can be worked out. But don't tell him it's okay until I've talked to Jace."

"Okay. I'll call Jeff and let him know the deal. Maybe he can find another place to board the horse."

"Good to have a backup plan."

Clint frowned as Luke walked away. Hopefully Luke's friend would make different arrangements and that would be the end of it. He'd call Jace and leave a voice mail. Chances were Jace wouldn't get back to him until later, but at least Clint would have followed through.

Clint stepped into the barn the next morning with a sigh, dreading having to tell Luke that Jace had nixed his request to board the horse. As he flicked on the light, a large black horse whinnied.

He stepped over to the stall and stroked the horse's muzzle, marveling at the animal's sleek coat. "Hey, when did you get here?" Sensing its calm demeanor, he opened the gate and ran his palm along its withers, then down one of its straight front legs. Then he checked him closer. He was a gelding. But where had he come from?

"I see you and Zorro have met." Luke came up to Clint as he was shutting the stall gate. "My buddy had to drop him off last night, as he was flying out at seven this morning. The house was dark and I didn't see a light in your apartment, so we didn't let anyone know we were here."

Clint winced and worked to bite back the not-so-nice words he wanted to say. Luke wasn't as responsible as they'd believed. "I thought the owner wasn't leaving until tomorrow," he said through clenched teeth. "I wasn't kidding when

I said Jace had the final word. I talked to him last night, and he said we couldn't accept the horse. We have to protect the health of our own animals and that of the two others that board here. Get him moved to one of the outdoor stalls, now. I'll call Doc Forster and have him come by as soon as he can."

Luke shifted his weight from one foot to the other and stared at the ground. "I blew it. I honestly thought he wasn't leaving until tomorrow. Then he pulled up in front of my place late last night with Zorro in tow. His vet did check him out, though."

"You got the paperwork?"

Luke grimaced. "In the rush, I forgot to ask for it. But I'm sure he's fine."

Clint narrowed his eyes at Luke. "Don't ever pull something like this again. And if you are a praying man, you'd better start praying Jace overlooks it and you still have your job." He stepped over to where the feed was kept and began mixing a nutrition grain supplement for the bulls. "Get Zorro out of here *now*."

"The guy knows his horses, and he wouldn't want for his own horse to be sick or cause others to get sick. Look at the horse. You can see for yourself he's fit."

Clint glanced over his shoulder at the new arrival. It wasn't the horse's fault he'd ended up here. He did look healthy, but without an exam to verify it, they had to take precautions. "I did give him a close look. But we need to know what's going on inside him, not just the outside. He's strictly a pleasure horse?"

"I think Jeff has competed with him, but he's mostly a trail horse."

"You have the responsibility of feeding and exercising Zorro. But I suggest that as soon as you can, you get in touch with his owner and advise him that he needs to locate another place and arrange for his transport ASAP."

Clint carried the bucket of feed mix he'd just prepared toward the door, stopping in front of Shiloh, located in the stall next to Zorro. "Morning, girl."

Shiloh bobbed her head and nuzzled his pocket.

He laughed. "Looks like you're feeling better. Nothing for you right now, but Luke will be mixing some grain and honey for you. I know you'll like it." He glanced at Luke. "I'll be out by the bulls. After you move Zorro, feed Shiloh and the other horses in the corral. We need to take a ride over to the far pasture later to check on the herd."

He walked away, shaking his head. They'd work together until he reached Jace with news of Zorro's arrival and Luke would be out of a job.

Chapter 9

One Week Later

Still unsettled by the ranch's stillness when people and animals were off to a rodeo he usually attended, Clint headed for the barn. It was the second time he'd stayed home from working a rodeo, and he didn't like it any better today than he had a week ago. Especially when he got stuck dealing with Luke's sneaking in his buddy's horse under the cloak of darkness. Jace hadn't been happy, but he cut Luke some slack and kept him on since the kid seemed to be an innocent bystander. What bothered Clint was the hold Zorro's owner had over Luke. The guy seemed to lose all reason regarding the situation. It wasn't adding up.

Even though Clint knew Jace didn't blame him for what had happened, he still felt guilty about it occurring on his watch. Doc Forster had had a family emergency out of town and wasn't available all week. So Jace decided to let it go since Zorro only spent one night in the barn and had been isolated from the other horses since then. Sadly, the owner had had a delay in his return and asked for the horse to stay longer. Tomorrow the unwanted equine guest would leave, and things would return to normal.

Clint stepped into the dimly lit aisle that cut between the row of horse stalls and paused. "What are you doing here?"

Lacy turned from the worktable. Her smile seemed forced. "Since Luke isn't coming today, I'm preparing feed for the horses. Why are you here?"

"Same reason as last weekend—doctor's orders. What happened to your determination to not miss any of the rodeos left on the schedule?"

She heaved a sigh. "Plans change sometimes."

He scowled. "Is Jennings bothering you again?"

"No. Haven't seen him since he came on to me that day."

Her answer came too quickly and sounded rehearsed.

"Come on, Lacy. Something says you're not telling the truth."

She lifted the pail she'd been using for a mixing bowl and sighed. "I said I hadn't seen him, and that's the truth. He called the other day, and I decided to make myself scarce this weekend." She headed for the door. "I'll take care of the horses. The bulls are all yours."

He laughed. "I think I got the right end of that deal. Only have three bulls here since Jace took the others to the rodeo. You've got yourself a half dozen horses."

"Nope, I've got seven. Remember? Zorro is still with us. I thought he was only to be here for a few days."

"He leaves tomorrow, and I say good riddance. Keep track of what he's eating. The tally is on a clipboard on Jace's desk."

Clint headed for the hay supply. A few minutes later, he wheeled a cart loaded with hay to the outside pen. The bulls trotted over, fully aware that he had their breakfast. "Morning, guys. Hope y'all had a good night." He began tossing the hay into the enclosure, moving along the fence at the same time.

Once finished with the task, he stopped and rested a foot on the bottom railing of the fence, then leaned his arms on the top rail, enjoying the way the bulls attacked the hay.

"Clint, something is wrong!"

At Lacy's shout, he turned.

She sprinted up to him, her chest heaving. "I think Shiloh has a temperature, and there's yellow pus in her nose."

A sinking feeling came over him. "Show me. We may need to quarantine, fast."

"She's in the pasture."

He took off in a jog toward the meadow.

She hurried along next to him. "What do you think it is?"

"I don't want to say, because I may be wrong."

"I decided to turn her out to the pasture since it's such a nice day, but as I unhooked the lead, I felt her withers, and she's really hot. I checked closer, and that's when I noticed the pus in her nose."

They reached the pasture, and Clint was relieved that Shiloh stood off away from the other horses. His heart pounded against his chest at warp speed. If it was what he suspected, the ranch would be in for a world of hurt, not to mention Lacy too. He should have brought examination gloves with him. Going back for some would eat up valuable time.

He approached the mare and felt along her neck. "She's swollen and struggling to breathe."

Lacy rubbed a circle under Shiloh's forelock. "I'm sorry, girl. She feels really hot, Clint."

He pulled his phone from his back pocket and tapped the screen. Jace answered before it rang twice. "Jace, we've got a problem. Shiloh might have strangles."

"You sure?"

"Swollen neck, feverish, labored breathing. I remember the signs from when we had a case on the Wyoming ranch."

"Where is she?"

"In the pasture, but she's standing off by herself."

Jace groaned. "Great. That's just great. Better call Doc. I think he should be back in town. He'll want to run tests. Get her isolated. I'm coming home now. I'll see if I can board Charley over at Bob Carsten's ranch."

Clint ended the call and glanced at Lacy. The tears streaming down her cheeks about did him in. "Do you know what strangles is?"

She nodded. "A rodeo I was to compete in a couple of years ago was canceled because a horse that lived on the grounds came down with it. I've never seen it in person. Where could she have caught it?"

He ignored her question. There was no use piling on blame until they were sure. He found Doc Forster's number in his contact list and tapped on it, then pulled Lacy under his arm and hugged her while he waited for the call to be picked up.

"This is Clint Palmer at the McGowan Ranch. We've got a sick horse, and I'm pretty sure it's strangles. How soon can you get out here?"

"Horse isolated?"

"Doing that now."

"Good. Better check the other horses. I'm on my way."

Clint disconnected. "We need to get Shiloh out of the pasture and isolated. We can use one of the outdoor stalls until we make room in one of the outbuildings for a quarantine zone."

"But Zorro is in an outdoor stall."

"He's in one at the end. Put Shiloh in the stall at the opposite end. I'll get the other horses corralled while you do that. Then we can put Zorro in the pasture. That will keep him isolated from the other horses since we've never gotten the paperwork from his vet." As soon as he said the words, a thought popped into his head. "I hope the lack of paperwork isn't because they already knew something about Zorro that they didn't want us knowing."

She looked at Clint through her tears. "Is Shiloh going to…"

He wanted in the worst way to rewind the calendar about a week and make all this go away. "I don't know, but I think we caught it early enough. After you get her into the outdoor stall, take some water and hay to her. She probably won't want to eat because the pustules are likely pressing against her throat and making things difficult, but try anyway. I need to disinfect my hands, my phone, and everything else, and then do a wellness check on the other horses. When you're done tending Shiloh, be sure to disinfect yourself. And from now on, use gloves when touching her. In fact, to be on the safe side, use gloves when handling Zorro too."

Lacy bit her trembling lip and nodded. "You never answered my question. Do you think she got it from Zorro?"

He grimaced. "It's bugged me all week that Luke never got the vetting paperwork. If he's the culprit, we're heading into a nightmare. Better not move Zorro to the pasture until I've checked him over."

"I'm not liking the sound of this, Clint."

"I don't either. Luke and I are going to have a talk."

In the barn, Clint went for the disinfectant and sprayed his clothes and phone, then scrubbed his hands and put on vinyl gloves.

Satisfied that he was as virus-free as he could be, he headed to the outdoor stalls. He approached Zorro and cursed under his breath at the telltale yellow pus draining from the horse's nose. No need to examine further. He'd deal with him after checking the other animals.

In the pasture, Clint approached his own horse, who was the alpha leader of the small herd. He clicked his tongue. "Jax, come here, boy."

The chestnut bobbed his head and trotted over to Clint, who pulled a horse treat from his breast pocket. He let Jax take it from his hand. "Time to head toward the barn, boy." He mounted the horse, grateful that he often rode Jax bareback. After getting a good grip on his mane, Clint signaled with his heels to walk toward the other horses. He then got Jax moving toward the gate that led into the small corral on the far side of the barn and was relieved that the other horses followed. At the gate, he slid off and undid the latch. Jax and the other horses trotted into the fenced-in area, and he swung the gate shut behind them all. He walked over and patted Jax, at the same time feeling along his withers. Everything felt normal. He'd already checked for pus when the gelding was busy having his treat. Hopefully, the other horses would check out cleanly as well.

He was shutting the gate to the corral when the sound of crunching gravel alerted him to Doc Forster's arrival. He walked over to where the doctor had parked in front of the barn door. "Glad you could come so fast, Doc."

The vet pushed his San Antonio Spurs ball cap back on his graying head. "When I hear the symptoms you described, I don't waste any time." He lifted his medical bag from the back seat of his vehicle. "Let's take a look."

Looking much more composed than before, Lacy walked up as they approached the outdoor stalls. "I'm glad you're here, Doc. I'm really worried about Shiloh." She blinked at the moisture gathering in her eyes.

They hurried alongside Doc, who kept up with them despite his uneven gait. The older man stopped at Shiloh's stall and set his bag on the ground, then put on a pair of vinyl gloves. He lifted a cotton swab from the bag and then ran his palm over the mare's neck. "There, girl, I can tell you're uncomfortable. We're going to help you through this. Hang in there." He turned and looked over his shoulder at Clint and Lacy. "She's pretty swollen. She eat anything this morning?"

Lacy shook her head. "Only little sips of water."

He stuck the tip of the swab into one of Shiloh's nostrils and dropped it into a specimen bag. "I'll run this through the lab at the office to confirm, but all signs point to strangles. Good call on that, Clint."

"Thanks. I've only seen it once before, but I remembered the signs."

Doc looked at Lacy. "Soak some hay in water to soften it. She may be able to take a few bites that way. You also should apply hot compresses to the neck and over her throat. That will help the infection to start draining. I'll leave some anti-inflammatory medicine to help reduce the fever. Is Jace around?"

"He was at a rodeo," Clint said. "He's headed home now. Should be here in a couple of hours. He plans to leave Charley at a neighbor's ranch until he knows the status of things."

"Good thinking."

"The black that I think caused this is down a couple of stalls," Clint said. "Same symptoms. Zorro is temporarily boarding and came in without being isolated until he was checked out."

The doctor sighed as he picked up his bag. "It's not like Jace to be so careless."

Clint nodded. "Jace had nothing to do with it. It's a long story. He was pretty annoyed that it happened."

"I'm sure he was. Let's see the other horse."

An hour later, Clint waved as Doc Forster's green SUV headed down the lane to the main road. It was going to be tough telling Luke that the horse he'd been given to take care of was already too far gone to survive the virus, unlike Shiloh. They'd have to find the owner and get permission to put him down. A gray Jeep pulled in at the same time and Luke climbed out, his eyes wide. "Was that the vet?"

"Yep. Your buddy's horse seems to have brought strangles with him." He pointed with his thumb. "Zorro is over there, as is Shiloh. They're the only two who appear to be affected right now. Since her stall was next to the one you put Zorro in that night, she caught it from him." Clint rested his fists on his hips and glared at him. "What were you thinking, bringing a sick horse to the ranch?"

Luke grimaced and muttered an oath under his breath. "I didn't know he was sick."

"If you plan to be a vet, you need to bone up on good practices. Right now, we need to turn one of the outbuildings into a quarantine unit for the sick horses. After that, I suggest you call your buddy and let him know what's going on and that his horse is not likely to survive. Jace will want reimbursement for the vet bills and for any horses that die from this."

"That's going to be kind of hard."

"How so?"

Luke jammed his hands into his front pockets and stared at his feet. "I can't get ahold of Jeff. The cell number he gave me is no longer in service. Looks like he used me."

Lacy zipped up her hoodie, then picked up the sleeping bag along with the duffel that contained her Kindle, a flashlight, a jug of water, and her pillow. Without even trying, she knew she wouldn't sleep if she stayed in the house. Besides, if she slept in the stall next to Shiloh, she could get up every couple of hours and put new compresses on the mare's neck.

She crossed the barnyard and started down the row of outdoor stalls. A dark figure suddenly stepped out of Shiloh's stall, and her pulse ramped up. It was already after ten. She glanced up at Clint's window. A very low lamplight shone from the living room—the one he always kept lit at night. He was probably sound asleep. The figure stopped and then moved toward her.

Her heart pounded. She needed to make her escape, but she couldn't get her feet moving.

A flashlight went on, its light so bright she couldn't see anything. She held up a hand. "Whoever you are, move that thing out of my face. If you've done anything to hurt my horse, I'll have you arrested."

The light went out.

"Lacy, it's only me."

"Clint! What are you doing scaring me half to death?"

He moved toward her. "I'm wondering the same about you. I was giving Shiloh one last check before I hit the sack. I put a fresh compress on her neck."

Her knees went weak, and she dropped the sleeping bag and duffel.

He caught her before she hit the ground. "Easy, girl. Your nerves must be getting to you. I'm glad you didn't have a gun. I may have been a dead man."

She chuckled. "You'd be safe. I've never fired a gun in my life. I doubt I would hit you if I tried."

He hugged her to his side. "That's a relief."

She loved how secure she felt in his embrace. Too secure. She stepped back. "Thanks for the catch, and thank you for taking care of Shiloh." She picked up her sleeping bag. "I'm going to sleep out here with Shiloh tonight and change the compress through the night."

"You're what?"

"You heard me. You go ahead and get some shut-eye. I'm fine."

"No way can I let you stay out here alone."

"And no way I'm going to let you stay out here with me. We'll have everyone wagging their tongues for sure."

He laughed. "No, they wouldn't. We're nursing a sick horse. It's not a setting for romance." He muttered something else she didn't understand and started toward the barn. "Be right back."

"Wait. What did you say?"

He kept walking and disappeared inside the barn's side door. Whatever he went to do, she'd send him back to his apartment. It may not be the most romantic setting, but knowing he was there with her, she'd get no sleep at all. She stepped into the stall next to Shiloh and spread out her sleeping bag on the straw before plucking a pair of gloves from a box in her duffel. She'd check on Shiloh once more and set the alarm on her phone to wake her in two hours. Her thoughts went to what he said under his breath as he was leaving. It sounded something like it would suit her fine. What would suit her fine? If she could remember what he said before that …

"I'm back."

She squinted to see what Clint was holding, but in the shadows, it was hard to see. "What did you bring me?"

"I didn't bring you anything. It's my sleeping bag. I'll sleep in the stall on the other side of Shiloh. We can take turns with the compresses. When do you plan to change the one that's on her now?"

"I was going to wake up in two hours."

"Then I'll get up in an hour, and that way she'll get the compress changed every hour."

She wanted to rush into his arms and hug him tight. But doing so would give him the wrong idea. At least he loved Shiloh almost as much as she did. Lucky Shiloh. Wait, that was it—the answer she'd been wanting. Before leaving for school, she'd give Shiloh to Clint. There wasn't a better person, outside of

Jace or Sydney, to have her.

"Does that sound like a good plan?"

Clint's voice startled her out of her thoughts. He still stood there. "Yes, that works for me. Thank you for being such a good friend."

He started walking away. "That's what friends do."

She slid into her sleeping bag and nestled her head against her pillow. This was no different than camping, right? A few minutes later, a soft snore drifted over. Men. They could sleep anywhere. She closed her eyes and felt her mind drifting. Suddenly a light flashed in her face, and she sat up. "What's wrong? Is she okay?"

"Is who okay, and why are you out here?"

"Jace? I'm no good worrying about Shiloh from inside the house. I decided to stay out here with her."

"I couldn't sleep either. Thought if I caught some sleep in the barn, I could keep tabs on the horses too."

Lacy giggled softly. "It's getting mighty crowded out here."

"What do you mean?"

"Hear those rustling noises on the other side of Shiloh's stall? Someone else couldn't stay away either."

"Who?"

"She's talking about me." Clint came up beside Jace. "We're taking turns so Shiloh gets the compresses changed every hour. We don't want her to have the same fate that Zorro appears to have."

Jace chuckled. "I love you both for your hearts. Between the three of us, we'll get Shiloh through this and make Zorro as comfortable as possible until we reach his owner."

Lacy stood and went to her cousin, and he pulled her into a hug. "Group hug. Get over here, Palmer." The threesome wrapped their arms around each other, and she blinked back tears. Maybe she was making too rash of a decision to move away. This was her family. If she moved to the East, she'd be there alone.

Chapter 10

During the hour-and-a-half service at the San Antonio Community Church the next morning, Lacy couldn't stop feeling guilty about leaving Shiloh while the guys stayed on duty after their long night. How she'd gotten her few hours of sleep in that horse stall, she had no idea. With the three of them taking turns, she'd only needed to get up twice—but she sensed the men were up more often than that, checking on Zorro and changing the compresses on Shiloh.

At the opening chords of the final song, she gathered her things and rushed for the door, only stopping to pick up a few brochures for an event that had been announced from the pulpit.

She raced through the parking lot and got her car moving toward the exit before others came and slowed her progress.

Heading out of town on a road so familiar she could have driven it blindfolded, she let her thoughts take over. She shouldn't feel guilty for leaving the ranch that morning. Jace insisted she go and said he and Clint wouldn't leave Shiloh alone. Her horse was well cared for. But for as much as she got out of the service, she may as well have stayed home. While her pastor's voice continued in the background, Lacy prayed for Shiloh and those taking care of her.

She could throttle Luke for bringing Zorro to the ranch that night when he'd been told not to. How many people had his actions affected, not to mention the horses? The one word she did hear Pastor Drake say again and again was "forgiveness." Could she forgive Luke? She wasn't sure. In time she supposed she could, but not right now.

At the ranch, Lacy zoomed into the barnyard. Across the way, Clint and Jace walked alongside Shiloh, leading her in the direction of one of the smaller barns. She skidded to a stop and jumped out of her car, not bothering to turn off the engine. Thankful she'd worn boots and not the high heels she favored on Sundays, Lacy raced across the gravel toward the men, her gaze fixed on her horse. "What are you doing? Is she worse?"

"On the contrary," Jace said. "She's improved since you left, thanks to the meds Doc gave her and our nursing her all night. We cleared out the small barn and set up some stalls for her and Zorro and any other horse that may come down sick."

Shiloh gave a soft nicker as Lacy approached. "Hi, girl. I'm glad you're better." She glanced at the guys. "Has she eaten anything?"

"A little water-soaked hay," Clint said. "Maybe later you could try giving her that honey-and-oat mix you make up special for her."

She looked at him. "I'll get on it as soon as I change." She reached out to massage under Shiloh's forelock then snapped her hand back. "Sorry, girl. I can't touch you until I'm wearing gloves."

"How was church?" Jace asked.

"Good. But truth be told, I didn't pay much attention to the sermon. My mind was on this girl right here. One thing y'all might be interested in though … Have you ever heard of Tim Steele?"

They looked at each other and then stared at her as if she were from another planet.

"I guess the answer is no."

Jace laughed. "On the contrary. We're just wondering what rock you've been living under."

"For someone who's been in rodeo as long as you, I can't believe you've never heard of just about the best bullfighter that has ever lived," Clint said.

She almost burst out laughing at the animated expression on his face. "I thought *you* were the best bullfighter."

He grinned and shook his head. "Not by a long shot. Steele has been my mentor ever since I took up bullfighting. Actually, before that."

"I guess he ended his illustrious career before I started racing. I've never heard of him. Do you know him?"

"Not personally," Clint said. "But I've read everything he's written about the sport and also watched his teaching videos."

"I haven't heard his name mentioned in recent years. Why do you ask?" Jace tugged at Shiloh's lead, and he and the horse continued walking, staying near.

Clint stood frozen in place, his expression suddenly serious. "I hope you're not saying he died."

Lacy shook her head. "No, nothing like that." She took the brochures from her purse. "I grabbed these from the table in the church lobby. He's speaking there next week." She held up the brochures.

Clint stepped closer and stuck out his gloved hand.

She jammed the handouts back into her bag. "Not until you've taken off those contaminated gloves and washed up. I'll give you one at lunch."

Jace laughed. "That will help him get the lead out. We still have to move Zorro."

"Good. Lunch is in a half hour."

Lacy had just set the last of the ingredients for make-your-own sandwiches on the kitchen island when the guys stepped into the room. Sydney trailed behind them. She still wore the aqua tunic top and stylish leather ankle booties Lacy had seen her wearing at church but now paired them with skinny jeans. Her blond tresses fell in waves over her shoulders.

Lacy gave Syd a hug. "Glad you're joining us."

"No sitting at the big table today?" Jace asked.

Lacy shrugged. "Sit wherever you want. We'll be at that table when we have our main meal at five. This is just to hold you over till then. Aunt Carolyn called to say she was going to lunch with some friends after church, so it's just us."

"Sounds good to me." Clint helped himself to a slice of whole-grain bread and laid a thick slab of leftover roast beef on top of it, followed by ham and a couple slices of cheese. The others came behind him. After they'd all served themselves, Lacy decided to follow Sydney's example of skipping the bread and only eating a slice of turkey, coleslaw, and fruit salad. Her jeans were a little too snug these days.

They settled at the round oak table tucked into the breakfast nook. Then Jace said grace and they dug into their lunches.

"You guys missed a great service this morning." Syd sipped her sweet tea and continued. "You'll have to be sure to catch it later online."

Clint rolled his eyes. "That reminds me." He looked at Lacy. "My hands are clean now. So where is that brochure?"

She held up a finger to indicate that she needed to swallow. "Still in my bag. I'll get it after we eat."

A short time later, after the talk had turned to how Luke still hadn't returned the calls they'd made to him yesterday, Lacy slipped away and went to find the brochures. Tim Steele's coming to speak at church had to be more than a coincidence, given how excited Clint was about him. On the way to her room, Lacy prayed that his enthusiasm at finally meeting his longtime hero would prevent him from being uncomfortable about the venue. She brought the leaflets to the table and handed one to Clint and one to Jace.

Clint studied the first page of the trifold, then flipped it over and continued to read. He scowled and opened up the rest of the flyer before staring at Lacy.

"This is at your church?"

"Yes. It's a talk he's giving to the middle schoolers, but it's open to everyone who's interested. I heard some of the older men talking about how they couldn't wait to hear him. Apparently he had quite a following in his day."

"He's been retired for a long while." Clint studied the man's picture. "He must be in his fifties. I'm surprised he's speaking at a church. You'd think he'd be at a rodeo event or something."

Lacy shrugged. "I guess our church qualifies as something. Maybe some of the kids mentioned wanting to get involved in rodeo." She caught Jace's eye and hoped he got her message not to say anything more. He gave a slight nod, and she relaxed.

Clint stuffed the brochure into his shirt pocket. "I assume y'all are planning to go, so count me in. I can't believe I'm going to finally meet Tim Steele in person, after all these years."

The next morning, Clint yawned and glanced at the clock in the ranch's office. Seven fifteen and still no Luke. He was supposed to start at seven and usually arrived at least fifteen minutes early. But since he hadn't returned their calls all weekend, they'd probably seen the last of him. Clint sighed. Best get to feeding the horses since the dude was AWOL. He turned to head to the feed supply and stopped short.

Luke stood in front of him, his hands jammed into his front pockets.

Clint tilted his head back to look him in the eyes. Sure tough to berate someone when they stood more than a half foot taller in bare feet. With boots on, the man seemed seven feet tall. But Clint was angry enough to get over the awkwardness. "About time you decided to join us."

Luke stared at the floor. "I almost didn't come."

"And you never returned our calls. Not the kind of guy we thought you were. Thought you were more responsible."

"I know." He looked up. "I lied about my buddy's horse being vetted. I hadn't gotten in touch with him to ask about it when he suddenly turned up the other night. I asked him then if the horse was vetted recently, and he said he was and that we needed to bring him here right away."

Clint let out the breath he was holding. "So even though you knew how adamant Jace is about that, you came anyway. Why didn't you wake me up, Luke? I was right up there." He pointed at the ceiling.

The ranch hand shifted his weight from one foot to the other. "It's a long story."

Clint drew in a breath and gave himself a moment to get his anger under control. "We don't have much time. The animals are hungry. Got a short version?"

"Jeff saved my life a couple of years ago, and I hate turning him down when he asks for a favor."

"How did he save your life?"

"I was feeding stock at a rodeo when several bales of hay fell and landed on my chest. Knocked the wind out of me. I couldn't breathe. Jeff came out of nowhere and lifted the hay off. I'd been lying there awhile and was about to suffocate. We exchanged phone numbers. I intended to call to see if there was anything I could do to repay him, but he called me first. I told him I was so grateful for his saving me that anytime he needed a favor done, I was his man. I only meant one time, but he's asked for several favors now. How can I say no? The man saved my life."

Jace stepped in from outside. "Whenever it is he asks or whatever he wants, you deliver, no matter if it goes against your principles." His piercing stare focused on Luke. "I've been listening outside the door. Didn't want to interrupt until now."

Luke stared at Jace.

Clint was losing his patience. "You haven't responded to his statement. You'll do anything he asks, no matter what?"

"Yeah. That's about right."

Jace heaved a sigh. "I thought you were more ethical than that. It's one of the reasons I hired you."

"How often has he asked for favors?" Clint asked.

"It goes in spurts. It's usually an errand like picking up a package at the post office or something similar. This is the first time it has involved his horse. I feel terrible about Shiloh." He glanced at her empty stall, and his face drained of color. "Is she …?" He looked at Clint, his eyes moist.

Clint's anger deflated a little. "Shiloh's in quarantine in the small barn, as is Zorro. Three of us were up most of the last two nights with Lacy's and Jeff's horses. We think Shiloh will be okay. Zorro isn't so lucky."

"In fact, he's worse," Jace said. "We've been waiting to talk to Zorro's owner to get permission to put him down."

Luke stared at Jace. "He's that bad?"

"Yes. Doc Forster will be here any minute to check on the horses, and we were hoping to take care of Zorro at the same time."

Jace held up his phone. "I'd like to talk to the owner personally. What's this dude's full name?"

"Harrison. Jeff Harrison."

Jace tapped on the screen. "Want to give me his phone number?"

Luke's shoulders slumped. "I already told Clint—the only phone number I had has been disconnected."

"Know where he lives?" Clint asked.

"Somewhere west of here, I think. He always comes my way." He looked from Jace to Clint. "I sure hope I haven't been played. There's got to be a good explanation for all this, right?"

"Let's hope so." Jace stuffed his phone into his pocket.

When Doc Forster drove his SUV into the barnyard, Clint and Jace were already waiting outside the quarantine barn. The vet parked at the edge of the gravel and climbed out. He waved at the men then reached into the back seat for his black bag and trudged toward them, his limp more pronounced than usual.

The threesome shook hands and then put on vinyl gloves.

Jace held up a hand. "Before we go in, Doc, you should know that there's a problem with getting hold of Zorro's owner. Luke gave us the name of Jeff Harrison, but the phone number Luke used to reach him in the past has been disconnected."

The vet's mouth turned down. "We can give it another day or two, but then we'll have to do the compassionate and reasonable thing."

Jace nodded. "I agree."

Clint followed the men inside, and Shiloh greeted them with a loud whinny. He walked over to the mare and rubbed her face under the forelock the way he'd seen Lacy do. "You're sounding much stronger today, girl. I bet you're hungry. Lacy will be glad to know that." He ran his palm over the length of her neck. "The swelling has gone down a lot."

Doc came over and swabbed inside one of Shiloh's nostrils, dropping the swab into a specimen bag. "Where is Lacy? Maybe she should be here."

Clint nodded. "I'd agree, except she's napping after staying up with Shiloh for the past couple of nights. I hate to wake her."

"No need to wake me. I'm here." Lacy walked up, looking refreshed and beautiful, wearing jeans, boots, and a plaid shirt.

Clint grinned. "Good news. Shiloh is stronger and asking for food. You want to do the honors?"

Lacy's eyes sparkled. "Is it okay to not wear gloves with her?"

Doc thought for a moment. "Let's wait one more day to be sure."

She grabbed a pair of gloves from a nearby box and put them on, then stepped closer to Shiloh's stall. The horse whinnied and bobbed her head. Tears cascaded down Lacy's cheeks, and she entered the stall. "Shiloh, my Shiloh. Girl, you had me worried." She looked over at the men. "She must be better. I want so much to hug her, but I'll wait until tomorrow for that."

Clint yearned to join Lacy in the stall and hug her in celebration but figured she'd push him away since the crisis appeared to have passed.

"Let's check on Zorro."

At Doc Forster's words, he joined the vet and Jace as they crossed to the makeshift stall on the other side of the barn. The gelding lay on the floor, his labored breathing coming fast.

Doc looked from Jace to Clint. "Something isn't adding up." He lifted his cap and scratched his head. "I should have brought my microchip reader. I want to see if Zorro has a chip, and if he does, maybe it will shed some light on things."

"You read my mind," Jace said. "I wish we had one. Something fishy is going on."

The threesome stepped outside as Luke approached the big barn with pail in hand. He waved across the yard, and Jace beckoned him over.

He ambled their way, looking much too at ease given the circumstances.

"Luke, this is Doc Forster." Jace looked at the vet. "Luke Barnes."

"I'd shake your hand, but I still have my gloves on," Dr. Forster said. "I'm glad to meet you, Luke, because you need to know that I'm going back to my clinic to get the chip reader. We ought to see if there's one in Zorro. He's in really bad shape, and something is odd about this situation."

Luke frowned. "I'm not sure I understand. There must be a reasonable explanation for Jeff's phone being out of service."

"You said yourself you hoped you hadn't been played," Jace said. "Something must have prompted that reaction. Did Jeff say where he was going?"

Luke looked at Jace. "I did say that. All he told me was that he had a business conference in Florida over the weekend and would be back last Monday to pick up the horse. Maybe I misunderstood and he meant today." He looked from one man to another. "Do you think something happened to him? An accident, maybe?"

Doc shook his head. "I doubt it. Let's hope we find a microchip and that it gives us a different way to contact Jeff."

Lacy walked up. "You'll be glad to hear that Shiloh ate the grain mix I just fed her and is acting like she wants out of her stall." She looked at the vet. "Is she well enough that I can walk her around the pasture?"

Doc frowned. "Let's wait until tomorrow. If she continues to improve, I'll run a test to see if the virus is still in her. If not, I'll give you the all clear."

Luke's shoulders relaxed. "I'm glad to hear that. Now I need to get to my chores, if I'm still on the payroll."

Jace's expression remained stoic. "You're still on the payroll. Start mucking the stalls in the big barn, and after that, tend to the tack room."

"I'm on it. This has been a lesson learned." Luke trotted toward the barn.

Doc opened the back door to his SUV and tossed his bag onto the seat. "I'll bring the reader within a couple of hours. Then maybe we can connect with the owner and put Zorro out of his misery. If Shiloh and the other horses test clean, the danger of a strangles epidemic erupting will be put to rest. Meanwhile, continue to keep an eye on the others. I'm afraid Charley will have to stay at the other ranch for a couple more days."

Jace nodded. "I figured as much."

As Doc drove out toward the lane that led to the road, Jace slapped Clint on his back. "Let's talk bull-stock business until lunch—a far more pleasant topic. What do you say?"

"Sounds good. I wanted to ask if you're planning to attend the Tim Steele event when he comes next week."

Jace's eyes widened. "Wouldn't miss it. But I thought you swore off ever entering a church building again."

Clint laughed. "I did. And it's not like I'm going to a Sunday service."

Jace frowned. "I guess it isn't. We'll plan on it for sure."

Lacy couldn't stop grinning as she worked in the kitchen to prepare the lunch meal. Seeing Shiloh doing so well this morning made the overnights with her worth the loss of sleep. She couldn't help but hurt a little, though, thinking about Zorro's fate. She hated it whenever an animal lost its life. Yet it was the humane thing to do.

As she was dishing up the chili, the men came through the mudroom and headed for the main dining table. She held up a hand. "Hold on, guys. Y'all need to wash up first."

"We already did, in the barn."

She caught Clint's gaze with her own. "And what did you touch between then and now? Twice can't hurt." She looked at Luke. "You too. I don't care if you weren't in the quarantine area."

He held up his hands, surrender fashion, his face void of expression. "I'm going, I'm going."

Jace looked around as he dried off his hands. "Where's Mom? She's not joining us?"

Lacy shook her head. "She's not feeling well. Probably overdid it yesterday. She asked me to heat up the leftover chicken noodle soup I had in the freezer, and she took it in her room along with a cup of tea." She wished her aunt would confide in the rest of the family as to what was going on. She wouldn't have any choice once the chemo started and her hair came out.

Jace winced. "Don't like the sound of that. I'll check with her before we head out. Maybe she's coming down with something."

"I don't know." Lacy turned away to keep him from seeing the moisture in her eyes. She'd have a talk with Aunt Carolyn after lunch. Her son needed to know the truth.

When lunch was finished, Lacy began rinsing the dishes and putting them into the dishwasher. Luke and Clint headed out to the barn while Jace walked to the master suite on the other side of the house to see his mom.

She'd just started the machine when Jace returned to the kitchen with a grim face. He rested his hands on his hips. "Mom told me about her cancer."

Lacy felt her shoulders relax. "I was hoping she would."

"How long have you known?" His eyes glistened, and he blinked. "I had no idea."

"A few weeks. Jace, she swore me to secrecy, not wanting to upset anyone until she knew all the details."

He closed the space between them and pulled her into an embrace. "That was a lot for you to keep inside. I'm sorry she didn't include us."

She stepped back and looked him in the eyes. "I didn't mind. I just wondered how much longer she was going to keep it from you. You needed to know. Is she going to tell your brothers and Sydney and Clint?"

He shook his head. "She asked me to do that. She had a hard enough time telling me. I'll call Corey and the twins tonight. We hugged and prayed. She seemed less tense than when I first joined her. I think she's glad she finally told me." He ambled toward the door. "I'd best get out to the barn."

The door shut behind him, and Lacy whispered a prayer of thanks.

Chapter 11

The next morning, Jace came up to Clint while he was tending their newest bull in the small corral they'd set up next to the larger one. "I just heard from Doc. He apologized for not getting back with us yesterday with the chip reader, but he'll be here within a half hour. It sounds to me like he suspects foul play."

Clint winced. "I sure hope Luke learned his lesson. I'm almost done here."

"I think he has. He's apologized at least a dozen times." They agreed to meet up when Doc arrived, and Jace headed back to the barn. Clint continued making notes on the bull's care schedule. It had been difficult to concentrate since Jace told him about Carolyn's cancer. At least now they understood why she'd been acting preoccupied and distant.

Last night when he should have been sleeping, he'd lain there staring at the ceiling. As healthy as Carolyn had appeared, he'd always assumed that she would be around for a very long while. She wasn't a drinker or a smoker, and she watched what she ate—so unlike his mother. From there, his thoughts wandered into questioning how the ranch operation would be affected if Carolyn didn't survive the cancer. He'd hated even thinking that direction … but he presumed there was a plan in place to take care of the situation.

He yawned and shook his head to bring himself back to the present. He looked at the bull again and scribbled another note. Someday he'd have to start using an iPad like Jace instead of sitting at the computer later and two-finger typing his notes into the software program.

By the time Doc's SUV rolled into the barnyard, the men were in the office.

The vet appeared in the doorway. He held up a small black case. "Gentlemen, shall we get this done?"

Jace stood and came around his desk. "Yeah. I just tried calling Jeff on the number Luke gave us, and it's still out of order."

They entered the quarantine barn, and Doc stepped into Shiloh's stall. "Good morning, girl. You're anxious to get out of this prison, aren't you?" He ran his gloved palm over her withers and down toward her throat before taking her temperature. "She's looking good. Temp is normal. How's she eating?"

"Great. She's had a healthy appetite since yesterday. Lacy is anxious to get her out to the pasture," Clint said.

Doc grinned. "That's what I like to hear. I ran the specimen I took with me yesterday, and it showed negative for strangles. She can be released from her quarantine. Tell Lacy to hold off riding her for a few more days until she gets her full strength back."

"Lacy will be glad to hear that," Jace said. "Does that mean once we put Zorro down, the ranch's quarantine will be lifted?"

"After I check the other horses to be sure there are no symptoms, yes."

They crossed the aisle to where Zorro lay on his side, breathing heavily.

"He was like this when I checked on him this morning," Jace said. "Can you read the chip with him this way?"

"His left side is facing up, and that's usually where a chip is inserted. Let's hope we don't have to try to get him up or flip him over." Doc pulled the scanner from its case and knelt beside the straining horse. "It's okay, boy. Just want to find out who you are and where you came from." He held the scanner between Zorro's ear and his withers, and the device beeped.

Doc stared at the screen. "Bingo. Let's see what the number tells us."

Minutes later, Clint peered over the vet's shoulder as he clicked through a couple of screens on the ranch's office computer. Doc typed in the number from the scanner and hit Enter. Once the screen responded, he read the results to himself.

"Just what I figured. The horse was stolen. He's owned by a training facility for jumping horses in Colorado. We need to call the owner and tell him we have his horse." Doc tugged his phone from his shirt pocket, tapped in the number shown on the screen, and put it on speaker mode.

A male voice answered. "Rocky Mountain Training Center."

"Hello. Is this Harold Warren?"

"You're talking to him."

"This is Doctor Jim Forster. I'm an equestrian vet here in San Antonio. We have a horse that belongs to you, according to the info on the horse's microchip. He's a black quarter horse, and the chip says he goes by the name of Jupiter."

"Well, I'll be. I figured he'd eventually show up. He was stolen out of our horse barn about six months ago. We finally stopped looking for him, figuring whoever had him had removed the chip. I just recently claimed him on my insurance. Got the check a few days ago."

"I guess the thieves weren't savvy enough to know to remove the chip. But I have bad news." Doc paused for a moment. "He's contracted strangles and needs to be put down. I'll need your permission."

Harold groaned. "That really stinks. He was one of our best jumpers. I don't have any say in what you do for him, not since I got the insurance money. I guess you can do as you have to. The cops have been looking for a stable hand we'd hired several months before Jupiter was stolen. Turns out the name he gave us was fake, but I'm pretty sure he had something to do with the horse's disappearance. He used the name Ryan Smithers, for what it's worth—though I doubt he'll use it again."

Doc frowned. "I figured it was something like that. I'll be reporting this to the authorities here and will pass on that information. If you have a picture of Jupiter, could you e-mail it just to make sure there's been no mistaken ID on him? Chips have been known to be switched out."

"Sure. Got one right here on my phone. Tell me the e-mail address."

Jace rattled it off, and a message popped into the ranch's e-mail in-box a minute later.

Doc clicked on the attachment and studied the photo. "I've got the picture, Mr. Warren, and it sure looks like the same horse in much healthier days. I'll be in touch with you later after I've reported this to the authorities." They said their goodbyes and disconnected. He looked from Clint to Jace. "Mystery partly solved. Now we need to let the cops find the horse rustler. Is your hand around?"

"I heard him come into the barn a few minutes ago. I'll get him." Clint headed for the door.

Jace and the vet still sat at Jace's desk when Clint returned with Luke.

Jace looked at the ranch hand. "Luke, we just learned from scanning Zorro's microchip that he's stolen."

Luke's mouth fell open. "What?" His eyes flicked back and forth and then settled on Jace. He raised his hands in the air. "Believe me, I had nothing to do with this."

"We didn't think you did," Doc said. "The horse is a jumper from a facility in Colorado. His real name is Jupiter. And, sad to say, his jumping days are over. He's going to be put down in a few minutes." Doc kept his eyes on Luke and then glanced at Clint and Jace.

"There's something more you should know. I have a friend on the police force, and he did some checking for me. Jeff apparently gave Luke a false name, and the phone number you have traces to one of those throwaway phones. Looks to me like Jeff, or whatever his name happens to be, is a horse thief. Luke, the horse's real owner just told us that an employee of the facility had used a fake name when he was hired several months before the horse was stolen. I have a feeling we are looking at the same person."

Luke's face paled. "This doesn't show me to be a very good judge of character. You've got to believe me—I didn't know. I feel like an idiot." He looked at Jace. "I guess you'll be terminating me. I'll grab my things and get out of here. I fed the healthy horses and the bulls too."

Jace drummed his fingers on the desk. "The man I used to be would probably fire you immediately. But I'm not that man anymore. Some people are really good at fooling others, and I reckon you learned a good lesson."

Luke dropped into a chair. "Thank you. I don't deserve it, but thank you. I feel so stupid."

Doc Forster rested a hand on Luke's shoulder. "Son, you aren't stupid ... just unaware of nefarious goings-on in the equestrian world. Like Jace said, consider this a hard life lesson."

Luke's shoulders relaxed. "Are the other horses still virus-free?"

"So far as we can tell." Doc picked up the chip reader. "After we take care of Zorro, I'll lift the quarantine on the ranch."

Jace grinned. "And Charley can come home." He looked at Clint. "You want to tell Lacy the news? I think she's out in the corral with Shiloh."

"Sure." Clint turned toward the door. Was it wrong to feel a little sad that the crisis with Shiloh was over? He'd sure miss those long nights nursing the mare with Lacy and her acceptance of his hugs when she needed one. At least he'd have those sweet moments to remember after she left for school.

Chapter 12

Clint sat next to Lacy in the back seat of Jace's Ford Explorer. He'd hoped his excitement of hearing Tim Steele speak and meeting him later would overshadow the uneasy feeling he'd had since the episode with Zorro began, but it was still there.

Next to him, Lacy leaned forward, chatting with Syd through the space that divided the two front seats. Who cared about a baby shower when they were about to hear the great Tim Steele speak? They should have put Syd in back with Lacy and him in the passenger seat up front; then he and Jace could have discussed the new bulls they were looking to buy or training techniques to use to help them become good buckers. Anything but baby showers.

Jace turned into the parking lot. No matter how much effort had been made to convert the former school building's appearance, it still looked more like a school than a church. After Jace got religion a couple of years ago, he'd convinced Clint to join him at a service. He enjoyed the music, though it was a far cry from what he remembered being church music, but Clint never could accept that God loved everyone. It was a cinch that God didn't love him. If He did, he wouldn't have been born to an alcoholic mother and a father who didn't want him.

Clint told Jace he wasn't interested in attending church again, and that was the end of Jace's pushing his new religion on him. During a weak moment right after Jace declared he was a Christian, Clint did question his reasoning. After all, Jace was no angel in his previous way of life. How could God accept Jace and not Clint? He told himself that as bad as Jace had been, he was worse, and he let the question drop.

After being greeted at the door by some excited middle schoolers, Clint and Lacy trailed behind Jace and Sydney, who walked hand in hand down the hall toward the auditorium. Along the way, several people who looked to be about his age spoke a greeting to them as they passed.

Inside the auditorium, they followed Jace down the aisle to the second row, who waited for Clint and Lacy to go in first. Clint was glad the two women sat next to each other while he and Jace bookended them. Already they were continuing the baby-shower discussion from the car, giving him the solitude he craved. The section across the aisle must have been reserved for the kids. The boys looked excited to see the famous bullfighter—and the girls anything but, as they stared at their phones.

Clint turned and surveyed the section behind him, recognizing a few of the men … locals who participated in rodeos, either in the past or currently. He scanned the front rows. No sign of Steele. He still couldn't figure out why the church was hosting the event. The man was a retired bullfighter, not a preacher. Not once had Clint heard Steele mention God in any of his interviews.

A man wearing jeans, boots, and a long-sleeved shirt came to the stage, and the chatter hushed. "I know y'all are as excited as I am to have rodeo legend and bullfighter Tim Steele here with us tonight. He has an amazing testimony that I'm sure will resonate with everyone. Let's have a moment of prayer, and then I'll introduce our guest speaker."

Stunned, Clint closed his eyes. He'd heard enough talk around the McGowan dinner table to realize that a testimony in church was a person's story of how they came to faith. He opened one eye first and then the other, glancing to his left and right. No easy way to escape without climbing over people. He kept his fisted hands out of sight of the others. The brochure didn't say anything about a testimony. If it did, it must have been in small print. Betrayed, that's how he felt. Betrayed by that brochure. Betrayed by the one man he'd always wanted to emulate and betrayed by his friends who let him think the event was to be about bullfighting and not God.

Hopefully, the testimony would only be a short part of the talk and the rest of it would be about bullfighting. He could still admire the man for his skills, just not agree with him so far as God was concerned—same as he did with Jace and the rest of them.

The prayer ended, and after a brief introduction, Tim Steele stepped through a side door and walked onto the stage. Wearing Wranglers, boots, and a black Stetson, his dark hair now more gray than brown, the retired bullfighter set a black book that had to be a Bible on the podium and waved to the audience. Clint sank deeper into his seat.

Steele released the mic from its holder and paced the platform. He thanked everyone for coming out and then said, "I began my career as a bull rider, but it didn't take long for me to realize I'd do better at protecting the riders rather than being one. I had enough bruises and a broken arm to prove that."

Clint chuckled along with the audience. This was what he came to hear.

The retired bullfighter scanned the audience. "For all you young ones out there who aspire to become bullfighters, don't think you don't need courage and intellect to be a bullfighter, because you do. When a rider comes off the bull's back, that's when you earn your paycheck. You have to learn to think like a bull and anticipate his next move, to get the animal distracted away from the rider. You also must be prepared to take a hit.

"One time a bull surprised me and got around to my backside. Next thing I knew, he'd lifted me and I was sailing through the air. I did not make a ten-point landing like those gymnasts you've seen on TV." He rubbed his behind. "I think the bruise is still there, and it's been years. There are things I wish I knew back then when I was a rookie bullfighter, but I had to learn the hard way by doing. I also wish I'd learned the things I know now about God a lot earlier than I did. But one of the things I know now is that God's timing is perfect. If He'd wanted me to know them sooner, I would have."

Clint rolled his eyes, hoping Steele would get back to his tales as a bullfighter, but instead, the man picked up his Bible and flipped it open. "One day I started reading a Bible someone had given me, and the first verse I came to …"

Clint closed his eyes and remembered how watching videos of Steele protect bull riders actually improved his own skills. Sadly, during that night last year in Illinois, he hadn't practiced what Steele had preached and suffered for it.

The sound of applause roused Clint, and his eyes popped open. Around him, people were standing. He scrambled to his feet. How long had he been asleep? He looked at his watch—at least a half hour. When Steele's talk turned to how he became a Christian, Clint's mind had drifted to the wreck that landed him in the hospital and how Lacy had stayed in Illinois a couple of extra days so he wouldn't be alone. That must have been when he'd nodded off.

"Wasn't his testimony amazing?"

He looked at Lacy … and saw her face glowing with the same joy she'd shown when she was told that Shiloh was going to be all right. "It was okay, I guess."

Her smile dissolved, and she turned to say something to Sydney.

He hated the hurt he saw in her eyes, but he wasn't going to lie. The night was a bust and he just wanted to go home. They started filing out into the aisle, and he trailed behind his friends as they chatted about how much they'd enjoyed Tim's talk.

At the Explorer, he climbed into the back seat next to Lacy as usual, hoping Jace wouldn't ask whether anyone wanted to stop for ice cream, like he usually did when they were in town on an evening out.

Jace pulled onto the street and Clint stared through the window at the homes whizzing by, imagining happy people sitting together and watching TV or doing whatever city families did in the evening.

"Wasn't Tim a wonderful speaker, Clint?" Sydney asked from the front seat.

"He was okay. I wish he'd talked more about bullfighting."

"He did talk about it," Lacy said.

He hadn't missed the sadness in her voice. Not because Steele didn't talk more about bullfighting, but because of Clint's response. "Yeah, for all of about ten minutes, and then the rest was about God."

"What did you think he was going to talk about at a church?" Lacy asked.

He shrugged. "Bullfighting. That's what he is—a retired bullfighter."

"A retired bullfighter who happens to be a Christian."

"I didn't know he was one of you."

Lacy jerked back. "You make being a Christian sound like we're in a cult or something."

"Isn't that what it is?"

"No." Jace's voice cut through the darkened cab. "Clint, you know better than that."

"You're right. I'm just teed off that he didn't talk more about bullfighting and less about his faith."

"I thought you knew he was a Christian. He's talked about it a lot in the later years of his career."

"Guess I missed those times."

"He mentions it on Facebook," Lacy said.

"I'm not on there."

The conversation died, and no one spoke until Jace drove through the ranch entrance and down the drive to the house to let Lacy and Clint out before he and Syd headed to theirs.

Clint stood looking down at Lacy, who hadn't moved since they said goodbye to the newlyweds. Unsure of what to do with his hands, he crossed his arms. "I'm sorry for being such a grump."

"And I'm sorry we weren't as forthcoming about the purpose of Tim's talk. It did mention his faith walk in the brochure."

"Didn't see that, and I'm not sure I even know what a faith walk is. I suppose y'all hoped that after hearing my role model talk about God, I'd get interested in the Almighty."

She nodded.

"Tim Steele has been my hero since high school because he's always been a stand-up guy and just about the best bullfighter ever. If he wants to believe like you, that's fine. It's just not for me. See you tomorrow." Clint turned and walked toward the barn, his boot heels making a crunching sound as they dug into the gravel. He'd never felt more alone in his life than right then, but no one was going to know.

Lacy plopped onto her bed. She should have known better than to think that by hearing Tim Steele's presentation, Clint would be drawn to see God in a new light. The time for moving on to culinary school couldn't come any faster. But what if she moved and her aunt's cancer returned after treatment and surgery? As always, putting others' needs ahead of her own, Aunt Carolyn had encouraged Lacy to follow through with her plans. The surgery was scheduled after a course of chemo, and the entire process would be done before Lacy would have to move. A verse from Proverbs came to mind. She needed to trust God with all her heart and not her faulty reasoning. To take it one day at a time.

A country and western tune suddenly broke into her thoughts. She looked at her phone and scowled. All she needed at the moment was a call from Austin. She hovered her finger over the disconnect button. But if she didn't pick up now, he'd only call again later. She sighed and swiped the screen.

"Hi, Austin."

"Hey, babe. Thought I'd check in and see if you've changed your mind about the PI. He's narrowed the search to a town in upstate New York, near Albany."

Her pulse picked up. Her daughter was in New York?

"Hold on." She took the phone away from her ear and went to a map app to search for Albany, New York. It looked to be less than an hour's drive from Schenectady, the area of one of the schools she was considering. She felt an internal nudge, the likes of which she always had attributed to the Lord. Would getting a picture of Alicia be that wrong? It wasn't like she was trying to contact her. She switched back to Austin's line. "I'm thinking about it."

"That's my girl."

She heaved a breath. "Let's get one thing straight. I'm not your girl, and my name is Lacy, not *babe*. Can you give me a reason I can trust the PI to be on the up and up? And how much is my share of his fee?"

"You drive a hard bargain. He's charging two grand. A thou each."

Her heart sank. If she took the money out of savings, even with a partial scholarship she'd have to lean on Dad to help with a larger chunk of her tuition than she'd told him. Was that nudge a warning from God to not give Austin's idea consideration? "Proof, Austin. I'll agree to nothing more unless I have proof."

"Okay, okay. I'll get back to you soon."

She pulled the phone away and stared at the screen. The creep had hung up without even a goodbye. She tossed the phone onto the bed. If she attended the school in Schenectady, she'd only be an hour away from her daughter. And if she stayed in the area after graduation and worked at a restaurant there, she'd be nearby when the child turned eighteen. She palmed tears away from her cheeks. "Is that asking too much, God, to be near her?"

A few minutes later, Lacy stepped into the shower and let the hot stream pound on her back. The lump that had been forming since she hung up from Austin pushed its way through her throat and erupted in a sob. Even though the kitchen and family room separated the sleeping wing from the master suite, and she and Aunt Carolyn were the only ones in the house, she pressed her washcloth to her mouth to muffle the sobs. "Why, God? Why am I losing all that I love so much? Aunt Carolyn's cancer, Clint, the ranch if I move away ... and I almost lost Shiloh. Thank you, Lord, that I didn't. And what am I to do about Austin? Reason tells me to not get involved, but if he's telling the truth ..." She left the sentence unfinished and turned off the faucet.

A short time later, Lacy climbed into bed and doused the light. Maybe in the morning she'd find the answer she was looking for. Never had she been so indecisive in her life.

Chapter 13

The next morning, Clint stepped into the ranch's office to look for the insulated water bottle he'd left there—and found Lacy instead. Wide-eyed, Lacy spun around and moved several inches to her left. "Clint. Hi."

He frowned. "What's going on?"

She averted her gaze. "Nothing. I was … um, just looking for something."

"Where? In the safe?"

"No."

"Then why are you trying to block my view of it?"

Her face reddened. "Aunt Carolyn asked me to get something out of the safe for her. She swore me to secrecy." She slumped and shook her head. "Forget I said that. It's not true." She looked past him into the stalls. "Is anyone else here in the barn?"

He shrugged and glanced over his shoulder. "Negative. Jace is at lunch with someone interested in buying a bull, and Luke is at school."

She dropped into the desk chair, revealing the open safe behind her. "If I tell you something, you've got to swear you'll never repeat it to anyone."

Thoughts—none of them good—pinged back and forth in his mind as he dragged a chair around the desk and sat beside her. "I'm not sure I can swear to something until I've heard what it is. I didn't know you had the combination to the safe."

"It was given to me for emergency use only."

He tensed. "What's the emergency?"

"I'm not sure *you'd* call it one, but it is to me. There's something about my past that you don't know."

He peered at her. Had she cheated on a test in college? Maybe got a speeding ticket? "Okay…"

Her lower lip trembled and she bit on it, then muttered something into her lap.

He leaned in. "Lacy, you need to speak up. It can't be that bad, whatever it is."

She kept her gaze on her lap and huffed. "When I was in high school, I got pregnant."

He blinked. He must have misunderstood. "Say that again?"

"I got pregnant the summer before my senior year of high school."

His chest tightened. He had heard her right. Never in a million years would he have guessed this. An ache as big as Texas filled his chest. He slid down into the chair. There had to be a logical explanation. "Did someone assault you?"

She shook her head. "No. It took some persuasion, but it was consensual. A very dumb and stupid mistake."

The ache turned into a sharp pain, like a dagger twisting. "I didn't think Christians did stuff like that."

"Christians aren't perfect, Clint. And I was a very shallow Christian back then. I got involved with a bronc rider when I began competing on the circuit and—"

"So, when you told me you were saving yourself for marriage, you were lying."

She rested a hand on his arm. "Clint, no. I wasn't lying. I've done nothing like that since then and don't intend to unless I'm married. The last dating relationship I had ended because of my stance."

He remembered the dude she last dated at least two years ago. A steer wrestler who was no longer on the circuit. He seemed a nice enough guy, but to stop dating Lacy because he couldn't get to first base with her? The guy's loss, not Lacy's. He wanted to push Lacy's hand away, but he couldn't bring himself to do it, nor could he take hold of it to comfort her despite the pain in her eyes. "Lacy, I don't know what to say."

"I know it must be a shock. I should have told you the whole story long ago when we had that conversation about waiting for marriage, but I was afraid you'd reject me and I'd lose the best friend you'd become. When you were in the hospital last year and we had those days together, I thought it would be a good time for my 'true confessions' speech. But before I could bring it up, you shared more than I ever knew about your mom's lifestyle and how your dad disappeared. It wasn't the right time to discuss my less-than-stellar past."

Clint looked at the clock on the wall. How long had they been sitting there? Probably no more than ten minutes. She'd made the right decision to not tell him back in Illinois. If she only knew where his thoughts immediately headed a few minutes ago. Lumping her in the same category as his mom was wrong, but that's exactly where they went, before she told him how she'd stopped dating the steer wrestler because he wanted more of her than she was willing to give. He needed to bolt and let it all sink in, but if he really cared for this girl like he thought he did, was that the right thing to do? He brought his focus back to Lacy. "I assume you were living in San Diego at the time."

She nodded. "Yes, but I was already spending my summers here on the ranch and barrel racing at rodeos. When I found out I was pregnant, it was already fall and I was back at school in California. My parents wasted no time in sending me here to live until the baby was born. Aunt Carolyn homeschooled me so I'd be able to graduate on time."

"That must have been the year I spent up in Wyoming at the ranch. Jace knows about this?"

"Yes. He was at college then but saw me in all my glory, big and pregnant, when he came home during school vacations. Since I was going to permanently stay on the ranch, the McGowans and I decided that because of the way some of the older people at church might feel about the circumstances, it was best to not tell anyone about the baby."

"I thought Christians were nicer than that."

"Many are, but there's a saying that we are all sinners saved by grace. In other words, because of placing our faith in Christ, we're forgiven, but we are still sinners. A lot has changed in the past thirteen years. A high schooler in our youth group became pregnant last year and everyone supported her and her family, both emotionally and financially."

"They all thought that what she did was okay?"

"No. She had to repent of her sin to God." Lacy smiled through her tears. "God promises to forgive our sin when we repent. What she needed was to be loved, and that's what we did."

"Did she give up her baby to adoption?"

Lacy shook her head and pushed down the familiar sadness that came over her whenever she compared her experience with the more recent one. "No. She kept the little guy, and she and her parents are raising him together. Perhaps if my parents had been more accepting ... but by the time Jace came home for the summer and you returned from Wyoming, I'd had the baby and given her up for adoption. As the years went by, my pregnancy was discussed less and less among the family. Unlike today, there was little social media for word to get out."

"Why didn't you return to San Diego?"

She hunched forward and stared at her feet, then looked up with her eyes watery. "My parents didn't want me back. Said they'd told their friends I moved to Texas to live on the ranch and loved it so much that I'd decided to stay. The part about loving it here was true. I'd fallen in love with horses and ranch life, but I'd have gone back in a heartbeat if they'd wanted me. My dad at least agreed to pay for my education, as long as I majored in business. The next year I went to college but came here for all my vacations." A tear trailed down her face. She palmed it away, then grabbed a tissue from a box on the desk and blew her nose.

Clint scowled and looked away, unable to bear any woman's tears. Two people within a week had let him down. First Tim Steele, and now the girl he was falling for had turned out to not have been as virtuous as he thought. How could she even think that God would be okay with what she'd done? Wasn't Lacy's giving away her baby the same as what his own father had done by abandoning him? He stared at her and felt a look of disgust forming on his face.

"It sounds like after you gave away your baby, your life went on as if nothing had ever happened. How could you do that?" He clamped his mouth shut but knew by the hurt on her face that it was too late.

"Oh, Clint, you have no idea how painful it was to give her away. From the moment I first felt life in my belly, I fell in love with the little person growing inside me—unlike her father, who dropped out of my life as soon as I said I'd never have an abortion. I sensed the baby was a girl and started calling her Alicia and fantasized about how I'd raise her on my own.

"When I told Aunt Carolyn I wanted to keep the baby, she helped me weigh the pros and cons of the decision. I was seventeen with no way to earn enough money to take care of her. As the due date came closer, I knew that the best thing was to surrender her to a couple who really wanted her and could provide for her in ways I couldn't." Her voice quivered. "When I handed her over to the social worker the day after she was born, I felt as if I'd given away an arm or a leg. A part of me went with her."

Okay, so it wasn't the same as what his father had done with him, but it still rankled him. "Do you know who adopted her?"

She shook her head. "It was a closed adoption, and I didn't want to know. I figured the less I knew of her whereabouts, the easier it would be to forget about her. I was wrong. Daily, I think of her and say a prayer for her. But it was the right decision to give her up, because my parents had all but disowned me by then and would be no help at all."

He opened and closed his fist, wanting to lash out, to find that good-for-nothing who deserted Lacy and his child, and then go tell off her dad. He needed to get away before he said something he'd regret. But she was the last person he should be angry with. If he felt that way, he must not love her after all. Love wouldn't want to desert her … right?

He stood. "Thanks for telling me."

"I thought you wanted to know why I was in the safe."

He lowered himself to the chair. "Oh yeah. It must have had something to do with what you just told me." He hated the evenness in his voice.

"The baby's father recently contacted me. He found out where our daughter is through a PI, and the PI offered to go to her home in New York and take a picture for us. I know it sounds a little crazy, but I can't contact her until she's eighteen. She's just thirteen now. Five years is a long time. Seeing a picture of her…"

He drew in a slow breath. "That's why you're so interested in going to school in New York."

"No." Despite her tears, her eyes sparkled. "That's the thing. I was considering the New York school before I knew my daughter's location. If I go to the school in Schenectady, I'll only be an hour from her."

Clint lifted his hat and ran his fingers through his hair, then replaced it. Where had the sweet, wholesome girl he'd known and loved for years gone? He had to get a grip, keep his head. "I don't know much about the laws concerning adoption, but if a PI is staking out her house to get a picture, isn't that stalking? She's underage, and if he's caught he could be in deep trouble."

Lacy straightened. "It's being handled by a professional who knows how to do these kinds of things. As I understand it, he's a former cop. I'm sure he will do the picture-taking in a way that is acceptable."

"How is sneaking a picture of a child you don't know *acceptable?*"

His question seemed to catch her up short. She stared at him for a couple of moments. "With all the news stories about child abuse these days, it's being responsible to check up on one's daughter to make sure she's well cared for."

He could see that there was no convincing her it was wrong, so he tabled the topic. "So why were you in the safe?"

She ran her gaze over his face with her reddened eyes. "I need a thousand dollars to pay the PI. I searched my room for my ATM card, but I can't find it. I planned to use the ranch's cash to get a money order today so I can send it off. I can replace the money on Monday when I go to the bank."

"Are you to send it directly to the PI?"

"No, I'm to give it to Aus—" She clamped her mouth shut.

He gaped at her. "Austin Jennings is the father? That creep whose been hitting on you at the rodeos?"

She nodded. "I only let you think he was hitting on me. We've been talking about our daughter and the PI."

He whacked the desktop with his palm. "I told you he was a no-good…"

"You don't have to remind me. I know he's a weasel, but he's never done anything criminal. And he *is* the father of my child. He says he loves her and regrets his walking away and causing me to give her up for adoption. If I could see a picture of her and be assured that she's having a good life, I can relax and Austin will crawl back into the hole he's been in the past thirteen years."

"How do you know he's being truthful about loving her?"

The tears reemerged. "I don't. But I think he's changed. At least I hope he has. Back then he was a self-centered jerk. A kid, actually. Barely twenty." She glanced at the open safe and sighed. "It was wrong to use ranch money for this. He'll have to wait until I can get to the bank. What's a couple more days?"

Lacy stood and slammed the safe closed, giving the combination lock a spin. She plopped back into the chair and stared at Clint. Her lower lip trembled. "Thanks for coming along when you did. You saved me from making a huge mistake."

If only he'd been around years ago to stop her from making an even bigger mistake. He longed to draw her shaking body into his arms, but he had to process the conversation and silence the voice in the back of his mind that kept taunting him, saying she was no better than his mom. Based on all she'd said, he knew that wasn't true, but he needed time to sort it all out. "Be careful and think twice before you do anything you'll regret. That's all I have to say for now." Without a backward glance, he strode from the room.

Chapter 14

Lacy sat in silence, not moving for a long while. She'd hated the hurt in Clint's eyes when she first mentioned the baby, but then after he got over the shock, he seemed okay. Maybe not understanding completely, but accepting. Before their conversation was over, though, he'd moved to disgust and then anger when he learned Austin was the father. By the time he left, even though he'd calmed, she sensed that the anger still lingered beneath the surface.

But wasn't that how he flipped the switch on his view of Tim Steele? Crazy about the guy one minute and done with him the next? It was a lot for Clint to process, but would he ever be able to accept her, flaws and all? If she were ever to marry, it would be to a man of faith. One who understood that the woman she was today was totally opposite of the young, impressionable girl who was swept off her feet by the most popular cowboy on the circuit. Today, her faith was much deeper and, like she told Clint during their conversation, she'd vowed to never engage in intimacy outside of marriage again.

She blinked at the moisture still burning her eyes as a dark thought dropped into her mind. Would Clint betray her confidence? He'd never promised to keep it to himself. As agitated as he'd become during the conversation, he might. No way. The Clint she knew wouldn't do that to her. If only she could move away from the ranch now and not wait till next year … But she had no money, nowhere to go, and no courage. She couldn't go back to San Diego—nor would she want to. She supposed she could look for another ranching job, one that would allow her to bring Shiloh. Of course, she wouldn't be able to disclose her plans to move out of state the next year.

Her heart sank. What was she doing, thinking about leaving the ranch while Aunt Carolyn's health hung in the balance? She placed her arms on the desk and rested her head on top of them as pain built in her throat. As much as her aunt had encouraged her to go ahead with her plans for school, how could Lacy leave the woman who was closer to her than her own mother?

The sound of footfalls drifted in from the stalls. Lacy looked up as Clint appeared in the office doorway.

Was he there to offer the comfort she craved? His stoic expression didn't give a clue. She offered a tight smile. "Come in. I'm glad you came back."

"Jace called and wants me to join him in town," he said without emotion. "Luke should be here in an hour to begin his chores. Have him start mucking and then take the four-wheeler out to the south pasture and check for new calves. The place is under your watch." Without waiting for her to answer, he spun on his heel and walked away.

She grabbed the stapler and hurled it across the room. It crashed into a plaque her uncle had received when he won Rancher of the Year. She circled the desk and ran her fingertips over the engraved metal plate. Not even a dent.

She looked at the plaque next to it: Jace's award for winning the top prize in bull riding at last December's NFR. Being at the finals and seeing him accumulate all those points over the competition had been a blast. When his win was announced, she, Clint, and Sydney leaped from their seats and hugged each other, jumping up and down. It was a wonder they hadn't fallen into the seats in the row below them.

She studied the framed photo next to the award of Jace receiving his buckle, award, and oversized check. The good times held on after that through Jace paying off the back taxes on the ranch, then finishing up the house he'd been building in time for his and Sydney's wedding the next May. But since then Aunt Carolyn had come down with cancer and Shiloh had almost died of strangles. Jace and his brothers had lost their dad only two and a half years ago. Lacy was beginning to feel like her only other option was to stay put and postpone school until Aunt Carolyn was feeling better. Serious prayer was needed, and without delay.

Clint pulled into the parking lot of Dee's Breakfast and More and rolled into the space next to the ranch's blue F-150. Jace sat behind the wheel, his thumbs tapping on his cell phone. He looked up and waved.

Clint jumped out of his truck and slid onto Jace's passenger seat. "Anything interesting in e-mail?"

"Wasn't looking at mail. Sydney and I were texting. One of her charges made a huge breakthrough this morning. Also while texting, I sold Rough Weather to the man from Laredo that we saw the other day at the ranch. Got the price we wanted on that bull, too. I wish you'd have agreed to come with me earlier. What was so important that you couldn't?"

Jace dropped the phone into his breast pocket and started the engine. He tapped on the dashboard screen until a map popped into view. "I already plugged in the address of where we're going." He put the truck in gear and backed up.

Clint frowned. "I wish I'd gone with you too. My morning didn't turn out so well. Didn't even get to work on the reason I stayed behind."

"Everything okay with the bulls?"

"Yeah. They're fine."

"Something with your mom?"

Why didn't Jace let up? Lacy's cousin obviously didn't feel the same way as he did about her questionable past. And at times Clint wasn't sure how he felt. One minute it was something he could accept and the next it wasn't. It wasn't right to disparage a man's relatives, either. "I'd rather not talk about it."

"Okay, bro. But if you ever need to get something off your chest, I'm here."

At the next intersection, Jace turned onto one of San Antonio's major thoroughfares. With each passing mile, Clint's gut burned hotter and hotter. If they were going to talk to someone about a bull, he needed to get his mixed emotions off his chest that were now leaning more toward a desire to dislodge his negative feelings and comfort her rather than judge. Jace was as trustworthy as they came. Clint only needed to keep his personal feelings out of the conversation. He swallowed hard and then glanced at Jace. "Lacy told me about the baby this morning."

Jace looked at him, surprise all over his face. "I figured you already knew." He moved his attention back to the road. "You two being such good friends, I'm surprised she didn't tell you."

"Well, I didn't know. Good thing I do now. Funny. Before I knew, I thought she was too good for me, and now that I know her past, I don't feel that way."

"Why is that?"

"One minute I'm okay with what she told me and I want to support her, and then the next I'm fighting thoughts in my head that she's no better than my mother. How am I to believe she's the Christian she claims to be and not been with others since then, like she said?" He pressed his lips together. *Way to go, Palmer. So much for keeping your feelings out of the discussion.*

Jace slowed the truck and pulled off to the side of the road. He faced Clint. "Whoa, dude. Let's back up. The baby happened to her back in high school, and I know she's square with God about it all. As for being no better than your mother, one mistake doesn't necessarily lead to a life of one bad decision after another. You can't paint anyone with a broad brush based on one misstep."

"But you don't know for sure. It's not like she would flaunt it."

"In all the years you've known her, has she ever given you reason to think she was sleeping around?"

He hated it when Jace made sense. He wanted to be mad at Lacy for how she'd deceived him. "No. But what she did is so out of character for her."

"For her now, but not so much when she was seventeen years old. I've watched her over the years, and I know she's been more than careful with the guys she's dated, which haven't been many. I didn't lead a chaste lifestyle until the past several years, and you never seemed bothered by it."

"That was before you signed up to be a Christian. I know what your life has been like since then. But Lacy has always been a Christian."

"No one is born a believer. She didn't come to a committed faith until after she had the baby. I think getting pregnant and suffering the consequences of the situation is what drove her to God. It was really hard for her to give up the baby, but she acknowledged that she was too young to raise a child and had no means to do it right. She's been very involved with a ministry at church for unwed mothers since then."

Clint blinked. "When she told me about her past, she mentioned something about a girl from church having a baby a couple of years ago, but I didn't know about her being involved that way."

"How would you, since you don't attend church with us? It's a ministry that is not openly talked about because of the sensitivity of some of the situations."

Clint stared out the window. He really didn't know Lacy like he thought he did. "Good for her. Did you know that the guy who'd been pestering her at the rodeos is the baby's father?"

Jace heaved a loud breath. "Yes. But she's a grown woman, and she's told me she has the situation under control. I have no idea why Jennings has a sudden interest in her after all these years. Hopefully he'll move on to someone else soon."

Clint yearned to tell Jace what Lacy was about to do with the money she'd been saving, but he couldn't bring himself to betray her. What he could do, though, was approach the creep at the next rodeo and give him a piece of his mind. A vision erupted in his thoughts and he smiled, imagining himself channeling his inner Chuck Norris and giving the guy a roundhouse kick, knocking him out cold. Of course, he'd need some martial arts training before that would ever happen.

By the time Jace turned into their destination and pulled the truck to a stop, Clint's innards didn't feel any better than they had earlier. If anything, he felt worse. He was in no frame of mind to discuss bull business with anyone. "I'm not feeling so well. Maybe I should wait here."

Jace snatched the keys from the ignition and opened his door. "No way. I need you in on this meeting."

He stared at the one-story brick home with its well-kept yard and colorful flowers in neat flower beds. If they were going to see someone interested in purchasing a bull, wouldn't the buyer be living on a ranch or a farm?

Jace glanced over. "We're expected, and we're right on time. Let's go." He climbed out of the truck and slammed the door.

Clint didn't move. Wasn't there a saying that bad luck happened in threes? He'd already had two bad things, and he had an uneasy feeling about this one.

Jace stood on the cement in front of the vehicle, his fists on his hips and giving Clint the stink eye.

He heaved a sigh and climbed out. They approached the small porch that held a pair of Adirondack chairs, and Jace pressed the doorbell. Chimes sounded from behind the six-panel wooden door.

Several moments passed. Jace shifted from one foot to the other. Why was he so antsy? Clint turned toward their ride. "The guy must not be home."

Just then the door swung open. Clint spun around and stared into the face of Tim Steele.

Chapter 15

Clint stiffened and glanced first at Jace and then at Steele. Unless Steele had an interest in buying a bull from them, they had no reason to be here. Though this could be Jace's way of arranging for Clint to meet his childhood hero in a setting where he could really hear from the master.

"Since you didn't have a chance to meet Tim in person the other night," Jace said, "I thought you'd like to meet him now."

Bingo. Clint wanted to wipe that smug expression off Jace's face—so proud of himself for fooling him into thinking they were there to talk about selling a bull. He cast about for words, but the only ones that showed up were ones he shouldn't vocalize. Before the event at the church, he would have been thrilled to have Jace arrange such a meeting. But now? Had Jace paid no attention at all to what Clint said on their way home that night?

Steele was looking at him with an expectant expression on his face. Clint had to deal and suck it up. He managed a smile and stuck out his hand. "Sorry, I'm in a state of shock. I'm glad to meet you at long last."

Steele gripped Clint's hand tightly. "Pleased to meet you, my man." He fixed his gaze on Clint for several moments as if memorizing his features.

He was about to tug his hand away when Steele released it and stepped back. "Sorry, I forgot myself for a moment. Come on in, guys."

Jace indicated that Clint should go first.

He followed Steele into a small entryway and then down a tiled hall toward the back of the house. They stepped into a large family room separated from a kitchen by a granite-topped island.

Steele walked to a trio of matching easy chairs arranged in front of a large river-rock fireplace. A colorful Southwestern-themed rug held it all together. Just the kind of decorating he'd expect of Tim Steele. Their host picked up a remote and turned off the TV above the wooden mantel before indicating the chairs. "Please, sit."

They all sat, with Steele between Clint and Jace. Clint narrowed his eyes at Jace, but the man looked everywhere except at him. Jace knew how much he hated surprises—same as Jace himself. This was probably payback for when he and Lacy snuck Syd down from Chicago after the couple had broken up. Of course, Jace was so tickled to see her, he never complained about being caught off guard. This situation was different. But he needed to forget his feelings, take advantage while he had it, and enjoy himself.

"My wife has gone out, so we can talk privately," Steele said, jolting Clint out of his thoughts. He looked Clint right in the eyes. "Jace tells me you've been a fan of mine for a long time and have considered me a kind of bullfighting mentor."

Clint nodded. "No better person to learn the sport from. I've seen all your online teaching videos, studied your methods during events, and read everything you've written that I could get my hands on."

The man grinned. "You flatter me. How long have you been bullfighting?"

Clint shrugged. "Since a couple of years out of high school. Rode bulls until then but took to bullfighting better. I was a lousy bull rider."

Steele laughed. "I hear ya. Sounds like we're wired the same way."

Clint squirmed in his chair. "Not entirely. I was at your talk the other night at Jace's church. I don't believe all your God stuff." He inwardly cringed. What had made him go and say that? Probably the end of any bullfighting tips now that he'd insulted the guy.

"I didn't either when I was younger." Steele grinned. "No worries. I'm not going to push any God talk on you. May as well get to the reason for your visit." He leaned to one side and pulled something from his back pocket. "I understand your mother gave you this."

Clint stared at the belt buckle and then pinned a glare on Jace. "I thought you were going to keep your inquiry private."

Jace nodded. "I intended to, but after I found a database that listed the Bullfighter of the Year winners at a rodeo that used to be held up near Tyler and saw Tim's name, I had second thoughts. Tim is the one I met at Dee's. As soon as we talked this morning, I had no choice but to tell him how I came to have the buckle and why."

"Mom was probably taking me down another rabbit trail and throwing me off from learning the truth. Not the first time she's done that."

"Clint, the buckle does belong to me." Steele's gaze locked with Clint's as silence fell between them. "Your mom was speaking the truth."

A shock wave greater than the one he'd felt earlier when Lacy divulged her past came over him. He couldn't mean… "Are you saying you're the original owner of the buckle? I'm sorry my mom dragged you into my problem."

Steele leaned forward and rested his elbows on his knees. His gaze searched

Clint's face. "I mean that I am ninety-nine percent sure I'm your father."

Clint blinked. The man was spinning a fairy tale. No way would Steele have been involved with the likes of his mom. "That's hard to believe. I know you hail from San Antonio, and Mom never lived around here until after I was born."

"I had a feeling you'd have trouble believing my story." He opened a wood-carved box from an end table next to him and took out a photo. "I've carried this around in my wallet since you were a baby. It's of me and your mom and you. You must have been about three months old there." He held out the photo to Clint.

Hesitant to take the picture because he didn't want Steele to see his shaking hand, Clint stared at the photograph a moment. Then he swallowed hard and took the photo by one of its frayed edges. The snapshot looked to be taken outside in a park. He recognized Steele, but if he hadn't been told the attractive woman was his mom, he'd never have believed it. Colorful hoop earrings peeked out from behind her blond hair that fell in long waves over her shoulders. She wore a colorful top that was probably the style back then—a lot baggier than what he saw women wearing now. The baby resting in the crook of Steele's arm sported a headful of blond hair and looked healthy and content. He'd never seen a picture of himself as a baby or a small child and had nothing to compare it to for verification. He'd have to take Steele's word for it. No matter if the picture was of him, it still was a lie. They may have looked like a young, happy family, but sometimes pictures weren't worth a thousand words.

Clint looked at Jace. "You want to see it?"

Jace shook his head. "Tim showed it to me at the restaurant. You haven't changed a bit."

"Well, my hair is the same style." He handed the photo back to Tim. "I had no idea my mom used to look like that. The alcohol has taken its toll. How did you meet her?"

"We met after a rodeo at a bar north of Dallas. I was a bit of a rowdy back in those days and enjoyed my beer too much. As you can see, she was a looker, and it didn't take long for us to hook up. Soon we were living together, and whenever I wasn't at rodeos, we spent our time swilling beer and sleeping the day away. I was gone a lot, though. I think that's when she took to drinking at home and not just when she was at a watering hole. I'd come home and find the trash full of bottles or beer cans and her sleeping off her latest binge."

"Some things never change. She's still the same."

Steele frowned. "I'm sorry to hear that. About a year after we were together, she told me she was pregnant. I first thought she was bluffing or maybe had someone on the side. But when I figured out the week you were likely conceived, it coincided with a couple of weeks I was home. She thought I'd want her to get an abortion, but I was excited.

"Knowing I was about to be a dad changed me. I cut way back on the drinking and told her she needed to stop for the sake of the baby. She held back, but she couldn't stop it completely. I was worried that when you were born you'd be addicted to alcohol, but you weren't." His face lit up. "You were the greatest thing that ever happened to me. I stayed home for a few months and changed your diapers and held you every chance I got. I even took you out to the rodeo grounds and showed you off when the circuit was in town."

At a vision of Steele changing his diapers, Clint's eyes watered. He couldn't get caught up in the emotion. He had to keep his head. It made a nice story, but it didn't line up with what he'd heard for years. "If you felt that way, why did you abandon us?"

Color drained from Steele's face, and he looked off toward the large window overlooking the backyard. When he looked back at Clint, his eyes were watery too. "Son, I never abandoned you. Is that what your mother told you?"

"Yeah. She said you left for a rodeo one day and never came back."

Steele's face twisted into a scowl. He shook his head. "I've been afraid she told you something like that. Truth is, when you were around six months, I came home all excited to see you after a couple of weeks away. Your mom was nursing you and drinking a beer at the same time. She was drunk, to boot. I yelled at her, then grabbed up her beer and poured it into the sink. She blew up and said I had no right to order her around and she'd do as she pleased. We got into a bad fight, and you started squalling.

"She tried to stand and nearly lost her balance. I reached to take you away from her, but she wouldn't let go and ordered me out of the apartment. When I refused to leave, she threatened to call the cops and tell them I was abusing her and trying to kidnap her baby. I figured I'd leave for a few hours to let her cool off. When I came back later, all my belongings were outside the apartment door and the two of you were gone. She'd managed to clear out of there in the hours I was away."

Clint fisted his hands, his nails digging into his palms. "You walked away without trying to find us? Without money, she couldn't have gotten far."

"I had a stash of cash in my dresser drawer, and it was missing. It wasn't a lot, but it was enough to buy her a bus ticket somewhere if she didn't spend it all on beer." Tears welled in Steele's eyes. "I tried to find you, but it was as if you two had vaporized. Several years later, I traced her to a trailer park down near Houston. I went to see her one night and demanded to see you. I told her that if she didn't let me, I'd get a court order. She still refused. I followed through on my threat, and after the court order had been served, I went back. She was gone."

Clint closed his eyes as the memory of a long-ago night exploded into his thoughts. "When I was five or six, I woke up to yelling coming from the living room. The trailer's walls were paper-thin. A man was demanding to see me, and Mom screamed that he'd never see me again as long as he lived. I wondered if it was my dad, but later she told me it was an old boyfriend who was delusional and she didn't know where my daddy was. I think that's when we moved to San Antonio to another trailer and she changed our last name to Palmer."

Steele winced and shook his head. "No wonder I couldn't find you. If she's never stopped drinking, how did she manage to pay rent and feed you?"

"By the oldest profession in the world."

Steele grimaced. "I'm sorry. I should have done more. That's no atmosphere for a boy to grow up in."

"It wasn't. Getting to know Jace saved my life." He glanced at his best friend. "I got interested in rodeo during high school, and that's where he and I met. He saw the squalor I was living in and talked his parents into taking me in. I've lived on their ranch ever since."

"It didn't bother her that you moved in with another family?"

Clint shrugged. "No. Not having to feed me gave her more money to spend on booze. She applied for disability, and with the help of a lawyer with questionable tactics, she qualified for a monthly check. I really doubt she could work anymore anyway. The booze has numbed her brain so much that she can't focus for more than ten minutes at a time before she's looking for something else to do. I only see her every couple of months. The McGowans are my family these days."

"You can count me in on that if you want. Being your family, I mean."

Clint stared at his feet. What was wrong with him? Here was his likely flesh-and-blood father sitting in front of him. A man he'd admired for years. And now he was almost hoping a DNA test would prove Steele to be mistaken. He could be, what with all the men his mother had been with.

Did it matter so much that his potential father was a Christian? Was that why he didn't want it to be true? Clint hadn't abandoned his friendship with Jace when he got religion, or Carolyn either, for that matter. An urge to throw caution aside, to give Steele the hug he'd been saving for his dad for most of his life, fought to be acknowledged. But he had to keep his emotions out of it—to not get too excited before he had hard evidence, no matter how Steele's story lined up with what he remembered. "I'd like you to take a DNA test. You willing?"

Steele's smile faded. "Sure. Whatever you want. You prefer to arrange it, or should I?"

"You can take care of it. Just tell me where to go to have it done."

"I'll check with my doctor and let you know. How can I reach you?"

He gave Steele his phone number, then faced Jace. He had to get out of there, to digest what had just happened. "Ready to go?"

His buddy nodded. "Whenever you are."

Steele stood along with the men and then looked at Jace. "Thanks so much for helping Clint during high school."

Jace smiled and rested his hand on Clint's shoulder. "My family has always loved Clint. He's like my brother from another mother."

Like a bolt of lightning, awareness of family came over Clint. His alleged biological dad and Jace, as close to him as a real brother. Not too shabby for a boy who grew up feeling cheated in that regard.

Clint glanced at Steele. "I almost forgot. One of the reasons I went looking for my biological father was to find out about any history of heart disease in his family. I have an enlarged heart, and my doctor wants to know."

Steele shook his head. "Not that I know of, but I also have an enlarged heart. It's a malady of athletes."

"That's what we were thinking, but we wanted to be sure." Clint grinned at Jace. "If the DNA proves I'm his son, it looks like I'll be back bullfighting again." He held out his hand to Steele. "Good to meet you."

Steele took his hand, but instead of shaking it, he pulled Clint toward him into the hug Clint had been holding back. "A handshake is too impersonal. You don't know how happy I am to see you."

They stepped out of the embrace, and Steele went to a bookcase and took down a brown book. "I'd like to give this to you. You say you don't believe the same as I do about God. You have no idea what I was like while you were growing up. I wasn't a very nice guy in private. This book changed all that." He held out the Bible. "Please, humor me, son, and at least take a look at it. I've underlined several verses that really spoke to me during my transition. Without God, I doubt I'd still be here today."

At being called *son*, a warm feeling rushed over Clint. All at once he sensed that Steele really was his dad. If the DNA said otherwise, he'd be devastated. He'd take the Bible, of course, but it didn't mean he'd have to read it. They could still be father and son without his worshipping a God who didn't want him.

Chapter 16

Clint approached the tiny run-down trailer. Its teardrop shape made it at least half the size of the two-bedroom trailer he'd shared with his mom until his junior year of school. This trailer was in no better shape. Rust spots and faded white paint covered the top half, while a garish lime green on the bottom probably concealed something worse than rust. Tucked away in a grove of small trees, making it difficult to see the neighbors on either side, Clint had to wonder if its placement was by design, given the mobile home's neglected appearance.

He stepped around a faded pink flamingo lying on its side on the only patch of grass and approached the door. Without Mom having a working phone, there was no way to call ahead, but given that it was only ten in the morning, he doubted she was even out of bed. Diane Palmer operated on her own timetable, her nights not usually ending until at least three in the morning.

He fisted his hand and banged on the metal door, waited a minute, then banged harder. The dingy curtain covering the window to his left fluttered. Probably her, kneeling on her lumpy mattress, checking to see who had the nerve to visit at such an early hour.

A minute later, the door swung open and the nasty blend of stale cigarette smoke and booze assaulted him. He retched and swallowed hard against the bile. The last time he saw her, she'd looked like something the dog had dragged home. Today she appeared even shoddier, with a ratty robe wrapped around her thin body, graying hair, and a sleep crease in her cheek. Nothing like the photo of what-had-once-been that Steele carried around for the past thirty-one years. She backed up so he had room to enter.

Clint stepped into the stifling space, and the heat and smell nearly caused him to gag again. He mentally ordered himself to stay calm.

Mom reached toward the dinette table on her left for a pack of cigarettes. "What are you doin' here so early?"

"It's after ten. It's not early."

She shook a cigarette out of the pack and stuck it into her mouth, then glanced around. "It is when you don't get to sleep until almost five a.m. There's some matches here somewhere."

He picked up a matchbook from the table and handed it to her. "Right under your nose. Where are your glasses?"

She grabbed the matches and lit the smoke, then tossed the spent match into an overflowing ashtray next to the sink. "They broke a couple of weeks ago. I need to wait to have them replaced. Do you know how expensive those things are?"

"You'd have the money if you didn't spend your disability check on booze."

Her dull eyes sparked. "I don't spend all my money on booze. I have rent and food to buy."

He shrugged and bit back the accusing words he wanted to say. "Well, you manage to feed your addiction somehow."

"It's not an addiction. I can quit anytime I want. Right now I don't want to. Why are you here? I'm sure it's not to see how your dear mother is doing. You haven't come around in weeks."

He pulled a handkerchief from his back pocket, lifted his ball cap, and blotted his forehead. "Your air-conditioning not working again?"

"Never got it fixed. You get used to the heat after a while."

Maybe she could, but not him. Not when it was ninety-five degrees in the shade. "Remember that belt buckle you gave me when I asked who my daddy was?"

She straightened. "Yeah. What about it?"

"I found him."

"Found who?"

"You know who. Why didn't you ever tell me that Tim Steele's my dad—or that he came to see me when I was a kid and you sent him away?"

"You have no proof he's your dad." She looked toward the window overlooking the table. "There were others."

She was right; she had had other men in her life. Lots of men. "Tim thinks he was the only one you were with while you were pregnant with me. He was living with you and not on the road."

Her shoulders slumped. "So? He deserted us."

"The way I heard it, you kicked him out when he wanted you to stop drinking around me."

"It was a long time ago. I don't remember."

"I think you do, Mom." He pointed to a waste can filled with discarded beer cans and a whiskey bottle. "Some things never change, do they? When are you going to get some help?"

He looked her in the eyes. Were those tears from remorse or from something else? "It's not too late to make a change, Mom. Do that, and you'd have enough money for a new air conditioner." He turned toward the door.

"How is Tim?"

Clint started and faced her. "Doing okay. He's married and a Christian now. Gives talks in churches. Also makes guest appearances at rodeos and sometimes teaches bullfighting at clinics."

"What's his wife like?"

"I didn't meet her. She gave us privacy the day we visited."

"How'd you find him?"

"Jace did."

"Well, now that you've learned the truth, you can leave me alone." She pushed the cigarette that had burned nearly to the filter into the ashtray, causing the ashes already there to spill over onto the counter. "I'm sorry I've made your life so miserable. See ya around." She shuffled toward the rumpled mattress at the opposite end of the tiny space. "I'm goin' back to bed."

Clint let himself out. He'd taken a shower before coming, but now he felt like he needed another.

Arriving back at the ranch, he headed straight for the barn. He wasn't kidding about needing a shower. All he could smell on the fifteen-minute drive was the odor of smoke. Not a good impression if someone stopped by about the bulls.

As he started up the steps to his living quarters, Jace yelled from the office, "Clint! That you?"

He reversed direction and walked to the office doorway instead. Jace sat at the desk, staring at the computer monitor.

He stayed put in the entrance, not wanting to permeate the air. "Can you wait a few minutes? I reek of stale cigarette smoke and sweat. I need a shower."

Jace sniffed. "Whew. I see what you mean. I take it your mom was home?"

"Of course. Her ten a.m. is our six a.m. I woke her up."

"At least you found her sober. I can handle the smell." He gestured to the chair in front of the desk. "Take a load off."

Clint stepped inside and sat. "I guess if you can stand the odor, I can too. What do you want?"

"First, how did she take your finding your father?"

"She was defensive and angry, but then as I was leaving, she seemed to soften some and asked how he was doing. I'm thinking I'll buy her a new air conditioner. That tin box she lives in had to be at least a hundred and twenty inside, and her old AC is broken." He grimaced. "I hate her for what she did to take away time from my dad when I was growing up, and for not letting us be a real family, but I can't let her stay in that oven."

"So you think that by buying her an air conditioner, you'll make it up to her for hating her?"

"She actually kind of apologized to me for messing up my life. I can't bring myself to accept the apology, but the least I can do is buy her an air conditioner."

Jace scrubbed his face with his palms. "That's gotta be hard. I'm not going to push my faith on you, Clint, but I can't help but encourage you to read the Bible Tim gave you. I think that if you do, you'll find the answer on how to forgive her."

Clint rolled his eyes. "You Christians think you have all the answers."

"No, but God does. Think about it. You'll know when the time is right to take a look."

"I'll keep it in mind."

Jace grinned. "That's all I can ask. Now, on another topic, we need to set up a plan for you to buy into the bull-stock business. I was thinking we could arrange a deduction from your paycheck. How does that sound?"

Relieved to not be talking about Mom or the Bible, Clint grinned too. "Now that's something I can buy into ... literally."

A wry smile took over Jace's features. "That's really a groaner. While you shower, I'll compose an agreement for both of us to sign."

After washing up and changing his shirt and jeans, Clint stopped back in the office, and he and Jace discussed what amount should be deducted from Clint's pay and for how long. Jace typed it into the computer and then printed a copy of the agreement. "I'll e-mail this to Syd to look over, to make sure I did it right. If she gets back to me before the day is out, I'll let you know, and then we can both sign it."

Clint grinned. "Nice having a lawyer in the family. Talk about roller-coaster emotions. Within a couple of hours, I've gone from shock to confusion to anger to euphoria."

Jace laughed. "Let's hope the roller coaster is now halted. We may not have the agreement signed yet, but I think, having come this far, that we can at least shake on it." He stood and came around the desk.

Clint jumped to his feet and took Jace's hand—and much like what Steele had done with him earlier that week, he pulled Jace into a quick hug.

After they separated, Clint had to keep himself from raising a fist in the air and pumping it several times, as he'd seen some bull riders do after a high-scoring eight-second ride.

He looked at the wall clock. Too late to head out to the bottoms before lunch. Instead, he walked over to the house in hopes of snagging Lacy for a chat.

Seeing his mom's squalor and unkempt condition helped assure him that Lacy wasn't like her at all and it was wrong to lump her into the same category. He needed to make amends.

He didn't have to like that she had become involved with a louse like Jennings, but she wasn't the first person he knew who'd made the same mistake. He'd seen some of those young barrel racers start on the circuit and be all starry-eyed at meeting rodeo stars they'd only seen from the stands. Every season, some of those guys boasted they could count on a hot night or two with the new crop of racers. He'd never joined in—and was glad of that a few years ago when cops showed up at a rodeo and arrested a bulldogger for sexual assault of an underage girl. Granted, the fifteen-year-old could have passed for at least eighteen, but that didn't make it right. They never saw the cowboy on the circuit again, and word was, he got time in prison and two years' probation.

Clint entered the kitchen. Lacy stood at the island, her blond hair pulled back into a ponytail. She looked up from mixing potato salad and offered a smile that didn't reach her eyes.

He glanced at a large platter filled with ham, turkey, and sliced cheeses. "Looks like a make-your-own-sandwich kind of lunch. Is that going to hold us over? We're heading out to check on the calves at the bottoms after lunch."

"I know it's not the usual big meal we do at noon, but it's too hot for anything else. It should keep you going, along with the potato salad and brownies for dessert."

He slid onto a stool. "I'm just giving you a hard time. I'm so used to your gourmet meals these days."

She smirked. "Even my chicken Marsala?"

"Even that."

"I hardly had time to get all this on the table. I took Aunt Carolyn to her first round of chemo today. There's enough here to make two sandwiches, one for now and one for later."

Feeling like a jerk for forgetting Carolyn's health ordeal, Clint grimaced. "I forgot that started today. How's she doing?"

"She did great through the treatment, but despite getting meds for nausea, she's not doing too well. They said that might happen. I think she's finally sleeping, though."

He glanced in the direction of the mudroom door. "Before anyone else gets here, I need to apologize for how I reacted when you told me about the … um … baby. I wasn't very understanding."

She pressed her lips together and looked away. "That's okay. I know it was a shock."

"No, it's not okay. You don't deserve that kind of treatment."

Tears filled her eyes, and Clint fought the urge to leap off the stool and take her into his arms. Why couldn't he gather enough courage to admit how he felt about her before she got too far into her plans to leave? "Lacy, we need to talk about something else. I should have said how I feel about—"

Voices sounded from the mudroom.

Lacy turned and scooted toward the main entry hall. "The potato salad is ready. Tell them to start making their sandwiches. I'll be out in a minute." The powder-room door slammed shut as Jace and Luke walked into the kitchen.

They looked around and then at Clint. "Is it only the three of us?" Jace asked.

Clint stepped over to the island. "Lacy will be back in a minute. We're to start making our own sandwiches. I plan to make an extra one to take for later. You guys might want to do the same."

While the men sat on stools at the island, eating in silence, Clint kept his focus on the entrance into the main hall … but Lacy never returned.

Jace finished his sandwich, then picked up his empty plate and carried it to the sink. After he stuck it into the dishwasher, he opened several cabinets and, finally, the fridge. "I was hoping there was at least a plate of cookies she forgot to put out."

"I think her mind has been on other things." Clint picked up the plate of meat and cheese, covered it with plastic wrap, and then stuck it into the fridge. He opened the freezer. "There are some brownies in here. I think she intended to serve them and forgot."

"Leave them on the counter," Jace said. "I'm going to check on Mom before I grab some for later. Meet you at the barn in ten?"

"Sounds good. Luke, help yourself to the brownies." Clint wandered across the main hall and into the study where Lacy sometimes liked to sit and read. Her favorite leather chair was empty. The opportunity to talk had evaporated. Had she sensed what he was about to say and had run before he could say it? Or was he reading too much into her actions? Between her aunt's health, her plans to head east to school, and Jennings popping back up in her life, she had a lot on her emotional plate. At least he'd gotten his apology out … but there was far more he needed to say before it was too late. Maybe he'd take a different route, one he was sure she'd like.

Lacy stood at her bedroom window. Across the way, Jace and Clint rode their horses down the lane toward the back pasture they called the bottoms. Good. Clint would be out of reach for at least a couple of hours. His wanting to have a talk beyond his apology had unsettled her. She shouldn't have avoided him, but with so much going on—as much as she'd been yearning to hear that he wanted to take their relationship to the next level—now was not the time. And it possibly never would be. After all she'd been through, she realized that because of Clint's lack of interest in God, he wasn't the man for her anyway.

Surely moving away from the ranch and not seeing Clint every day would snuff out what was left of the flame of emotion she still felt for him. Moving would help ease her into a life without Clint around, but other factors had to be considered: Aunt Carolyn's cancer … and the reality that she'd have to leave her beloved Shiloh behind. Moving was seeming less the answer, more and more.

The obvious solution was to attend the culinary school in San Antonio part-time. But then, going to the New York school would put her close to where her daughter lived—if Austin was speaking the truth, not lying about a PI and looking for a fast buck. She should tell him to get lost and have nothing more to do with him. But the ache for information about her child kept pushing her toward taking a chance on him. She dropped to her knees and stared up at the ceiling. "Lord, help me in this, please. Show me what I should do."

Chapter 17

Lacy stood from her kneeling position, frustrated that no answer seemed forthcoming. What she ought to do was confront Austin and get his assurance that she wasn't throwing good money after bad.

She scanned the room for her phone and then remembered she'd left it in the kitchen. She needed to go there anyway, to clean up from lunch. Stepping into the kitchen, her mouth fell open. The dishwasher rumbled through its wash cycle, the sink sparkled, and the island had been cleared off. She crossed to the fridge and opened it. A small plate containing several brownies sat next to the platter holding the leftover meats, tightly covered with plastic wrap. Even the condiments were tucked into their usual places on the door.

Her heart swelled. She loved those guys for doing this. Now she had time to make that call. She grabbed her phone and headed for the back door, seeking a spot far enough from the house where she wouldn't be overheard. Her aunt had no idea what had been going on with Austin, and she didn't need to know— ever. Anywhere near the house was taking a risk if Aunt Carolyn decided to take a walk.

She saddled Kip, the paint gelding she'd been using since Shiloh had taken sick. With Luke mucking stalls and Jace and Clint checking on the herd, she was certain she'd have her favorite leafy spot next to the water all to herself. Lacy took the trail to a portion of the river that crossed through ranch property. Easily accessible by car from the ranch's main entrance, over the years the family had kept up a clearing next to the water for bonfires and picnics. The last event had been the celebration of Jace and Syd's engagement that ended with the happy couple being tossed into the water—something of a tradition done to the guests of honor no matter the circumstance.

Unlike the party that day, today the river offered Lacy the peace and quiet she craved. At the clearing, she tied Kip to a sapling and tapped on her phone's screen several times.

Austin picked up. "Hey, Lacy. You got good news?"

"Aren't you the one who is to have good news for me?"

A low chuckle came through the connection. "Not until I see a thou in my checking account."

She grimaced. "Yeah, about that thou. I need to be assured that this isn't one of your ill-fated schemes. I don't want to take the money from my school-tuition fund and not have something to show for it."

"School? I thought you already went to school."

"That was for a business degree. Now I'm going to study something else— something I've wanted to do for a very long time."

"And what is that?"

"Culinary school."

"Isn't that a glorified cooking school? What do you need that for?"

She hated the sneer in his voice. "To learn about being a chef and then maybe own a restaurant."

She waited through several moments of silence. "Austin, you still there?"

"I'm here. Just surprised at how you think I've remained the same guy I was back when we were together, when it sounds like you've changed a lot yourself. I'm different now too, Lacy. The guy I was then isn't the man I am today. You can't know how much I regret the way I ignored our child and you."

"You have a funny way of showing it."

"What? Aren't I making a way for you—for us—to be able to check on our little girl and make sure she's doing okay and in a safe place? If I could arrange for you to go to her house and see her in person, I would. But you know that's not possible. You can save more money for your education. Knowledge about your daughter surely must be more important than school. It is for me."

"You're not planning on going back to school."

"How do you know? I could be. But the money I'm using was earmarked for a custom-made saddle."

Custom-made saddles were pricey, and he sounded sincere. But was he? "Give me the PI's name and contact information, and I'll send the money straight to him."

"Can't. I promised I'd keep it between him and me. He has to be extremely careful. He could lose his license if word got out about what he's doing."

A chill ran down her back. "I don't like it, Austin."

"We all have to take risks sometimes. PIs often take risks to serve their clients. It's for the greater good. He won't be hanging around their house long. He'll go in the morning about the time she's leaving for school and take a couple of shots. Mission accomplished."

Her heart swelled at the thought of seeing what her baby girl looked like. The all-too-familiar pang of guilt for giving away her daughter filled her chest.

It was bad enough that Austin had stirred the flame that was low enough to ignore most days. Now it was a roaring fire that refused to be stifled. And to rub it in, she had stumbled across a television program last night about the joys of birthing and raising one's child. It had been all she could do to not show emotion with Aunt Carolyn right beside her.

She heaved a breath. "Okay, I can have the money for you on Monday." She clicked off the call and stared at the river. She was doing it for the greater good, wasn't she? If she was, why did she feel so uneasy?

Chapter 18

Clint mounted Jax and then joined his new business partner, who waited outside the barn astride Charley. Together, they headed out on the trail that led to the bottoms. At last check, several calves had been born, and they needed to tag the babies to identify them with their mothers. They'd intended to do this sooner, but shortly after they started out, Jace got a call from someone who wanted to look at a bull they had up for sale, and that brought them back to the barn. After a half hour of negotiation, the man walked away empty-handed.

They rode in silence for a short time until Jace spoke. "Wonder what was up with Lacy. She never did join us at lunch."

"I know. I was wondering too. By the way, before you and Luke came in for lunch, I apologized to her for the way I reacted when she told me about the baby. After hearing Tim's side of how it was for him and my mom, and then going over to Mom's place this morning, I realized that Lacy is nothing like her. I was wrong to lump her in that category."

"Good to hear. How did she respond?"

He looked at Jace and shrugged. "Okay, I think. You and Luke came before we finished the conversation."

"Maybe you can finish it now. Look who's coming up the trail."

He turned his focus from Jace. Had Lacy been out here the whole time they were at lunch?

She reached the men and brought her horse to a halt. Between her forced smile and her reddened eyes, it was all Clint could do not to take her aside and try to comfort her. But if he'd been the cause for those tears, that wouldn't go over too well.

Lacy looked from Clint to Jace. "Fancy meeting you guys out here. I was just at the river to reflect and pray. I thought you headed to the bottoms long ago."

"We did, but something came up and we had to head back," Jace said. "We think we've got a couple of calves that need tagging. Want to join us?"

She shook her head. "No thanks. I've got something I need to do in town."

Clint wanted to ask what was so important in town. Anything to do with her tears? "We missed you at lunch."

She nodded and fiddled with the reins. "I know. I'm sorry. Just wasn't hungry. Got a lot on my mind right now."

He wanted to tell her he was there for her, but her evasiveness made him uncomfortable. She wouldn't be planning to give Jennings that money after all, would she? Not after agreeing with him that the guy was not to be trusted. No doubt her child's adoptive mama loved her a lot, but the girl likely had no idea how much her biological mama loved her too. Probably figured that if she did, she wouldn't have given her to someone else to raise. If she only knew. While he was growing up, what he wouldn't have given to experience even half the love Lacy seemed to feel for her child.

Jace clicked his tongue, and Charley started to move. "We gotta get to the pasture. We'll see you later, Lace. Let's go, Clint."

Clint got Jax trotting. Once Lacy was far enough down the trail to be out of earshot, he looked over at Jace. "Got any idea what's bothering Lacy?"

"I was about to ask you the same thing. Do you think she's upset about my mom's cancer?"

"I'm sure she is concerned about that—we all are. But I think it's got something to do with Jennings."

They came to the clearing that opened onto the pasture.

"Ha! I see a calf." Jace got Charley moving toward the newborn, and Clint and Jax followed.

As they approached the calf, its mother stepped closer, determined that nothing was going to hurt her baby. Sometimes the mama cows got real feisty. This one let out a long, low bellow, and Jace spoke softly to her. An unwanted thought popped into Clint's mind, one he'd had before when tagging calves. The motherly instinct wasn't lost on most animals. He'd bet this bovine would fight to the death for her baby.

He stuffed down the wave of sadness and signaled Jax to stop. No need for them all to approach the calf. Jace already had his rope circling as he slowly brought his horse closer. When he flung the loop toward the calf, it landed softly around the animal's small head. Charley halted, and Jace stopped him from stepping back to tighten the slack. There was no need for that because the calf was so young. The animal stood frozen, looking bewildered.

Clint grabbed the tagging gun from the leather pouch affixed to his saddle and dismounted. He slowly approached as Jace gently lifted the calf and laid it onto the ground. While Jace straddled the small animal to keep him secure, Clint slipped a tag into the device, making sure it was in the right position. He knelt beside the calf and, in three short maneuvers, attached the tag to the little one's ear.

By now the unhappy mother was bellowing constantly and coming closer.

"It's all good, Mama. We didn't hurt the little guy." Jace let go and the calf stood, taking a moment to regain his balance. His mama ran her nose over him and then looked at Jace as if to say, "Try that again and you'll answer to me." She gave her baby a little push with her nose, and he trotted after her.

Jace scanned the pasture. "I see another new one over there." He pointed across the grassy field. They mounted up and headed that direction.

After tagging two more calves, they inspected the rest of the herd and determined that they had five pregnant cows, and two appeared to be ready to deliver within the next few days. Over the next several weeks, they'd need to check for new calves daily. Jace said they'd do the next check with Luke, and then after that, Luke would accompany either Jace or Clint while the other would tend to the bulls.

Jace attached the rope to his saddle. "Hopefully soon you'll be able to scratch tagging off your to-do list, except for when we start impregnating some of our own cows to produce new bucking bulls. I know that's a job you like better."

"What made you think I don't enjoy tagging?"

"I've noticed the grimace on your face whenever we do it."

"I hadn't realized you'd paid attention. It's not the procedure I dislike. I hate the reminder that cows care more for their offspring than my own mother ever cared for me. That really bites."

Jace stared at him. "Bro, I had no idea your pain went so deep."

"Of course you didn't. You have a mom who loves you and would act just like those mama cows back there if any of her sons were in danger."

"I think you can count yourself with me and my brothers as far as my mom is concerned."

"I don't know about that."

Jace's eyes widened. "Dude, after you got injured at the rodeo in Illinois last year, you should have heard her carry on when I made that trip home with you still in the hospital. She knew the circumstances here required me to come, but if Lacy hadn't stayed behind to be with you, I think she would have flown up there to do it herself."

Clint stared at him. "Really?"

"Yes, really. She loves you like a son."

They continued riding, Jace behind Clint through a narrow portion of the trail. Clint welcomed the hush as he digested what he'd just heard.

Jace's phone ringing intruded on the silence, and Clint halted his horse and twisted to look back to see whether Jace would take the call or send it to voice mail.

Jace took the phone from its holster, glanced at it, and then swiped the screen. "Hi, honey." After a pause, he laughed. "Thanks, but I'll stick to ranching and running a bull-stock business and leave the lawyering to you. See you tonight. Love you too."

Jace grinned. "Syd says the contract looks good, no edits needed. When we get back to the barn, I'll print it up and we can sign it. Let's get going."

Clint grinned back at his friend and business partner and nudged Jax into a trot. The first thing he planned after they signed the contract and he got cleaned up was to say hello to Carolyn. He had to admit, since her diagnosis, he preferred avoiding her, unable to bear the thought of her suffering. If she'd ever expressed parental feelings toward him, they must have gone right over his head. But that didn't matter. Jace had said all the words Clint needed to hear.

Lacy parked her Renegade in front of the bank but didn't turn off the engine. She'd planned to wait until Monday to make the withdrawal, but after giving more thought to her discussion with Austin, she'd made up her mind to take the risk. Best to get the money today. By Monday she might chicken out. She could attend culinary school in San Antonio and then transfer to the New York school down the road. Staying at the ranch and attending classes on a part-time basis would be more economical, and she could help her aunt through her illness that way.

Jace had called while she was on her way to the bank—Doc Forster had stopped by and checked on Shiloh. Her horse was strong enough to be ridden … and that gave her yet another reason to stay. Shiloh meant the world to her, and to go off and leave her behind would be torture.

If the PI was successful in snagging a picture of Alicia, she'd have that and Shiloh to keep her going until her child turned eighteen in five years. As far as Clint was concerned, she still had feelings for him, but she'd done okay up to now with keeping their relationship in the friend zone. Maybe that was all they were meant to be anyway—friends only.

A blast of icy air hit her as she stepped into the bank's small branch office. Wishing she'd grabbed her denim jacket from the back seat, she rubbed her bare arms. A young man, who looked to be barely out of high school but wore the bank's staff uniform, approached her. His megawatt smile could have lit up the room on its own. Too bad it seemed insincere.

"Hi. How can I help you?"

Feeling as if she were in the middle of a clandestine operation, she avoided looking him in the eyes. "No help needed. I'm here to make a withdrawal." Not bothering to acknowledge his response about being there if she needed anything, she made a beeline to a small table to fill out a withdrawal form.

She held the pen over the blank amount line and drew in a breath. Although a thousand dollars was a lot of money to her, in today's economy, it was not that big of a deal. But it had taken her almost a full year to save that much. In all the years she'd attended the NFR in Las Vegas, she'd never once gambled—but this gamble offered a big payout.

Before she could stop herself, she scribbled the amount she needed on the form and then moved to the line snaking its way forward as one of the two tellers became available.

She checked the time. Coming on Saturday, a half hour before closing, was a bad idea. Maybe she should wait until Monday. Or talk it over with Sydney first. Even though she wasn't practicing law anymore, Syd was still a lawyer and would have good judgment.

"Next, please."

Lacy snapped out of her reverie. How had she moved to the head of the line without realizing it? She stepped up to the window. She'd take the money out now but talk to Syd before she gave it to Austin. She handed the withdrawal slip to the teller. "I'd like to make a withdrawal, please, in cash. One hundred dollar bills."

After a quick stop at a tack-and-feed store for some special horse treats, Lacy pulled into her usual parking place in front of the ranch house and climbed out. She hooked her crossbody bag over her head and gripped the purse as if she were carting around a gold bar. Her first order of business was to find a safe hiding place for the cash and then contact Syd to set up some "girl time" before Monday.

Inside, after a quick glance into the empty study on her right, she turned left and entered the kitchen. "Hey, I'm back. Anyone here?" Satisfied with no response, she crossed through the family room and entered the bedroom wing.

Lacy strode down the hall, past the twins' room and then Jace's old room— now serving as a guest room—to her suite at the end of the hall. She stepped into the room and let out the breath she'd been holding. Then she chuckled. What was with all the drama? She was safe. She hadn't stolen the money. It was hers to do with as she wished. So why did she feel like a kid stealing from the cookie jar? She pushed the bedroom door shut. It didn't quite close, but no one was around. And even if they were, they'd have no idea what she was doing. She opened her underwear drawer, pulled the bank envelope out of her purse, and slid it under the things into the far corner.

"I thought I might find you here."

She jumped and spun around.

Chapter 19

Her heart pounding like a jackhammer, Lacy placed her hands behind her back and pushed the drawer shut. "Who let you into the house, Austin, and why are you in my room?"

Austin pushed his Stetson back, allowing a dark blond curl to fall over his forehead, and smirked. "I saw you enter the house as I was driving up. You left the front door unlocked, and no one answered my knock. I called out your name, but you didn't answer. I figured you must be in your bedroom."

"The door is always unlocked. We've had no trouble here until now."

He glanced around. "Nice house. I don't remember it being this large the last time I was here. This big room yours? Looks more like a master."

"It used to be, until they added the wing on the other side of the house." What was she doing chatting like it was a normal thing for him to be in her bedroom? "You should have waited until someone came to the door, instead of barging in like you did. But you never did have good manners. You need to leave now."

He snickered. "You're cute when you get riled up. As I was saying, this was the only bedroom door that wasn't wide open, and I'd already looked in the other rooms. Figured this one had to be yours. Did you get the money?"

Never had she considered shooting someone until now—not to kill, but a good shot to his leg to show she meant business. She clenched her jaw. "I meant what I said. No one invited you into this house. Get out of here now, or I'll …"

He chuckled. "You'll what? Shoot me?" He glanced around. "I don't see any weapons. Come on, Lacy. Just tell me. Did you get the money?"

She drew in a breath to calm herself and then, using wide steps, moved around him and into the hall. "I refuse to have a conversation with you in my bedroom. We can talk on the front porch."

He gripped her arm and squeezed. Pain shot through her bicep. She wrenched her arm toward herself, but he tightened his grip. She swallowed a scream.

"You're friskier than a calf. I may have to use my roping skills on you. I think it might be better to speak about our matter privately and not outside."

His stage whisper could have awakened the dead. She'd never been more thankful that her aunt's master bedroom wasn't on the same hallway. She needed to get him outside. And he had to be distracted if she was ever going to break loose.

"I think it's nice that you're finally interested in Alicia."

"Who?"

"Our daughter. I'm sure that isn't her name now, but it's what I've always called her. Alicia Jennings sounds nice."

His hold loosened. "It does at that. I bet she's as pretty as the name too."

She yanked her arm out of his grip and stepped back several feet. "There will be no discussion unless it's held on the porch. Besides, I haven't yet made up my mind."

She marched toward the front door, assured by the sound of his boot heels hitting the wooden floor that he was following.

He grabbed her arm once more. "Not so fast, little lady. I meant what I said. It's better if we have our discussion inside."

She jerked around, the motion snapping her arm out of his loose grip, and glared at him. "We talk in here and my aunt will hear us, and she'll call 911 if she thinks I'm in trouble."

He nodded toward the front of the house. "Go on, then. Make it fast."

She didn't stop until they stepped through the front door and onto the porch. Then she faced him. "I don't know why you came all the way here from town without checking with me first. I'll let you know Monday or Tuesday whether I'm going along with your plan."

Fire lit his eyes. "You little hypocrite. If you're messing with me, you'll be sorry. If you change your mind, don't think I'm going to show you the picture of our daughter after I pay the guy from my own funds."

She narrowed her eyes. "You haven't given me any guarantee the guy will even get a picture. Seems to me he shouldn't be paid in full until he delivers. Or is the two grand only part of his fee?"

He looked toward the porch ceiling. "He'll probably ask for more."

"Another reason I have to think and pray about it."

He sneered. "As if God cares. Aren't you on His condemned list?"

"There's something called forgiveness. We all need it, including you." She glanced toward the barn. "Here comes my cousin. You know Jace, don't you?"

He started for the steps. "We've met. But I need to get going. I'll call you on Monday morning. I trust by then you'll have come to your senses."

She didn't move until he'd climbed into his truck and headed toward the road. His tires spit gravel as he sped down the lane.

"Was that who I think it was?" Jace asked as he mounted the porch steps.

She faced her cousin. "If you're thinking Austin Jennings, the answer is yes. He had the nerve to come into the house uninvited and found me in my room." Trembling, she fell into his outstretched arms and briefly pressed her face against his chest. "It was so scary. I looked around for some kind of weapon to knock him out. Then I mentally asked God for help and got the courage to stand up to him. Managed to move him out here."

She stepped back, fighting off the urge to tell him what Austin was really after. "Were you coming to the house for something?"

The skin around Jace's eyes tightened, and he fisted his hands. "The dude doesn't trespass on our property and get away with it. We need to press charges."

"No!"

He gaped at her. "What do you mean by that?"

"I mean, not yet. Jace, please give me time. I know this sounds dumb, but I'm to give him my answer to something on Monday. If it's no, then you're free to do whatever you want."

He rested his fists on his hips. "I don't understand."

"I know. You will in time. Trust me. Were you coming to the house for something besides checking on me?"

He shook his head. "No. We just got back from tagging calves, and I noticed y'all standing here. Your body language looked as if my presence might be needed."

"He really is a creep, Jace. I'm glad now that he wanted nothing to do with the baby. What if he had and I'd married him?"

He grimaced. "You'd likely be divorced by now. I know how hard it was for you to give her up to be adopted, but you did the right thing."

Her eyes ached as pressure built, and she squeezed them shut. If she'd kept Alicia, would her daughter have loved horses too? Maybe she'd be interested in chasing barrels like her mom.

"I need to get back to the barn. You going to be okay?"

Jace's voice broke into her thoughts. She nodded. "I'll be sure to lock all the doors from now on. You'll have to knock when you come back for supper." She paused and then asked, "Is Syd around today? I might stop over later and see if she'd like to go for coffee."

"She's busy preparing the stalls in our new barn so we can start keeping our two horses over there. She'd enjoy having a good reason to stop."

As he strode over the gravel, his phone rang. He put the instrument to his ear as he entered the barn.

Lacy turned and went inside, locking the door behind her and feeling safer than she had over the last hour. She tugged her phone from her pocket and hit Syd's name on her contact list.

As Clint was removing the saddle blanket from Jax, voices sounded from the office. Seemed Doc was back. Curious, he positioned the saddle on the stall railing, walked down the aisle to the office door, and leaned against the doorframe.

Doc sat in front of Jace, who sat behind the desk. "The guy is worse than I thought," Jace was saying. "He's been hitting on Lacy and had the nerve to show up and come inside the house uninvited. What if Luke had been around and recognized him? No telling what he might have done to cover his tracks. I hope the cops catch up with him fast before he does more damage."

He looked up at Clint. "Glad you're here. Have a seat. You aren't going to believe this. Harold Warren, Zorro's owner, sent this photo to Doc of the stable hand he suspects stole the horse." He held out an image printed on photo stock paper.

Clint settled in the empty chair next to Doc and took the photo. His jaw dropped. "This for real? I'm surprised he let his picture be taken."

"He didn't know it was," Doc said. "It was during an employee picnic and Harold was casually taking photos of the event. On a hunch, he started looking through his pictures and found it."

"You can't make this stuff up." Jace looked at Clint. "Can any more surprises happen around here?"

Clint studied the picture. Jennings's hair was shorter than he wore it now. In the photo, the cowboy attire had been replaced by a horse-stable uniform of maroon polo shirt and khakis, no hat.

Doc looked from Clint to Jace. "I already sent the picture to the police, and they ran the info through their database. Turns out the man has quite a history and they've been looking for him a long while. Jennings and his partner have been moving around and using different aliases. One of them would take a job at a horse farm or training facility, and after he'd had time to observe the horses, he'd select one that would be easy to sell at a good price. Then they'd come in at night, trailer the horse, and be long gone before the owners were awake.

Clint glanced at Jace, whose expression matched his thoughts. "Luke must be the partner."

"The cops don't think so." Doc looked at Clint. "The police immediately verified with the college that Luke is enrolled there and has not missed any classes. They also verified that he was working in Wyoming before he moved here last year for college. If he were part of Jennings's operation, he'd have missed quite a few classes.

"When the thieves realized the horse they'd renamed Zorro had been exposed to strangles, they decided to dump him. Jennings was already using Luke as his lackey and knew Luke had just been hired on here. Got him to inquire about boarding Zorro. When y'all threw a curveball by wanting the horse vetted first, he told Luke he was leaving town right away and needed to drop Zorro off here in the middle of the night."

Jace sighed. "Luke's naivety played right into Austin's hand. And that's not all, Clint. While we were out tagging calves, Jennings showed up here, having followed Lacy back from her errands. He let himself inside, uninvited, and walked in on her in her bedroom. Scared the you-know-what out of her. But our girl handled it well and got him back onto the porch. I spotted them from the barn door and walked over. He made his exit pretty fast when I showed up."

Clint tensed. "Good thing it was you who saw him and not me. I'd have likely given a hard right to his left jaw."

"Not that I didn't want to." Jace started to stand. "We've got to let Lacy know all this. I'll go talk to her."

Clint jumped up. "Let me tell her."

Jace paused. "Fine by me." He looked at Doc. "We'll keep you posted as we hear something."

"You bet, and I'll do likewise." Doc stood and started for the door. "Meanwhile, I have another call to make before I can quit."

The three men reached the barn door as Lacy's Jeep crunched over the gravel toward the lane to the main road. Clint's shoulders dropped. "Too late. She's already leaving. Now where can she be going?"

Jace pulled out his phone. "I think I know." He stabbed a finger at the screen. "It's going to voice mail." He spoke into the phone. "Lacy, give either Clint or me a call ASAP. It's very important. Thanks."

After a quick trip to the nearest Starbucks on the outskirts of San Antonio for a couple of caramel macchiatos, Lacy turned into the lane that led to Jace and Sydney's home. After a short drive through a stand of tall pines, she turned into their driveway. Instead of immediately getting out of the car, she studied the one-story river-rock-and-cedar-sided home. Jace had done a lot of the work himself. Then after the rooms had been framed out, it sat for over a year while he struggled with a tax mess his dad had left when he passed away. Jace was finally able to finish the construction after his big win at the NFR.

Lacy had once dreamed about living on the ranch property in her own home and raising a family there—private and yet connected to the ranch by a lane leading to the ranch house, same as Jace's home. Of course, the dream included a husband. At first, the husband had no features at all, and then Clint's handsome face began appearing in her daydreams. Now, she'd not only erased his face but the house and family too.

With that thought, she dropped her phone into her purse and began gathering up her bag and the coffee carrier. She'd check later to see who had called as she was leaving the ranch. A conversation with Sydney was more important. With her hands full, she climbed out and slammed the door with a shove of her hip. Time for some girl talk.

Sydney opened the door before Lacy reached it. With no makeup, her long, blond hair pulled back into a ponytail, and wearing one of Jace's T-shirts with her jeans, she looked more like a teenager than a lawyer turned therapeutic horse trainer.

She eyed the drinks and grinned. "A girl after my own heart. You sounded like you have some serious stuff to discuss. Shall we head to my 'she shed'? Jace won't bother us there if he comes home before we're done."

Not sure what Syd was talking about, Lacy followed her friend into a great room, its open-concept design including a tricked-out kitchen and the large farmhouse table where they'd all enjoyed a family dinner a couple of months earlier.

They walked through the kitchen and out the back door to the deck. Talking outside would be okay as long as Jace wasn't home. Lacy began moving to one of the chairs situated at the umbrella table.

"Not there. We're heading over that way." Sydney pointed to a small building painted a soft green and sporting flower boxes under its two small windows.

Lacy had forgotten Syd wanted to repurpose an ordinary prefabricated garden shed for her office and hangout space. "Syd, I love it. When you mentioned doing this, I couldn't visualize it."

Syd led her down the steps of the back deck and across the grass. "Well, I can't visualize a recipe and build it from scratch like you. It's been great fun fixing it up. Not like the work I've been doing in the barn today." She unlocked the door and let Lacy step in first.

Lacy wanted to squeal like a teenager. Could she move in here tomorrow? Done in soft pastels, it was made complete by a small fireplace flanking a pair of facing love seats. A flat-screen TV hung above the fireplace. Lacy wanted to curl up with a good novel or maybe a movie under the afghan draped across the back of one of the sofas. "Did you design this yourself?"

"Much of it with the help of online websites and a friend from the equestrian center. Jace built my desk over there." She pointed toward a white desk nestled between a pair of tall bookcases. One held what looked to be about two dozen law books, and the other, novels and decorating manuals.

Syd crossed to the desk and picked up a closed laptop computer. "If you have legal things to talk about, I'll need this. Let's get settled." They sat on one of the love seats, Syd with her laptop and both of them with their macchiatos.

After a few minutes of chitchat about how great it was to have Shiloh healthy again, Lacy looked her friend in the eyes. "Syd, there's something about me you probably don't know. From what I can tell, Jace has never told you what happened to me in high school."

Sydney's eyes widened. "No. This sounds like a conversation that demands no interruptions." She took her phone from her pocket and tapped on the screen. "Whoever calls me can wait until later."

"Good idea." Lacy brought her phone out too, put it on Do Not Disturb, and then tossed it back into her handbag.

"Jace has never told me anything other than that you've been living on the ranch since high school, much like Clint has," Sydney said. "I've always loved how the McGowans welcomed you both in."

Lacy nodded. "Yes." She sighed. "I got pregnant the summer before my senior year, and my parents wanted me out of the house before I ruined their reputations. Coming to the ranch was their solution—far away from their circle of friends and secluded out here, not knowing anyone. I was pretty much out of sight for seven months until the baby was born."

Sydney set the computer on the floor and scooted close enough to be able to wrap her arms around Lacy. She sat back with her dark eyes full of concern. "You must have been how old? Seventeen? Eighteen?"

A lump was forming in Lacy's throat, and she swallowed against it. "I turned seventeen just before the baby was born. Aunt Carolyn homeschooled me after I came to the ranch, and my daughter was born at the end of April. I held her only once before a social worker took her away to give her to her new parents." She brushed a tear from her cheek, then took her wallet from her purse and fished out the picture. She handed the photo to Sydney. "I named her Alicia. I can't have any contact with her until she turns eighteen, but I think about her every day." She looked up and was surprised to see tears in Sydney's eyes as she gazed at the picture.

"She's beautiful, Lacy. I'm so sorry this happened to you."

Lacy took a tissue from a box on the coffee table and dabbed her eyes. "Thank you. But the good news is, I'm sure she's well-adjusted and cared for and has both a mom and a dad—something I couldn't give her. I was a child myself when I had her."

Sydney handed the photo back to Lacy. "You remember that I had a difficult time myself during high school."

Lacy nodded. "Your dad had that horse accident and died. I remember."

"When we have something catastrophic happen during those impressionable teen years, it can overshadow us for a long time to come."

"You haven't asked me about the father."

"That's your business unless you want to tell me." She smiled. "The lawyer in me knows to not ask questions unless it's for information I need to have. Do I need to know this?"

Lacy took a sip of her drink. "The father is the reason I'm here."

Syd reached for her laptop. "Maybe I should take notes in case we need them later."

"I'll tell you, and you can decide."

Lacy intended to give Sydney the CliffsNotes version, but several sentences in, Syd asked one question and then another. Lacy threw up her hands. "I was trying to spare you the ugly details."

Sydney offered a wry smile. "I'm an attorney, raised in Chicago. Nothing much surprises me. Start over. You met the baby's father at a rodeo."

"Yes. Austin already had a following of buckle bunnies. He's never lacked in the looks department. I fell for him hard. I never expected to give myself to a boy at least until we were engaged."

Sydney nodded. "I was raised as a Christian but drifted away as I got older. The majority of the world believes 'If it feels right, it's not wrong.' I presume that when you found out you were pregnant, he wanted nothing to do with you or the baby."

"Yes. He wanted me to get an abortion, and I refused. He just about blew a gasket and said to never count on him for anything. As far as he was concerned, the baby and I didn't exist. After I had the baby, I called to tell him we'd had a girl and that I'd already given her up for adoption. All he said was that he was glad to hear it. I think he was afraid I'd keep her and nail him for child support. I heard soon afterward that he'd moved to Oklahoma. Meanwhile, I committed my life to the Lord and made a promise to remain celibate until I married."

"Don't tell me he now wants back into your life."

"Yes and no. Here's where you might want to make notes."

Sydney opened the laptop and typed a couple of things, then looked up. "I'm ready when you are."

"I need to say first that Jace knows nothing of what I'm about to tell you. He thinks Austin has only been hitting on me, wanting to start something again. I plan to tell him what he's really after when I see him next."

Lacy gave her a blow-by-blow account, starting with the first time he approached her at the rodeo and told her about the chance to see a picture of their daughter. She ended with how he had come into the ranch house uninvited and found her in her bedroom.

"That's trespassing. You can press charges."

"I know. Jace fumed when I told him what Austin did. I think he's ready to report him to the police. I'm so confused. I almost didn't take the money out of the bank. Then I thought, 'What if he's telling the truth?' If I could see a picture of my girl, it would mean more to me than anything."

"What this investigator is suggesting is highly illegal. If he's caught and arrested and it's found out that you paid him to do what he was doing, you can be liable too. Do you want to take that kind of risk? To be in prison when your daughter turns eighteen and unable to try to connect with her?"

"I suspected as much. I've been really stupid about this. I know what I need to do when I talk to him on Monday. He's not going to be happy when I tell him I've changed my mind."

"Lacy, don't come down on yourself about what you almost did. You were acting on emotions and your love for the child you carried for nine months and then gave away. Totally understandable. Did you already set a time and place to meet with the father?"

"No. He's to call me on Monday. But what's to stop him from coming back to the ranch and pressuring me into giving in?"

"He won't get far if we put Jace and Clint on guard. That is, if Clint knows about it."

"He knows everything." She rolled her eyes. "Hearing about the baby didn't go over too well at first. The guy had me on a pedestal. You should have seen the look on his face when I told him. He figured out Austin is the father and had to apologize later for his reaction."

Sydney looked up from typing. "I'm glad you told him."

"I planned to tell him a long time ago, but every time I decided to, something came up."

"Would it help to hear that I have a hunch there is no PI and no chance of seeing a picture of your child? You've said he's a lowlife and is no good. That he has a bad rep in the rodeo circuit. My guess is he's looking to con you out of the thousand dollars, maybe try to get more, and then get out of Dodge before you can report him."

Lacy shook her head. "I can't believe he'd go to so much trouble for a thousand bucks."

"He would if he's tapped out and owes someone a lot of money. You don't know how many others he's scamming besides you."

A loud knock on the shed door sounded. "Syd, are you in there?"

Sydney jumped to her feet. "We're here, Jace." She rushed to the door and opened it. "Hi, hon. Lacy and I wanted privacy. What's going on?"

"I've been trying to call you and Lacy for the past hour." He stuck his head in and looked at Lacy. The look in his eyes scared her. "Lace, I'm sorry to break this up, but you're needed back at the house right now. A Texas Ranger is on his way over to talk to us." He pulled out his phone and put it to his ear. "Clint, I found her. She's on her way."

Chapter 20

After giving Jace a quick update on what Austin's sudden interest in her was actually about, Lacy followed his SUV down the lane that connected Jace's home with the main part of the ranch. A Texas Ranger vehicle sat next to Clint's truck in front of the ranch house. Clint and the Ranger stood a few feet away in conversation. They looked over as Jace and Lacy pulled up and parked.

Clint met Lacy as she was getting out of her car. His face was grim. "We've been looking all over for you. Did Jace tell you why the Ranger is here?"

"He said something about finding Luke's so-called friend Jeff."

"I wish we had more time to fill in the details for you, but Doc found out that Jeff Harrison is not the guy's real name."

"I'm not surprised. What is his actual name?"

Clint kept his eyes on her, his face void of emotion. "Brace yourself. It's Austin Jennings."

Her mouth fell open. She couldn't have heard him right. "No way. Austin may be a lowlife, but he wouldn't be stupid enough to get involved in horse stealing."

"Apparently he is."

She bit on her trembling lower lip and blinked at the moisture building in her eyes. "I feel so dumb."

Clint wrapped his arm around her and pulled her to his side. "You're not dumb. He's been playing to your emotions, and you reacted like he expected you to. The Ranger wants to interview all of us. Since you saw him when he came here a couple of hours ago, the Ranger would like to take your statement first. They're getting a warrant for his arrest right now."

She stepped out of the comfort of Clint's arm and heaved a sigh. "I hope they throw him in jail and toss the key. Let's get this over with."

They walked over to where the Ranger was talking with Jace, and the officer extended his hand to Lacy. "Miss Roberts, Ranger Tom Girard. The Ranger Division is working with the San Antonio Police to find Austin Jennings in connection with a horse-thieving ring. I understand you've been in contact with the suspect as recently as today."

She nodded. "Unfortunately, I have."

"May we speak privately inside?"

"Yes. My aunt isn't feeling well, and I should check first to be sure she's in her room. I think we can sit at the kitchen table without disturbing her."

"Was she involved when Jennings entered the home?"

"No. I doubt she even heard us, since the master suite is on the opposite side of the home."

"I'll check on Mom and fill her in." Jace headed for the front door.

The Ranger looked at Clint and then at Luke, who stood off to the side. "Can you both wait on the porch? After I talk with Miss Roberts, I'll want to talk to you also."

They agreed, and Lacy led him inside to the kitchen. She indicated the table. "We can sit there. Do you want something to drink?"

"Water would be fine. Thank you."

Grateful for the time it took to retrieve two bottles of water from the fridge, Lacy prayed for the strength to get through the interview. She'd have to lean on God and take each moment as it came.

She carried the water to the table, where the Ranger was already setting up a small recorder and a laptop.

Ranger Girard removed his gray Stetson and placed it on the table. "Do you mind if I record your statement?"

Did she have any choice? She nodded. "That's fine."

He turned on the device and spoke the date, time, and case number. He looked at Lacy. "Let's start with how you know Jennings."

She swallowed against the lump in her throat. She'd managed to keep that chunk of her past buried from most everyone she knew, and now one person after another was learning her secret. At least these days most people hardly blinked at a girl having a baby outside of marriage. "Some of the facts are quite personal to me. Will all this be made public?"

"It doesn't have to be. We'll do our best to keep things redacted from any info given to the media, but I can't promise confidentiality. Newshounds have a way of digging up dirt."

"I know. Well, I met Austin at a rodeo about fourteen years ago." She continued the story in bullet-point style, listing each step of their relationship in single sentences.

"That brings us to today." She described how she'd gone to the bank and was hiding the money in her dresser when Austin surprised her by coming into her room.

Girard looked up from typing. "What did he say to you?"

She squeezed her eyes closed, trying to remember, but nothing came to her mind. She shook her head. "I don't remember exactly. I think I was so shocked, the conversation didn't even register. I do remember him saying that he saw me going inside the house as he was driving up the lane from the main road. He must have been following me."

The Ranger stopped typing. "How did you wind up on the porch?"

"I remember telling him I wasn't going to discuss the matter unless we went outside. He grabbed my arm real tight and fussed about not staying inside, but I was determined. I didn't want my aunt hearing our raised voices and coming to see what was going on. He finally agreed, and we moved to the porch."

"Then what happened?"

"We talked for another minute or two. He kept pushing me to give him the thousand dollars I was to pay for my half of the PI fee. Then Jace walked over from the barn. As soon as Austin saw Jace, he hustled to his truck and took off."

"He didn't know you were putting the money in your drawer when he walked in on you?"

She shook her head. "If he had, he wouldn't have agreed to leave the room without it."

"Probably not." He typed for several minutes and then frowned. "Did he brandish any kind of weapon when he was in your bedroom?"

"No. Just gripped my arm like a vice. He did say something about causing me bodily harm if I backed out, and when I mouthed off, he squeezed tighter."

The Ranger typed on the keyboard. "Looks like we can include trespassing and assault to the warrant."

"But he didn't beat me."

"He gripped your arm tight enough to cause bruising and kept you from moving. It doesn't have to escalate to a beating for it to be an assault."

"Okay." She rubbed her arm and winced. "I'll probably have a good bruise."

He typed for a couple of moments. "Before I leave, I'll have to ask you to show me that arm. If there's a mark, I'll need to take a picture. After you managed to get him out to the front porch, did he say he'd be back for the money?"

She thought a moment. "No. I told him again that I was uneasy about the plan since what the PI wanted to do sounded like stalking. He insisted it wasn't because it was only a one-time thing. He'd wait for the child to leave for school and snap a couple of photos and leave. He said he'd call me again on Monday morning to tell me where to meet him. That's when Jace showed up and he made a fast exit."

"So, as far as you know, he'll be calling you on Monday?"

"Yes."

He stood. "That's all for now. I need to speak to the men, and then I'll probably want to finish with all of you together and take that picture I mentioned. Please ask Luke to come in next."

Clint waited until Luke had stepped inside, then glanced at Lacy; she'd taken the chair next to him. She looked wasted. "Was he rough on you?"

She shook her head. "Not at all. It's everything combined. Jace interrupted Sydney and me at the end of an intense conversation, and I came right into this. I confided in Syd for a legal opinion. Never did I dream Austin was in more trouble than his small-time harassment to try to get money out of me." She faced him, her eyes watery. "I've been so conflicted the past couple of weeks with you and Jace telling me not to trust Austin. What you said made sense, but the idea of possibly seeing a picture of my daughter had a power over me that I can't describe. I wanted what he was saying to be true more than I cared whether he was scamming me. He sure got my motherly emotions going." She pulled a tissue from her pocket and dabbed her eyes.

"There's a positive to all this, as far as I'm concerned."

She frowned. "All I see are negatives."

"Until I observed the fierce love you have for a daughter you only saw for a brief time more than thirteen years ago, I assumed all women who had unplanned babies disliked their child because of how my own mother made me feel all my life. She never gave me up for adoption, and in a way I kind of wish she had. Then I could have grown up with a family who loved me and wanted me." He paused. Had those words really come out of his mouth? He'd thought them often enough but had never spoken them. He glanced at her, then reached over and used his thumb to wipe a tear from her face. "Hey, girl, don't cry for me. You've got enough of your own troubles to deal with."

"Clint, I had no idea it was that bad with your mother. Of course, you've said before how hard it was growing up with an alcoholic mother and no father."

"I didn't expect you to understand. No one does. When my dad told me the other day how he'd never forgotten me even though my mom made sure he didn't see me again, I wouldn't have believed that to be true if I hadn't seen how you are with your own child."

"I'm glad you told me."

He hunched over and kicked a pebble with the pointed toe of his boot.

"It's not something I like to talk about. There's an element of embarrassment. And fear that people will think that something must be wrong with me, to be rejected by my own mother."

She grabbed his hand. "Most people wouldn't think that. There is absolutely nothing wrong with you. You are one of the most caring and patient people I've known." She squeezed his hand, then wove their fingers together. "You've been my rock to lean on during some tough times. I don't know why I tried to shut you out these past few weeks."

He huffed a sardonic laugh. "I know why. I wasn't exactly the rock to lean on when you first told me about the baby. I don't know how you've managed with Jennings nagging at you and messing with your emotions like that."

She let go of his hand and drew in a long breath. "You aren't going to like my answer."

"Try me."

"I've had my moments of anger with God, but I've always known that He is right there with me. He's given me the strength I've needed when I had no more of my own."

"I admit I've admired you for your faith. Believe it or not, I'm kinda jealous of it."

"You don't need to be jealous, Clint. He's there for you too, waiting for you to turn to Him."

"For you, maybe, but not for—"

The door next to them opened and Luke stepped through. "He's ready for Jace."

So deep in his conversation, Clint had forgotten Jace sitting on the other side of the porch. Had he been listening to them? He glanced at the chair Jace had been occupying. "Where did he get off to?"

"There he is." Lacy pointed across the barnyard to where Jace stood next to the round pen.

"Jace, get over here! The Ranger is ready for you!"

At Clint's shout, Jace trotted across the gravel and up onto the porch. He looked from Lacy to Clint. "Thought you two needed some privacy." He opened the door and slipped inside.

Luke stood a few feet away, appearing puzzled. "I'm to stay on the ranch, but I don't need to wait right here anymore. I'll be in the barn doing chores."

Clint watched the ranch hand walk toward the barn, then turned to Lacy. "I'm glad we had that conversation."

She nodded. "Me too. Now I need to change into a short-sleeved shirt so the Ranger can take a picture of my bruised arm."

He tensed. "I thought you said his abuse was emotional, not physical."

"It was until earlier today when he grabbed my arm as I tried to get out of the bedroom. It felt like it was trapped in that vice on the barn's workbench. It's sore to the touch, and I'm assuming there's a visible bruise."

"I sure hope they find that piece of scum before he hurts anyone else, man or animal."

"Me too. See you later." She stood and stepped inside, and the door clicked shut behind her.

Clint relaxed and settled against the back of the chair. He'd be the next one called. He pulled out his phone and clicked on an e-mail from Dad. It felt funny thinking of Tim Steele as *Dad*, but he loved calling him that. Even though the DNA test hadn't yet confirmed their relationship, he had no doubt he'd reconnected with the right man. It would take a while, but in time, he'd be able to call him Dad to his face. Just not yet.

Chapter 21

"I'm glad someone is around to talk to."

Clint shook his head and tried to open his eyes. He blinked and stared up into Carolyn's face. "I must have drifted off. How long were you standing there?" He tugged his phone from his pocket and checked the time. "Couldn't have been sleeping more than ten minutes."

"Just got here." She adjusted the scarf tied around her head like a turban and plopped into the chair Lacy had vacated. "The only way I could escape was to go through the door from my hall to the side deck and walk around."

"Jace told you what was going on, didn't he?"

"Yes. My heart breaks for what poor Lacy has been through. I never did like that Jennings boy. He only came around once after she moved in with us. He was participating in a rodeo nearby. By then she was showing real good, and it was obvious her appearance made him uncomfortable. Served him right. After all, he was the one who got her that way. He couldn't have cared any less about that baby, and I could say the same for how he felt about Lacy."

All the more reason to dislike the piece of... He stopped himself from thinking the word he said often. Now that he was part business owner, he should clean up his speech. "It wasn't all his doing. It does take two to make a baby."

"Of course it does. Lacy bore some of the fault, but she was only sixteen at the time she got pregnant. Had her seventeenth birthday while she was pregnant." She paused and looked at Clint. "Did she tell you she started kindergarten a year sooner than she should have? Her parents got the school district to approve it."

He shook his head. "She must have been a smart kid."

"Smart, maybe, but not mature otherwise. Now here she was entering her senior year at the age of sixteen. She may have been at the age of consent, but a young girl starry-eyed over a rodeo hero can lose all sense. Especially if they're not properly grounded. Austin told her he loved her and said if she loved him too, that was the way to show it. Oldest line in the book."

Clint made a fist with his right hand. Jennings was lucky she was at the age of consent, or he could have been charged with rape like that bulldogger was years ago. Oh, how he'd love to knock the daylights out of him for what he did to Lacy, not to mention to the horses by bringing Zorro to the barn.

"They got into a terrible row the day he was here," Carolyn continued. "He walked out, saying it wasn't the time of his life to be a dad and that for all he knew, he wasn't even the father. It was the last we saw of him. He was three years older than her. And he was right; it wasn't the right time for him to be a dad, but at that point he had no choice but to cowboy up. Major failure on his part. Others may have thought she'd put the past and her daughter behind her, but many a night I heard her crying when I walked past her room." She faced him. "How long have you known about everything?"

He worked to tamp down his anger. "I thought he was hitting on her. He's had a bad rep around rodeo for a long time, and I wondered why she didn't just tell him to get lost. She eventually told me about having the baby with him, but I had no knowledge of his scheme involving a PI and seeing a picture of the girl until later."

Carolyn sighed. "And then to find out he's involved with horse thievery and conning poor Luke into bringing that sick horse to our ranch. What a piece of scum."

Clint jerked his focus from his anger to her. "That's a pretty strong word for you, Carolyn."

"I save my choice words for those who deserve them. He's fortunate I'm a God-fearing woman, or you'd be hearing stronger words than that."

He chuckled and studied her profile while she stared across the yard at the barn. Her face had thinned in the past several weeks, and her skin reminded him of tissue paper. To see her now, one would think her a frail woman, but he knew that beneath the surface she was as strong as ever. Texas-born and raised on a ranch over near Houston, she'd met Jace's dad when they were at the University of Texas. Married him a week after their graduation from UT and moved onto the ranch, where she raised their family. Nursing her husband through his own cancer and learning after he passed of his hidden gambling addiction had been a lot for her to bear.

The gambling debt just about cost them the ranch property that had been in the McGowan family since Jace's great-granddaddy staked a claim on the land over a hundred years ago. Some mornings after Ted McGowan had passed, when Clint came over to the house at dawn to fuel up on one of Lacy's breakfasts, he'd see Carolyn in the study, her Bible on her lap and her head bowed. She'd not been that religious before then. But she apparently found solace in God during that rough time, and before long Jace did too.

He never heard her say a cross word or express anger toward her husband for leaving them in such a dire situation. He knew without asking that she'd forgiven him. He admired her faith and how God gave her strength because she was a good woman. Him? Not so good, and God always looked away whenever he called out to Him.

"How are you doing, Clint? I hear you found out that Tim Steele is your daddy."

He blinked and snapped out of his thoughts. He couldn't help but smile. "Yes. We still need the DNA test results to prove it, but I'm certain I've finally found him."

Her face lit up. "That's wonderful. You've had a rough go of it, haven't you?"

"Yes, ma'am. If y'all hadn't taken me in when you did, I would probably be doing time somewhere. You know I've always thought of you as the mom I never had."

She waved a hand. "Oh, but you have a mama. What would she think if she heard you saying that?"

"Nothing much. She was happy to be rid of me. She's always been much happier nursing a bottle of booze than her own son."

Her brows rose. "I've never heard you talk so bluntly."

"It's time I faced reality. Meeting Tim has shown me that I have at least one parent who has loved me since the day I was born. And that's more than some people have. He's actually carried around my baby picture all these years."

The door opened, and Jace stepped onto the porch. "Clint, he's ready for you, me, and Lacy together."

"Not me alone?"

"Guess not. Where's Lacy?"

Clint tugged out his phone and tapped on the screen. "In her room. I'm calling her now."

Lacy settled into one of the four chairs around the kitchen table Ranger Girard had been using as a kind of interview desk and offered the Ranger a closed-lip smile as she held out her bare arm.

He frowned and picked up his phone from where it sat on the table. "Looks like you're going to have a good bruise by the time it's done forming. Hold your arm right there a sec." He held up his phone, aimed it at her arm, and snapped a couple of shots.

She slipped into the denim jacket she'd brought with her as Clint and Jace settled on the two vacant chairs; then she pressed her hand against the cross hanging around her neck, a gift given to her several years ago by her aunt and uncle when she was baptized at church. She hadn't worn it for a while but decided when changing a few minutes ago that she needed it there today to remind herself that she had God on her side and would get through this with His help.

The Ranger looked at Clint. "I didn't ask to interview you directly because you've had minimal interaction with the suspect. Is there anything you recall that might go toward helping us piece together this man's unlawful attempt at scamming Lacy?"

"What about that time you interrupted us at the rodeo?" Lacy asked.

"Yeah, I was thinking about that. From a distance, Jace and I saw Jennings talking to Lacy, and we discussed how he was probably up to no good with her. I had no knowledge of their history together. I went over there, and Jennings got visibly agitated and ordered me away." He looked at Lacy. "Lacy also asked me to leave them alone, but in a nicer way, and I left."

The Ranger looked at Lacy. "Why did you ask him to leave?"

Lacy dropped her gaze to her lap. "Because Austin was telling me about finding our daughter, and I was hoping that for once in his life he was being truthful. Clint didn't know about my having a baby with Austin. I didn't want him to hear about it that way."

Ranger Girard made a note on his laptop, then looked up and acknowledged Lacy with a tip of his head in her direction. "Before Jennings left Miss Roberts's presence earlier today, they'd agreed she would let him know on Monday whether she was going to go along with his scheme. He assured Miss Roberts that the investigator would know the exact time her daughter leaves for school, to keep his time of observance to a minimum. He'd snap a couple pictures of her and then go. Jennings is to contact Miss Roberts on Monday morning and tell her where to meet him with the money." He looked around the table. "Any additions to what I've just said?"

Jace shook his head, and Clint did the same. Lacy raised her hand. "Not an addition, but are you going to go to the place he tells me and arrest him when he shows up?"

"Not exactly, but you're on the right track. The only person we'd like to meet him is you."

A chill raced down her spine. "Me? What if he takes my money and we never see him again?" She rubbed her palm over the sore place on her arm. "Or when I refuse to give him the money, he hurts me worse than he did today?"

The Ranger offered her a sympathetic look. "The money you'll have on you will be marked bills from us. You'll wear a listening device, and we're hoping you'll engage him in conversation that causes him to admit what he's doing. You'll flash him the money and demand he show you he's telling the truth about the PI—and how he knows for certain that your daughter is in Albany, New York. If he insists on being given the money, you'll need to comply. He'll probably inspect it to make sure it's real and to try to see whether it's marked. But the way bills are marked today, he won't be able to tell with the naked eye."

"Where will you be?"

"We're hoping he'll suggest a public place to meet like a restaurant, but wherever it is, we'll be outside in an unidentifiable van, recording and listening to the conversation. If something dangerous happens, we can be in there in a nanosecond."

He leaned back in his chair before continuing. "Miss Roberts, has he ever been known to carry a weapon like a gun or a knife?"

She clasped her shaking hands and rested them in her lap. "No ... but I've spent little time with him in the recent past. If he's into stealing horses, there's no telling what else he's doing."

"I think we'll place an undercover officer near you that day, for safety's sake. If he suggests a private place, you need to convince him it's better done in public. Hopefully he'll agree."

Lacy looked at Jace for assurance, and he nodded. Easy for him to do. He wasn't the one wearing a wire and trying to entrap a horse thief and scammer. If Austin received a short sentence or never even saw jail time, who was the first person he'd come looking for? What if she had to go into the witness protection program ... leave everything she knew and loved behind forever? "I'm not liking this one bit. Can I have some time to decide?"

The Ranger's lips flattened into a thin line. "No more than a couple of hours. We need to start setting things up."

She clutched the cross. "I need more time than that."

"Lacy, let's go outside and talk this out." Clint stood and looked at Jace. "You want to come too?"

She looked from Clint to her cousin. "Yes. Both of you come." She needed Clint for emotional support but Jace for spiritual strengthening.

The Ranger returned to his laptop. "While you're talking, I'll get started on my report."

Once outside, the guys headed for the barn. Lacy walked between them, surprised that they didn't stop on the porch.

"Let's go up to Clint's apartment where we have some privacy." Without waiting for the others to agree, Jace increased his stride, causing Lacy to almost run to keep up with him.

When they entered the apartment, Jace indicated that she should sit on the leather couch. He and Clint sat on either side of her.

Jace leaned forward and looked at Lacy. "Let's cut to the chase. You're scared. I get that. What is the worst that can happen?"

"The thought occurred to me that I might have to go into the witness protection program if he gets out of jail early, or maybe he'll pay someone to kill me if he's behind bars."

"I think you've been watching too many cop shows lately. That program is for protection from big-time gangsters," Clint said.

How could he dismiss her fears like that? "This is big-time enough for me. You don't think my fears are valid?"

Clint took her hand and squeezed it. "Of course they are, but maybe you are overthinking this. The man is going to a lot of trouble for a thousand bucks. He's small potatoes."

"Or he'll ask for more later after he pulls her deeper into his web." Jace looked her in the eyes. "Lacy, if you don't do this, think of how many other people he's going to scam, how many horses he'll steal to make a fast buck. Horses that might suffer the same fate as Zorro. What if he tries to get to your daughter and take her for ransom, bringing her adoptive parents into it? You're leaving God out of this right now. He's got your back, and He promises to never leave you or forsake you."

She nodded. "I know all that. But what do I do with this fear? I'm afraid I'll be so shaky that I'll give myself away."

Jace closed his eyes for a moment and then opened them. "Fear can be healthy, but it can also be an enemy. One of our US presidents said that the only fear we have to fear is fear itself. I'll go a step further and say that we have Someone greater than our fear. Man may take away our earthly possessions, people, job, whatever, but he cannot take away God. He is with you now and will be with you on Monday and all the days following. Let's pray about this."

She glanced at Clint, who sat there staring off to the side. Were Jace's words touching his heart right then?

"Clint, where is that Bible Tim gave you?"

Clint blinked and looked back at them. "In the bedroom. I'll get it."

Jace grabbed Lacy's hand as Clint disappeared into the other room. "I have no idea whether he's looked at the Bible, but if it's in the bedroom, maybe he's been reading it."

She made a face. "Or maybe it's there but put away out of sight in a drawer."

Clint returned and handed the book to Jace. Lacy loved the crinkly noise the Bible's pages made as Jace flipped them, seemingly intent on finding a certain verse. In an unexpected way, the sound brought her comfort.

"Found what I was looking for," Jace said. "Listen to this from Psalms: 'In God I trust and am not afraid. What can man do to me?' "

Lacy relaxed for the first time since they'd left the meeting. "I like that. What can man ... what can *Austin* do to me? With God on my side, he can't do anything. I will trust in Him." She stood. "Let's go tell the Ranger I'm ready to do what needs to be done."

Chapter 22

Lacy's phone rang on Monday morning as she cleaned up from breakfast. She checked the screen and froze. She'd been hoping ever since Saturday that Austin would somehow realize the cops were on his tail and go underground. It felt as if her heart had risen to her throat. She swallowed against the pulsing and uttered a two-word prayer—"Help me"—before putting the phone to her ear. "I didn't know you woke up this early."

A low chuckle came through the line. "I do when I have an important appointment to keep with my daughter's mama. Have a good day yesterday?"

She bit back the snarky words that sat on the tip of her tongue. "It was good, and I'll make your day better by telling you I've decided to go along with the deal. Thanks for giving me the time to think it through."

"That, my dear, is like the eight-second buzzer going off while I still have a seat on the horse. A lovely sound."

"You haven't ridden broncs in years."

"But bronc riders still remember their last ride as if it were yesterday. Okay, here's the deal. Meet me at one o'clock at the 1745 Café in New Braunfels, on the frontage road off I-35. Remember the name and you'll know the street number."

"I'm not very familiar with the area."

"Then look it up on your GPS. Be there with the dough. I'll be waiting in a booth. Look for me."

The line went dead. She put in a call to Ranger Girard.

At twelve forty-five p.m., Lacy parked her taxi-cab-yellow Renegade in a slot several storefronts down from the 1745 Café. She'd questioned whether she should drive a car that was so noticeable, but Girard said Austin would suspect that something was up if she came in a different car.

Before parking so that her car faced the café, she scanned the lot in front of the coffee shop. Not a single truck there like she'd seen Austin driving. She pushed away the thought of him stealing a car to avoid recognition by the cops. Of the several vans in the lot, each displaying the name of a company on their side panels, she had no idea which one held the electronics that would hear every word of her conversation with Austin. She cut the motor, then grasped her cross necklace, closed her eyes, and prayed for the umpteenth time, giving her fear to the Lord.

She checked the time: five minutes to one. "I'm about to get out of the car. Am I coming through okay?"

"Loud and clear." Ranger Girard's baritone voice came through her earbud. "Now start following the procedure we discussed."

"Yes, sir." She stuffed the earpiece and her personal phone inside a cloth bag and slid it under the driver's seat, then patted her jeans pocket to assure herself that a different phone was still there. The new device had been tricked out to look like the one she personally owned, complete with a contact list and apps she used, in case Austin asked to look at it. Hidden inside was an app that would record and transmit her entire conversation with Austin to the Rangers listening in a van. She opened the door and climbed out.

Walking up to the building, Lacy opened the café's glass door and stepped through. The warm vibe of the rustic décor seemed out of place with what was about to happen. Several people stood in line in front of the ordering bar. She hadn't been told whether she should get a drink first, only to act naturally. Since it hadn't been mentioned, she presumed she didn't need to, although the thought of throwing a steaming hot coffee in Austin's face did cross her mind. But that was too tempting.

She glanced down a row of booths that ran along the eatery's waist-high front window, and a hand shot up toward the end of the row. She took tentative steps across the hardwood floor. When she was still several booths away, Austin leaned out into the aisle and waved. She nodded, walked over, and took the seat across from him.

He stared at her expressionless. "Right on time. Glad to see you found it okay."

"Yes. Thanks to my GPS."

"Did you bring the money?"

She patted her purse. "It's right here. But can you humor me one more time and run through the process this PI is going to do once he's paid? How soon will I be able to see what she looks like?"

He rolled his eyes and lifted the tall paper cup in front of him to his lips. "Like I said at least a dozen times already, after I send him the payment electronically, he'll travel up to Albany. The next morning, at the time he knows our girl usually leaves for school, he'll be hidden in place with his camera ready. He told me she walks several houses down to where she waits for the bus with a couple other kids. He should get a good shot of her as she walks by."

She grinned, hoping the expression appeared to be genuine. "I can't believe I can even know this much about her. Has he described her at all from what he's already seen?"

He shook his head. "Only that she appears to be in good health and seems to be of average height for a kid her age. Didn't occur to me to ask for details. I suppose you want to know her hair color, what she was wearing, stuff women always want to know. But we'll have a picture by Wednesday or Thursday." He offered the smile he'd used for years to charm people. "You can see for yourself what she is wearing then. It's unbelievable that we'll soon see our little girl. Well, not so little anymore … a teenager."

She nodded. He was good. No wonder she was sucked in at first. "Actually, it's a motherly thing to want all the details. What kind of neighborhood is it that he can hide himself and not get caught?"

He heaved a breath. "I thought I told you already."

"Maybe so. I'm sorry, Austin. This was a huge decision for me, and I'm looking for assurance that he'll be able to do this."

"Don't you think I need that assurance too? The house across the street from hers has a lot of bushes in front near the sidewalk, and he'll hide in there. He plans to wear clothes that make him look like he's a gardener and will have gardening tools with him if anyone is around to see him."

If she hadn't already realized he was scamming her, she would now thanks to the detailed explanation that he rattled off as though he'd rehearsed it a dozen times. She smiled. "Sounds like he's got it all planned out."

"He's good at his job."

"Will we have to wait for him to get back to his office before he sends the pictures?"

"He'll email the shots to me from his hotel later that same day. Then I'll forward them to you."

"And that's it?"

He nodded. "Unless he has extra expenses and asks us for more money before he sends the pictures."

The Ranger had warned Lacy he might try this tactic. "How much more?"

"I don't know. Maybe a half stack."

She frowned. "I have no idea what you're saying."

"Five hundred smackers. Can you handle that if he asks?"

"I don't know, Austin. I'm not exactly rolling in the dough."

He drained his cup and crumpled it with his hand. "Well, hopefully he won't ask for more. But be warned that he might." He held out his hand, palm out. "It's time, Lacy Lynn. Show me the money."

It was all she could do not to slap his mouth for uttering both names. She reached into her purse and drew out the envelope. "You know I hate being called that."

He took the envelope from her. "That's why it's so much fun saying it. Your daddy still call you *Lacy Lynn?*"

"No, he doesn't."

Austin pulled out the ten one-hundred-dollar bills and held one up to the light above their heads. Then he did the same with another bill.

"Come on, Austin, don't you trust me? They're real."

He looked at her with narrowed eyes. "I wouldn't have expected it of the girl I once knew, but people change."

"I've changed for the good, not the bad."

He reached over and flicked her cross necklace so hard the pendant hit her on the nose. "Got religion, did you? What makes you so sure God's forgiven you for what you did with me?"

"My faith. You know I would never have gone that far if you hadn't lied to me."

His eyebrows shot up. "It seems to me you were a willing participant in our sinful act of passion. So how did I lie?"

She'd hardly call it an act of passion. "Saying you loved me and that sleeping with you was the best way to show my love. That we were going to be married as soon as I was out of school."

He chuckled. "Works every time. You still fought me off for a while until that night, when I found a way to break down your resistance."

"What do you mean?"

"Slipped a little vodka into your soft drink, and you never noticed it." He flashed her a grin. "After you got tipsy, you were like a show horse responding to my touch."

She'd never mind being compared to a well-trained horse, but he'd gone too far. She wished she *had* bought that hot coffee. What joy it would have been to toss it into that prideful smirk of his. She slid from the booth. "You are disgusting, and I hope we never have to meet again."

"Me too, but if the PI needs more dough, you know we will."

She turned on her heel and stomped to the door.

A soft rain fell as she stepped outside. It felt good as it hit her face, as though she was finally being cleansed of her past. She walked to the Renegade and climbed in, then found the Bluetooth device and hooked it over her ear. "Did you get it all?"

"Every word. He's coming out now. Gotta make the move."

A *click* sounded in her ear, and the connection went dead. As instructed, she quickly removed the phone from her pocket, turned it off, and stuffed it into the bag. After retrieving her personal phone, she jammed the bag back under the seat.

Shouts came from the direction of the coffee shop, and she slumped down and peered over the dashboard. Ranger Girard had his knees flexed and both arms extended, pointing his gun at Austin, who stood a short distance away with his hands casually held up.

"To the ground, now, Jennings."

Austin didn't move. "Why? I just stopped in for some coffee. You've got the wrong man."

"We have the right one. There's a warrant out for your arrest. Drop to the ground now."

Austin shook his head. "Like I was saying …" His hand went to his back pocket, and he pulled out a pistol.

The door to the coffee shop flew open, and a man wearing jeans and a leather jacket rocketed through it, grabbing the gun from Austin and tossing it to the ground. He kicked it farther away and forced both of Austin's arms around to the back. In one swift movement the cowboy was on his knees, and Ranger Girard lowered his gun. He approached Austin and cuffed him while the undercover Ranger recited the Miranda rights. Girard yanked Austin to his feet and walked him to a waiting black-and-white police car.

Lacy let go of the breath she was holding and wiped her brow.

After a few minutes, Ranger Girard approached her vehicle, and she lowered the window. "That was more drama than I ever want again in my life."

A wry smile emerged on his face. "In other words, you have no plans to join the Rangers."

"You got that right. Did you get enough information to indict?"

He grinned. "You were amazing. He should be locked up for a long time."

"But some of that happened so long ago. Doesn't the statute of limitations apply?"

"Not for the horse-thief ring and his scamming you. As far as sexual assault goes—there's no limit on it. Listen, I need to go to the office and fill out reports on all this. I'll pay the ranch a visit soon to wrap it up with you and the others."

Lacy handed him the black bag holding the fake iPhone and the earbud.

"I'll look forward to that."

After Girard headed to his unmarked van, Lacy called Clint. "The deed is done. He's arrested, and he's not only going to be indicted for horse thievery and scamming me, but also for sexual assault back when he made me pregnant."

"I didn't realize the incident could be called assault."

"He admitted to spiking my soft drink with vodka to get me drunk and more agreeable to his advances. I don't even remember feeling out of it. Wouldn't I have tasted the alcohol?"

"Vodka doesn't have a taste like whiskey. It's a good thing I didn't hear him admit to that. I'd have given him something to knock him out cold for a day or two."

"I'm glad you weren't here. You'd be going to the slammer along with Austin."

"I know. Teaching him a lesson with my fists only happens in my dreams. I didn't realize he could be charged for such an old crime."

"I didn't either, but if it sticks, he'll be put away for a long time. I'm shaking, Clint. I'm going to sit here awhile until I've calmed down. Then I'll drive home."

"Want me to come get you?"

Her heart warmed at his offer. "Thanks, but you've got your work to do. I'll be fine. See you soon."

Later that afternoon, Clint approached the practice arena and stopped at the rail to watch Lacy take Shiloh through a run with the barrels. They'd already circled the first barrel and were shooting across to the second. Shiloh hadn't lost her speed despite having been sick. They cleared the barrel and raced to the third at the top point of the cloverleaf pattern. They made a tight turn, and Lacy flung the reins from side to side, shouting, "Go for home, girl!" Shiloh sped up. Lacy's long blond hair lifted in the wind. They arrived at their starting point, and the horse halted next to the fence.

She spotted Clint and grinned. He gave her two thumbs-up, then opened the gate and stepped inside the arena. "Looking good, both of you."

She patted the horse's withers. "I'm thrilled she's not lost the speed she had before the strangles hit."

"Now that you have no worries about Jennings bothering you, are you planning on rodeoing this coming weekend?"

Lacy's eyes twinkled. "I'm thinking about it. Jace is going. Are you?"

"Not sure. I got the okay from my doc to go back to work and was asked to be a backup for the bullfighters. I need to work out for a few weeks and to get myself to where I was before, though. You want me to time you on another run?"

She patted her horse's neck. "She was a little sluggish the first time we ran the pattern, but with each one she's improved. I think we're done for today, but I'll take you up on timing me tomorrow. You should go to the rodeo, even if it is only to observe. You need to make your presence known again, and you'll soon be ready to work."

Clint studied his feet. Knowing Lacy was planning to be there, he suddenly wanted to go. "You're right. I should go. I'll let them know I'll·be there." He waited a moment, and when she didn't respond to the comment, he decided to change the subject. "You've had a rough morning. You doing okay?"

Her smile gone, she dismounted and faced him, hands on her hips. "It was very scary, and I'm glad it's over. It's weird. Although I'm in a better place now, I'm a little sad because I'm back to knowing nothing about my daughter's whereabouts. I just need to be patient for five more years, and maybe then I'll be able to contact her." She palmed sudden tears from her face. "I need to unsaddle Shiloh and get her dried off before I turn her out to pasture. Then I'm going inside for a good cry."

He could no longer resist and tugged her into his arms. "I'll take care of Shiloh. I'm sorry this happened to you, Lace."

Her hat dropped to the ground, but she made no move to retrieve it or step out of his embrace. To the contrary, she pressed her face against his chest. A sob burst from her throat as she wrapped her arms around his waist. "Thank you. I'm sorry I didn't confide everything to you from the beginning."

Could they stand there like that for the next hour? She felt so right in his arms. He ran his palm over her head, loving the softness of her blond waves against his skin. "That's okay. I think I understand now more than ever."

She leaned back and looked at him, her beautiful eyes seeming to search his face. "Why is that?"

"It's too long a story. Maybe we can go out some night when we can talk longer?"

"I'd like that."

His heart felt as if it were going to burst. Best to seize an opportunity when it presented itself, for tomorrow it might not be there. "Is tonight okay? Or do you have to stick around for the meal?"

She offered a small smile. "Not knowing how today would pan out, I already have a casserole in the fridge that just needs to be put in the oven. But if Aunt Carolyn is the only one eating, I can save the casserole for tomorrow and get her set with the leftover veggie soup she prefers."

"Then tonight it is." His gaze focused on her lips, and he brought his face closer to hers. She didn't pull back. She rose up on her tiptoes instead. His pulse racing, he lowered his lips to hers. Soft and tender, he let the kiss deepen, not caring that they were right there in the open. She brought her hand to his neck and tugged him closer. His pulse went into overdrive, and he ran his fingers through her hair. Her lips were as soft as he remembered that night they danced. A tiny moan from her throat was all the response he needed to let the kiss linger. When the kiss ended, he leaned back and stared into her eyes. Moisture glinted on her eyelashes. He caressed her beautiful face with his gaze. If he was dreaming, he never wanted to wake up.

He reluctantly released her. "Go on inside. I'll see you tonight."

"I should be free to go by five or five thirty."

"Let's make it five thirty." He waited until she crossed the gravel to the house, then grabbed Shiloh's reins. "Come on, girl. Let's get you walked out and into the pasture." What had just happened? It was best to not jump to any conclusions. Her emotions were ramped up after the morning and Shiloh's good runs. For all he knew, she'd change her mind about dinner after she'd sorted everything out.

Chapter 23

A bit later, Lacy entered Aunt Carolyn's bedroom carrying a tray that held a bowl of steaming hot vegetable soup and a whole-grain roll. She set the tray on the overbed table they'd bought when her uncle became ill and then lifted the lid on the antique flowered teapot. "I think the water is about the right temperature. Do you want me to start your tea steeping?"

Her aunt offered the first smile Lacy had seen on her face since chemo day. "Yes, please. You are too good to me, dear niece, making me a separate supper." She sat up and slowly swung her legs over the side of the bed. "You know, I'm feeling stronger today. I think the worst of the reaction to the chemo has passed. I'm going to sit over there in the chair." Without waiting for Lacy to assist, she slipped her feet into her house slippers and moved with measured steps to the chair.

Lacy rolled the table over and handed the cloth napkin to her aunt. "I'm really encouraged that you're feeling better. Maybe by tomorrow you can take your meals at the table with the rest of us."

"I don't know if I'll be ready to eat your delicious food so soon. I can only eat well-done meat and none of your beautiful salads. There's so much I need to be careful of. What are y'all having tonight? Tell me so I can enjoy it vicariously."

Lacy chuckled. "Nothing."

Aunt Carolyn's eyes widened. "What? Why?"

"Syd and Jace are eating at home tonight, Luke is meeting a buddy for burgers, and I'm having dinner out with a friend."

Her aunt's blue eyes twinkled. "By the smile on your face, I presume it's not a girlfriend. Do you have a new beau?"

"Well, not new in the sense of having just met him."

"Someone from church?"

"No, but I wish I could say yes, because he doesn't go to church." She held up a hand. "I know. Not a good idea."

"Do I know him?"

"Yes."

"Does he work on the ranch?"

Lacy giggled. "You're getting warmer."

"Is it Clint?"

"Bingo!"

Aunt Carolyn clapped her hands. "Finally."

"Finally?"

"You two have been sweet on each other for months. I wondered who was going to make the first move."

Her stomach tingled. He sure did kiss as though he had deep-down feelings. "I've liked him for a long time, but I never got the sense he felt the same. But if the way he just kissed me over at the practice arena means anything, maybe he does." She brought her fingertips to her lips and then pulled her hand away, suddenly feeling self-conscious. She blinked at the tears that welled up as her face heated.

Her aunt offered her a gentle smile. "You young people are so different now than in my day. We sometimes didn't kiss until we'd had several dates. Now you kiss before the first date. But then, you two have known each other since you were teenagers. That's a long while. I think he struggles with thoughts that he's not good enough for you. Maybe his learning about your past has helped him to see himself as worthy enough to be with you."

She shrugged. "I don't know. Maybe I shouldn't have agreed to go out tonight. As much as I'd like to be with him, he doesn't feel the same way about God as I do. Can we go to dinner and still keep it in the friend zone?"

"Not if you keep kissing each other like you did today."

Lacy nodded. "I know. I've been praying about it, but I don't have a clear answer. He's coming for me at five thirty."

The tears that had been pushing against her eyes broke through, and she pulled a tissue from her jeans pocket and blotted her face with it.

Her aunt pushed the meal table away, then took Lacy's hand and tugged her onto her lap. "Come here, you sweet girl. You're not too old that I can't cuddle you like I did when you first came here to live."

Lacy snuggled her face into the crook of her aunt's neck, loving the scent of the jasmine lotion the woman favored. She was thankful the chemo hadn't made Aunt Carolyn sensitive to the scent. "I feel weird now, going out with him, about how to act. I wish we'd never kissed."

"If it makes you feel any better, I'm willing to bet he feels the same way. Just be yourself and let things happen naturally. Now stand up so I can see how cute you look. I wondered why you were wearing that tunic top with those skinny jeans and sandals."

Lacy stood and smoothed out her top. "I wasn't sure what to wear since he didn't tell me where we're going."

"Well, wherever it is, I'm sure you'll have a good time." Aunt Carolyn pulled her table back over, then dipped her spoon into the soup and lifted it to her mouth. She swallowed and gave Lacy a thumbs-up. "Perfect. Now go have a wonderful evening. And relax. Remember ... let things take their natural course."

Clint strode up to the ranch house, wishing the butterflies in his stomach away. All afternoon he'd second-guessed himself for kissing Lacy the way he had. But she *did* kiss him back. Still, he shouldn't expect that her kiss meant she wanted a dating relationship. Even though he felt better about his situation by becoming a business partner with Jace, there was one very big obstacle only he could take away, and becoming a Christian to get the girl was something he'd never do.

He first headed to the side door as always and then stopped himself. If this was a date, he should be using the front door. But maybe she didn't think of it as a date. To be on the safe side, he went to the front and pressed the doorbell.

The door swung open and Lacy stood there, wide-eyed and adorable. He loved her non-Western outfit that showed off shapely legs covered by skintight jeans. Oh, so appealing.

She tilted her head. "Why are you at the front door and ringing the bell?"

He shrugged. "Isn't that how it's done?"

She grinned and pushed open the screen door. "I like that. Come on in, and I'll get my things."

He stepped past her, and a light, flowery scent tickled his nose. They stood staring at each other for a moment. What was he supposed to do now? He stepped back and took in the whole of her. "You look nice."

"I can look like a woman and not a cowgirl when I try. You look nice too."

He glanced down at his plaid shirt, black jeans, and black boots. "Still look like a cowboy, though."

She offered a slight smile. "And a very good-looking cowboy, I might add. Wait a sec. I'll be right back." She stepped into the family room and headed for the bedroom wing.

With Lacy's words echoing in his thoughts, Clint wandered into the study and toward the wall of awards won by Jace's dad in team-roping competitions. Did she really think he was good-looking? He'd never think to use those words to describe himself. He wasn't ugly, but not celebrity handsome either. He gave himself a mental shake. *Focus, Palmer, focus.* He studied one of the awards. Ted

McGowan hadn't been gone for more than three years, and his presence was still felt strongly all over the ranch, as it should be. He was the third generation to run the ranch, and Jace was doing a fine job of becoming the fourth.

"There you are. I'm ready."

She stood in the study's doorway, her purse over her shoulder and a sweater draped over her arm. He ached right then to kiss her like he had earlier, but he refrained.

As they walked to Clint's red Chevy Silverado, he glanced down at her. "I thought we could go to a steak house I like. That okay with you?"

"Sounds great. You know I like a good steak dinner."

"It's not one of those chain places. It's locally owned by a former bullfighter."

"Anyone I know?"

"Don't think so. He didn't work our circuit. Name's Carson McGraw." He opened the passenger-side door and waited until she buckled herself in, then closed it and went around to his side. Good thing he'd remembered his manners. It had been a long time since he'd taken anyone on a date. He slid behind the wheel and smiled at her. "Doing okay?"

She gave him a funny look. "Yeah. Why?"

"I dunno. We've known each other for years, but I feel like a kid on his first date."

She laid her hand on his arm, sending tingles clear up to his shoulder. "Is that what this is? A date?"

He slanted a glance at her. "I think so. That okay with you?"

"Yes. It's fine. We've gone out together many times for supper and movies and concerts, but it feels different this time."

"It is different, isn't it?"

"Yes, and yet it feels as natural as breathing to me." She removed her hand from his arm. "Now, drive. I'm starving."

He laughed, wanting her to put her hand back where it was. He'd heard someone say that their spouse completed them. Having Lacy sitting next to him did give him a sense of completion, yet there seemed to be a feeling that she was holding back.

By the time they arrived at Carson's Steaks and Chops, they were chatting like the old friends they were. Without even thinking about it, he almost took her hand as they crossed the parking lot, but just in time he caught himself and made an awkward gesture of sweeping his arm around as he said, "Look at all these cars. I hope we don't have to wait long."

After they were seated in a booth, he asked the waitress who came for their orders, "Is Carson working tonight?"

The ponytailed girl looked to be barely out of high school. She nodded. "Yes, he is. You know him?"

"Yeah, I do. Tell him Clint Palmer is in the house and ask him to stop by to say hey."

"Will do."

They both ordered rib eyes medium rare, baked potatoes, and a tossed salad. Lacy glanced around the room after the waitress left. "Nice place."

"You'll like it even more after you taste the food." He picked up his sweet tea and sipped.

"Well, knock me over with a feather. Look what this pretty lady here dragged in."

Clint looked up into Carson McGraw's round face. "Yeah, I thought I should come by and check up on you." He patted his friend's protruding paunch. "Been eating a bit too much of your own food, I see."

Carson laughed. "And it looks like you got your head caught in a lawn mower. What happened to that hair you swore you'd never wear short?" He looked at Lacy. "Pardon my friend's manners here and let me introduce myself, since he won't." He stuck out his hand to her. "Carson McGraw. Welcome to my house."

Lacy laughed and gave him her hand. "Lacy Roberts."

He indicated Clint with a tip of his head. "How'd a nice gal like you end up with this one?"

She looked at Clint and flashed him a smile that would light up the sky on a cloudy night. "We both work on the same ranch."

"And her cousin, the rancher, is my best friend," Clint added. "What she didn't tell you is that she is one of the best barrel racers around." He smiled at Lacy, loving her mock displeasure at his words.

Carson nudged Clint on the shoulder. "You've got good taste, bro. Better hang onto her. You still bullfighting?"

"I hope to, in answer to your first comment. As for your question, for now I'm still bullfighting, but maybe not for much longer. A bad wreck last year messed up my leg pretty good. I'm partnering with Jace in his bull-stock business now."

"That so? I may be interested in investing in a bull to satisfy my girls. Got about fifty head and need to increase it. I'll give you a call soon. Still have the same phone number?"

"Sure do."

A busboy appeared with sizzling steaks on a tray, and Carson stepped back to make room. He looked at Clint. "The steaks are on the house. I'll tell your server."

Clint opened his mouth to protest, but Carson held up his hand. "Next time you can pay."

He nodded. "Deal. Thanks a lot."

As they finished up their meals, Lacy's phone rang. She made a face. "I meant to silence the thing. Let me send it to voice mail." She found the phone in her purse and frowned. "It's from Jace. He wouldn't call unless it was important." She tapped the screen. "Jace, what's up?" Her smile faded. "When did that happen? ... Where is she now?" She began gathering her things. "You staying there awhile? ... We're finishing up here. We'll be there fast as we can."

She clicked off and looked at Clint, who was already placing a tip on the table. "They took Aunt Carolyn to the hospital with heart-attack symptoms."

Adrenaline coursed through him as he slid out of the booth and pulled his keys from his back pocket at the same time. Without speaking, they scurried through the restaurant. He spotted Carson as he passed by the front desk and waved at him. "Family emergency. Thanks again for the steaks."

His friend waved him on, and they soon arrived at the truck and climbed into their seats. He got the motor started and spoke to Lacy for the first time since she had hung up from Jace's call. "Which hospital are we going to?"

"University. That's where her oncologist is. She went by ambulance." She tapped on her phone and put it to her ear. "Jace, we're on our way. Is she in a room? ... Okay, I'll call when we get there."

Clint pointed the truck toward downtown and the hospital. "I hope they did the right thing, bringing her there and not to the hospital that's closest to the ranch."

"Me too. Jace said the doctor is examining her now. They aren't sure it was a heart attack after all."

He eased his foot off the accelerator. No sense in getting a traffic ticket and arriving later than they would at normal speed.

Sydney met them at the ER entrance. "They just took her up to a room. She suffered a panic attack, not a heart attack. They want to keep her overnight for observation. Jace is with her. I'll take you up there."

A few minutes later, they stepped into a private room on the cardiac floor. Clint acknowledged Jace, who stood on the far side of the bed, and stepped closer. Carolyn had seemed so tiny in her large king bed at home but now appeared even smaller in a narrow hospital bed surrounded by an IV pole and wires coming from the neck opening of her hospital gown that looked to be three sizes too big.

Carolyn opened her eyes and looked at Clint. "You didn't need to interrupt your dinner date for me and my silly panic attack."

"Oh, yes, we did," Lacy said. "We can go out anytime. There's only one you, and if you're being taken to the hospital in an ambulance, that's where we need to be. If it was a panic attack, why are you on this floor hooked up to surveillance?"

"Just a precaution. They're going to monitor me overnight. If nothing more is amiss, I'll be home by lunchtime."

Clint rested a hand on Carolyn's shoulder, the only spot that didn't seem to have a wire attached. "If it makes you feel any better, we'd already finished our steaks. All we missed was dessert."

Carolyn turned her head toward him and managed a soft smile. "Well, then, I owe both of you a gooey dessert when I get home."

He laughed. "It's a deal. How are you feeling?"

"Much better now that they gave me a relaxant. But it's making me sleepy."

"I don't remember you having panic attacks before," Lacy said.

"Years ago, when the boys were small, I had one. Never since then. I don't understand why one came on now. I was resting in bed, watching a movie, and my heart suddenly started racing. When my chest pains started, I called Jace. He called 911 and came over right away. The ambulance must have driven at top speed to get there so fast."

"That's why they have lights and sirens, Mom." Jace grinned at Clint. "You guys have a good dinner?"

"Yep. We went to Carson McGraw's. He may be contacting us soon about investing in a bull."

Jace's brows rose. "Is he going into the stock business too?"

"Negative. He's acquiring a small herd and wants one for stud." He looked at Lacy. "I think we need to give this lady some rest."

She nodded then turned to Carolyn. "I can bring you home tomorrow if you get released. No need for Jace or Clint to leave their work."

After they got back on the road, Clint took Lacy's hand. "Want to stop somewhere for the dessert we missed?"

"Not unless you want to. It's been a long day, what with going undercover, our wonderful dinner, and then the scare about Aunt Carolyn. I just want to go home." She squeezed his hand, and he decided to leave it there.

"Probably best. We can both get to sleep early and be ready for the day tomorrow."

"But we still haven't had dessert. There's a cherry pie sitting on the counter at home. I made it this morning to get my mind off meeting Austin. How does that sound? A little something sweet to sleep on?"

His spirits soared. "That sounds perfect. I love your pies." He almost added that one of her kisses would be all the sweet he'd need to sleep on, but he held his tongue. Maybe he'd get both the pie and the kiss.

Chapter 24

Lacy placed a generous slice of cherry pie in front of Clint and then set a smaller slice in front of her stool at the island. She slid onto her seat. The evening had been so topsy-turvy emotionally that she was glad she'd suggested they have pie together before the night ended. She watched as Clint forked his first piece and put it into his mouth.

He smiled and looked at her. "This tastes awesome." His gaze went to her untouched serving. "Aren't you going to eat yours?"

"Yes. I was waiting to see your verdict first."

He stabbed his pie with his fork and cut off another bite. "You know I always like your pies. I like anything you cook."

"This was baked, not cooked."

He held up his forkful and shoved it into his mouth. Then he set the fork on his plate. "I'm not eating any more until you eat some yourself. In fact, this reminds me of a mystery I saw on TV once. A person put some poison into food he'd just cooked and then served it to another person, never taking a bite of the food himself. After several bites, the other person dropped dead."

Lacy burst out laughing. "If I were going to poison you, I'd have better ways of doing it."

Clint laughed, forked another bite, and held it up. "Just to be sure, eat this." He offered it to her.

Lacy giggled and closed her mouth around the bite, letting the sweetness of the syrup and the tartness of the cherries mingle for a delicious moment on her tongue. She'd knocked it out of the park with this new recipe.

"Um, can I have my fork back?"

She let him slide it away from her lips. "Just enjoying the taste awhile before I swallowed."

His gaze went to her mouth. "I see you didn't quite get all that gooey syrup off your lips. Let me help you." He ran his thumb over her lower lip, sending goose bumps down her neck.

Their gazes locked and held. "Did you get it all off?" she asked.

He leaned in closer and peered at her mouth, so close that she felt his breath. "Nope, there is one tiny crumb right there. Let me get it for you."

The sensation of his lips covering hers sent shivers through her. She slipped her arms around him as the kiss deepened, causing a warm sensation to flow through her. Who needed pie when she could enjoy kisses like his? They slowly separated and laughed at the same time. "Cherry-flavored kisses are the best," she whispered.

He chucked her under her chin. "No better way to have dessert." He ran his eyes over her face as if he were going to kiss her again but turned and continued to eat his pie.

She did the same. Where was her determination to keep the evening to friendly banter without even a good-night kiss?

She finished her serving and laid her fork on the empty plate. "Outside of Carolyn's emergency, it's been a wonderful evening."

He stacked their plates then leaned her direction. "I agree. The steak was great and the company stupendous. I couldn't ask for a tastier dessert. But, I have to say, the best part was your kiss."

Before she could answer, his lips were on hers. Tender and soft, they let the kiss linger. Then they separated, and Clint pulled her closer. "Can we do it again soon?"

She'd been crushing on him for so long, and now that it was obvious he had feelings for her … "I'd like that, cowboy."

"Good." Clint gave her a quick kiss and a hug before he stood. "Me too. See you in the morning. Sleep well." He headed for the mudroom. "I'll let myself out. Get yourself to bed. It's late."

Clint threw off the covers and planted his feet on the floor. He'd known he'd not fall asleep easily after the full day and the sweet time he had with Lacy, both before Carolyn's panic attack and after. He smiled at the memory of their cherry-pie kisses. He was definitely falling for her. Correction—had fallen for her.

As much fun as they had together and the developing mutual affection they seemed to feel, one strong insurmountable problem remained: her faith—or, he should say, his lack of faith. It might not come between them now, but he knew over time it would become a wedge. He didn't care how much Jace told him he was wrong in his opinion—or the pastor at their church, or Lacy. He could never be good enough to be loved by God. Period.

He flicked on the lamp, and his gaze went to the Bible his dad had given him. Instead of putting it back into the drawer after he'd let Jace use it the other day, he'd left it out on the nightstand. The thing had seemed to take on a life of its own the past couple of days, beckoning him to open it and read, but he'd resisted. Now the pull was back.

He lifted it and set it on his lap. It weighed heavy on his legs. He gripped a chunk of its pages between his thumb and index finger and watched them flip past. Underlined verses and, in some cases, full paragraphs highlighted in yellow popped out at him. One caught his attention, and he let the page fall open. He stared at the words: *"Can a mother forget the baby at her breast and have no compassion on the child she has borne? Though she may forget, I will not forget you!"*

A handwritten note in the margin cut to his heart: *Nor will I ever forget my son. God, watch over him, wherever he is. TS*

He read the verse along with Dad's note several times. He'd finally accepted that his dad loved him even though Tim hadn't seen him since he was a baby, but was this saying God loved him too?

He tried unsuccessfully to swallow the lump that felt like the size of Texas. How was it he came to these exact words? He pressed the heels of his hands against his eyes, but the tears escaped anyway. He wanted to pray, but how? He'd heard others pray before a meal, seemingly unrehearsed, but right then he had no words. Clint grabbed his phone from the nightstand and tapped the screen. The ringtone sounded in his ear, followed by a sleepy voice saying, "Hello?"

"Tim? This is Clint. I've been reading the Bible you gave me, and I have some questions. This a good time?"

His dad made a sound that sounded like a yawn. One a.m. was not a good time.

"Look, I'm sorry. I lost track of the hour. I'll call in the morning."

"Son, anytime you call is a good time."

Lacy put the last of the breakfast dishes in the dishwasher. Aunt Carolyn had just called to say that the doctor had left a few minutes before and she'd be ready to come home by the time Lacy got there. And Clint had left her a text while she was in the shower, saying he wouldn't be at breakfast and was grabbing something at the apartment. Without an explanation why, her imagination wanted to go wild with speculations that he wasn't interested in her after all—but she wasn't going there. She'd texted him back, but he'd never responded.

She was gathering up her purse and keys when her phone dinged. She checked the screen and smiled at Clint's words.

"Sorry I missed your text back. Last night was the best night ever."

"Aw. I feel the same way too."

"I'm glad you said that. Are you going to bring Carolyn home this morning?"

"Yes. She's very happy to be released."

"That's great. My dad and I are getting together in a few minutes."

"To talk bullfighting?"

"Maybe a little, but…"

"But what?"

"I want to talk to him about something I saw in the Bible. I'll tell you more when I see you."

Lacy clicked off the phone and tossed it into her purse. Her grin had to be ear to ear. Could she feel any more joy than right now? They had both enjoyed last night, Aunt Carolyn was coming home, and best of all, Clint was reading the Bible and talking to Tim about it. She stepped out the front door as Clint drove by in his truck. She grinned and returned his wave before all but skipping to her car.

A half hour later, Lacy entered the hospital room and smiled at how her aunt was already propped up on the bed against a pile of pillows, her eyes closed and wearing the jeans and T-shirt she must have come to the hospital in the night before. Her heart squeezed at how thin and faded Aunt Carolyn's dark brown hair had become after just two sessions of chemo. They'd have to make a trip to a wig store soon.

Her aunt's eyes popped open.

"Good morning." Lacy crossed to the bed. "Looks like you're ready to leave."

Her aunt shifted position. "The nurse told me to go ahead and get dressed, but I can't leave until the doctor officially signs the release document. He's due here anytime."

Lacy frowned. "I'm surprised, since he saw you already."

"The paperwork wasn't available, so he has to come back. I'm sorry to make you hang around. I know from experience—it may be a while. I'm sure you have something else to do."

"I do, but Shiloh can wait. If you are still doing all right by the weekend, I'm planning to rodeo. She and I ran the pattern yesterday, and that horse of mine hasn't lost a beat even being sick."

Aunt Carolyn waved a hand. "Of course I'll be fine. Now that we know that what I had wasn't a heart attack. Outside of this nuisance of cancer, I'm more than fine. Tell me, how was that date of yours last night? I was dying to ask but didn't want to with the others there."

Lacy dropped into the chair next to the bed. "It was wonderful."

"By the looks on your faces last night, I could see you two are smitten."

She giggled. "Smitten? Isn't that an old-fashioned word?"

"It's been around awhile. But it still fits the occasion. I presume you'll be having more dates in the future."

Lacy felt herself grinning. "Looks that way." She glanced off to the side and then back at her aunt. "Is it too soon for me to feel so certain that I'm falling in love?"

Her aunt beamed. "It isn't like you met him last week. You've known each other for years. Look how fast Jace and Sydney fell for each other with just one day together."

Lacy laughed. "Yeah, and a couple of years between that date and the next." She thought back to the rough start her cousin and his wife had. Syd had been so adamant about not ever leaving Chicago—and when she and Jace parted company at the end of the rodeo weekend, it seemed they'd never work out their differences. But Lacy would never forget the joy on both their faces when Sydney showed up at the ranch unannounced, declaring her love for him. Was that the kind of joy her aunt saw on hers and Clint's faces last night?

"I heard you say he took you for a steak dinner."

Lacy snapped out of her reverie. "Yes, and the food was great. He's being very affectionate with me too, and I'm loving every minute."

"I'm happy to hear that."

She felt her smile fade as a dark thought overtook her joy. "I never intended to fall for someone who didn't believe the same way about the Lord. Tim Steele gave him a Bible, and I'm hopeful that, in time, the wall around Clint's heart will crumble enough to let God in. Actually, he's with Tim right now, discussing something he read in that Bible."

Aunt Carolyn clapped her hands. "Lacy, that's wonderful. Nothing is impossible with God. But it's important you not get too serious until he's solidified his belief about the Lord. I'll pray for both of you."

A tall, balding man in scrubs stepped into the room just then. He nodded at Lacy, then focused on her aunt. "I know you're anxious to blow this joint, Carolyn. I just signed the release."

Aunt Carolyn scooted off the bed. "You bet I'm ready. This beautiful young woman is my niece, Lacy. She's my transportation."

The doctor looked at Lacy. "I'm Dr. Browning. I've told Carolyn there is nothing else she can do except follow the protocol set by her oncologist. Just try to keep her free of stressful situations as much as possible."

Lacy stood. "We'll do our best. The most stressful situation we were all in is over now."

"She mentioned that."

After shaking Lacy's hand, he left, and a nurse pushed a wheelchair into the room. "No arguments, Carolyn. We provide this for all our patients." She looked at Lacy. "If you bring your car to the side entrance, we'll be there."

Lacy headed for the elevator. She had to keep her head here, but in reality her thoughts kept wanting to focus on that meeting Clint was in with Tim.

Chapter 25

Clint pulled into Tim's driveway a few minutes before eight. He'd hardly slept since he called his dad at one a.m. Tim had encouraged him to come over right then, but he would have felt terrible about keeping the man up when he had a flight to Oklahoma City at noon, so he said he'd be over first thing in the morning.

Tim opened the door before Clint could ring the bell. Wearing pressed dark blue Wranglers, boots, and a blue Western-style shirt, he looked as if he was ready to leave the moment he and Clint finished their discussion. "Been watching for ya. I'm good to go to the airport except to pack, and Nancy is working on that for both of us now." He grinned as his gaze went to the Bible in Clint's hand. He opened the door wider and stepped back. "Come in."

Clint followed him into the kitchen. A woman with graying shoulder-length hair, wearing jeans and a crisp white shirt, stood at the counter. She turned and held out her hand, her dark eyes twinkling. Her smile revealed deep dimples. "You must be Clint. I'm Nancy. Nice to meet you. You want some coffee?" She indicated Tim with a tilt of her head. "I know this guy does."

Her easygoing demeanor put Clint at ease, and he returned her smile. "Coffee sounds great. I take it black."

She laughed. "I figured you did. Seems most bullfighters and bull riders do." She lifted a pot of steaming brew from the drip maker's hot plate. "French Roast suit you okay?"

He nodded, and she grabbed a red mug from a hook on the wall and poured the fragrant dark liquid. She handed him the steaming cup. "I'm happy to finally meet you. Tim has been beside himself with joy since you two found each other. No worries about me hanging around. I'm finishing up our packing and then off on errands until it's time for us to go to the airport."

The men said their goodbyes to Nancy and settled in the same chairs from the last time Clint visited.

Tim took a sip of coffee and looked Clint in the eyes. "You may as well have come over after you called. I didn't sleep much after we hung up."

"That makes two of us. I'm sorry I called so late."

His dad grinned. "Hey, I meant it when I said I was happy you did. I'd been hoping I didn't overwhelm you with all I told you before."

"It took a while to wrap my head around it. I probably would have called sooner, but we've been involved in helping catch a horse thief who was also causing trouble for my girlfriend." He paused. The word *girlfriend* rolled off his tongue naturally, and it felt good saying it.

Tim's eyes twinkled. "I don't know which question to ask first, the one about the horse thief or the one about the girlfriend. I don't think you've mentioned having someone special in your life."

Clint felt a smile emerging. "That's because the last time I was here, she wasn't officially my girlfriend. And she still isn't yet, but hopefully she will be. We've been good friends for a long time, and we had what we're calling our first date last night. Her name's Lacy. She is Jace's cousin and lives and works on the ranch too. Chases cans on weekends."

"At least she understands what a time-suck rodeoing can be."

"That she does. We're often at the same rodeos. That is, until I hang up bullfighting for good. I'm not sure how much longer I can do it with this bad leg."

Tim frowned. "If you're in the stock-contractor business, you'll still be taking the bulls to rodeos. Tell me about the horse thief."

Clint settled back in the chair. "Our new ranch hand was asked by a friend to board his horse at our ranch. The horse became sick with strangles shortly after that, and we found out through his microchip that he was stolen. There's much more to the story, but that should wait until another time." He held up the Bible. "This is the reason I'm here today."

His dad's face lit up. "I was about to get to that." He reached for a Bible resting on the side table and set it in his lap.

Clint opened his own Bible to the passage he'd called about. "For the past several days, I've been sensing a nudge to look at this. When I opened it last night, I was surprised at first to find all the underlining, and then I remembered how you said you'd marked it up some."

"It was the only copy I had that day. I was prompted to give it to you, notes and all." His dad patted the Bible resting in his lap. "Got me a new one now."

Clint shrugged. "Maybe we should trade so you can have your notes back."

Tim shook his head. "Keep it. You never know when something I've written will grab your attention in a good way."

"It already did. You highlighted a verse that said even though a mother may forget her child, God won't abandon him." He stared up at the darkened television and worked to put his thoughts together. "I never felt a mother's love until I moved out of that wretched trailer and started living with the McGowans. Jace's mom is more a mom to me than my own mother." Unbidden moisture gathered in his eyes.

He continued, "When you told me how you thought about me every day and I saw your note in the margin next to that verse … well, I've always believed God exists, but I felt I wasn't good enough for Him to love me, no matter how many times someone has told me that He does. I read those words and realized I might be wrong." He palmed the moisture on his cheeks away. "Sorry for the tears. Not very manly."

Tim reached over and gripped Clint's arm. "Son, it's very manly. Read the psalms and see how often David, a warrior, shed tears because of the Lord's love for him—even after he had failed God."

Warmth washed over Clint as he mulled Tim's words. "I've got a lot to learn. Everyone who is part of my life has a faith like yours. I've never admitted it until recently, but I've been a little jealous of them. Even so, I'm having trouble coming to grips with my past and how that fits in to things." He looked toward the fireplace for a moment and then back at his father, startled at what he saw. "I didn't mean to make you cry."

"Tears of joy, tears of joy." Tim flipped through his Bible. "Can you find the book of Romans in that Bible of yours? Let's look at some passages I know will help clear away the confusion."

A couple of hours later, the men embraced. "Now we're more than father and son," his dad said. "Welcome to both families."

Clint's eyes widened. "You've lost me there."

"Like I told you earlier, you've got siblings you've never met, meaning my daughter and son and their families. I hope to remedy that within a few weeks when they are here to celebrate Nancy's birthday. And after turning your life over to God this morning, you have another brand-new family that extends around the globe."

Not exactly sure what he meant, Clint smiled and gave him a quick hug. "It's nice to know I'm not an only child anymore."

"No, you're not. I'm just sorry I'm scheduled to fly out so soon. We'll talk more about it all as soon as I get back." His dad's grin was infectious. "And I can't wait to come to the ranch and see that bull-stock operation. There's so much to catch up on." Then his smile dimmed a little. "I hope it goes well when you talk to your mom."

"Me too. I'm going there right now." He waved the brochure that Dad had just given him.

Clint drove out of his father's neighborhood in a state of euphoria mixed with disbelief over what had happened that morning. Who should he call first, Jace or Lacy? He pulled over and called Jace.

"Hey, bro, I know you'll be glad to hear the news. I did what you've been after me to do for several years. I turned my life over to God."

He laughed at Jace's whoop.

"That's awesome news, Clint. Does Lacy know yet?"

"I'm calling her next. I hope you don't mind if I ditch work the rest of the day. After discussing Mom's situation, Dad and I think it's best if I do a one-man intervention with Mom and get her into rehab. He gave me information on one he's familiar with over in San Marcos. If she agrees, I want to take her over there right away before she changes her mind."

"Hey, you do what you need to do. We're fine here. Lacy and I got all the animals fed, and she's inside fixing lunch. Keep us posted."

They disconnected, and he called Lacy.

She answered with a "Hey there."

"Hey there, yourself. I've got some news you're going to want to hear. I've been talking with my dad for the past several hours. He answered my question and then took me to a book in the Bible and showed me how much God loves me no matter how imperfect I am. I now know that's true because Christ took my punishment in place of me on the cross." He drew in a breath. "I prayed with him, Lacy, and it looks like I'll be heading to cowboy church with you and Jace at the rodeo this weekend. I can't believe how free I feel." He waited to hear a whoop like Jace's but heard nothing. Was she not happy? A loud *sniff* filled the connection. "Are you crying?"

"You big oaf. Of course I am. I'm working very hard to not let out a huge squeal of joy. I'll wait until we hang up."

He laughed. "I may not be home until later this evening. I'm on my way to Mom's to insist she go to rehab. If she agrees, I need to take her immediately. There's one in San Marcos Dad told me about."

They talked a few minutes more and ended the call. He started the truck moving, feeling as though he could fly to Mom's unaided.

He pulled into the parking space outside her trailer and then said a quick prayer before approaching the residence and pounding on the door. He glanced at the window to his left, waiting for the curtain to move. It didn't, and he raised his fist to knock again—but before he could do so, the door swung open.

Mom stood there looking much the same as she had the last time he visited. She yawned and scratched her head. "Don't you believe in late-afternoon visits?

If you want to know how the new AC you ordered is working, it's fine. Now can I go back to sleep?" She swung the door to shut it, but he'd already stuck his booted foot between it and the doorjamb. "You're not going to shut me out, Mom. I'm coming in." He pushed at it, and she allowed it to open.

He stepped inside. "It feels a lot better in here than last time."

"I already told you the AC works. Can you leave so I can go back to bed?"

"I came to tell you something important, and I'm not leaving until I do."

She raised her hands in surrender and stepped back. "Guess I don't have any choice. But make it short."

He took a few more steps, and his stomach lurched. "The AC has cooled off the air … now what are you going to do about the stench?"

"I don't smell anything bad."

"I don't suppose you would." He had to get her help. He moved to the table and sat. She wrapped her ratty-looking robe tighter around her thin body and sat across from him. "I suppose you saw that creep you think is your dad since you were here last."

Instead of the usual feeling of disgust at her attitude, love and compassion welled up inside him. "I did, but it wasn't the first time I've met with him."

She picked up an empty cigarette pack and stuck her finger in as if looking for a smoke. Not finding one, she pulled an overflowing ashtray across the table and stirred around in it with her finger until she fished out a butt that still had a bit of white showing above the filter. She took a disposable lighter from her pocket and lit the stub. After a long draw she expelled the smoke, and its putrid odor seemed to make a beeline for Clint's nose. He swallowed back the bile, trying not to gag.

She leaned back. "I remember now. He told you the buckle was his. So why did you go back to see the loser again?"

"Mom, he's no loser. Like I told you last time, he spends a lot of time helping kids and keeping them straight and out of trouble. He's helped me to see that I needed God in my life—and that I need to forgive you for keeping him away from me. He and my stepmom are heading to Oklahoma City to see my half sister and her family." He paused and waited while she snuffed out the butt. "This isn't easy to do, but I forgive you, and I want to help you get that monkey off your back. Dad told me about a rehab center in San Marcos that sounds like a good place, and they will take in addicts at no charge."

She fished around in the ashtray and pulled out another almost-spent butt. "I don't need no handouts from nobody. When I decide I need help, I'll pay my own way. I ain't no charity case." She lit the butt and inhaled. The smoke trailed from her nostrils. She leaned over and opened the tiny fridge under the sink.

"Looks like I drank all the beer. I don't suppose you'd get me some before you go home."

His heart sank, but he wasn't giving up. "No, I won't, Mom. There's no shame in admitting you need help. People are doing that every day to get clean. Please think about it." He took the rehab brochure from his pocket and opened it. "Here's some information about the place. You aren't going to live much longer if you don't get help, and I want you around to see your grandchildren someday."

Her eyes grew large. "You don't even got a girl. It may be years before you get hitched."

"You're wrong. There is a girl I've loved for years, and I'm finally willing to admit it. Her name is Lacy. She's Jace's cousin—the barrel racer I've talked about. We're not anywhere near to talking engagement yet, but she's real special."

She narrowed her gaze. "You're not joshing me, are you?"

"I wouldn't joke about something like that."

"How are you going to support a wife on a ranch hand's salary?"

"I'm not a ranch hand anymore. I'm part owner in Jace's stock-contracting business."

"You never told me this before."

"I did, but you were too drunk to remember." He nodded toward the brochure that still sat on the table. "What do you say?"

She picked up the flyer and unfolded it. "I always liked San Marcos when I visited there, before Tim left us."

He bit back angry words of correction. It didn't matter. He only wanted to get her into rehab. "Are you saying okay, you'll go?"

"When would I have to leave?"

"I'll drive you there this afternoon, if you agree. It's only a little over an hour away. Mom, I love you and want to help you get sober. Please agree to this. They already know I might be bringing you in today. They have a bed and people there to care for you and help you through detox."

Tears filled her eyes, and she buried her face in her hands, letting out a loud sob. "How can you love me after all I've done?"

"I don't know, but I do. Same as how Christ loves us no matter how rotten we've been. So much that He gave His life for us. That's what I couldn't understand until today." He stood and helped her stand. "Let's get a bag packed and be on our way."

Chapter 26

Lacy's phone rang as she was saddling Shiloh to practice the cloverleaf pattern. She smiled at Clint's picture on the screen and put the device to her ear. "Hey there. How did things go?"

"Great. Mom's right here beside me, and we're on our way to San Marcos to the rehab center. I'll have to stay to get her registered and settled, but I'll call when I'm on my way back."

Lacy couldn't help the squeal that erupted from her mouth, and she clamped her lips together. "I hope she didn't hear that."

He chuckled. "I don't think she did. She fell asleep as soon as we got on the road and hasn't moved a muscle. You're not too excited, are you?"

"Oh, Clint, I am very excited. First your own news, and now your mom is finally going to rehab."

"I feel the same, but I don't want to get ahead of things here. One day at a time."

"I know. But this is the most positive thing that has happened with her in a long while."

"How is Carolyn doing?"

"She actually came to the table for lunch with Jace and Luke and me. Will you be back in time for supper?"

"I may not be home until closer to six. Maybe you should go ahead and serve at the regular time. I'll grab something at a drive-through when I hit town. I wouldn't mind the company while I ate."

"Don't do that. I'm making spaghetti and meatballs. They warm up nicely."

"Deal. Mom's stirring. I'll talk to you soon."

After the call ended, Lacy finished saddling her horse and mounted her. "Let's go, girl. I know you're itching to get those legs of yours moving."

Clint parked under an overhang at New Life Rehabilitation Center and helped his mother out of the truck. "Mom, you're shaking."

She sneered at him. "Wouldn't you be if you were going to prison?"

"Is that what you think? This isn't prison."

"May as well be."

The shaking was probably due to her not having had a drink in a while rather than the fear of what she was about to do. He reached into the back seat and grabbed the duffel, which contained the cleanest clothes he could find in the pile on her closet floor. After she was settled, he planned to run to the Walmart they'd passed a few blocks back to get her some clothes and toiletries. It felt good to be doing something positive for her. Strange, since until today, all he'd wanted was to be free of her.

A pair of doors slid open as they approached, and they stepped into a sunny room decorated in a Southwestern style. He led her to a counter on the far side of the reception area.

A middle-aged woman looked up from her computer and smiled. "Welcome." Her gaze went to his mom and back to him. "Are you here to check in?"

"Yes," Clint said. "I called a couple of hours ago and spoke to Margaret Currington. She's expecting us. I'm Clint Palmer, and this is my mother, Diane Palmer."

The woman nodded and pointed to a couch a short distance away. "Please have a seat, and I'll let Margaret know you're here."

Clint sat on the couch next to his mom and draped his arm over her bony shoulders. "The next several days might be rough, but these folks seem really nice, and they know how to get people through the worst of withdrawal."

She patted his leg and left her hand there. "You're a good boy, Clint."

He shut his eyes and let the words wrap around his heart. Why couldn't she have said stuff like that while he was growing up? He gave himself a mental shake. No more whys and what-ifs allowed.

A door across the room opened, and a woman about Clint's age stepped through. Tall, her red hair clipped short, and wearing navy slacks and a white shirt, she approached them. Her gaze went to him. "Clint Palmer?"

At his nod, she focused on his mom. "You must be Diane. Nice to meet you. I'm Margaret, but the people around here call me Maggie. We have your room ready. After a brief time of registration, we'll get you settled. I know you're very uncomfortable right now, and that's to be expected. Your son did the right thing to get you the help you need."

Mom looked at him. "I just told him he was a good boy."

He helped her up, and they followed Maggie back through the same doorway. His mom might think she was the only one who was scared, but she wasn't. After so many life-changing decisions in the past twenty-four hours, he was terrified but confident, because for the first time in his life he had God to lean on.

Lacy sat in the study so she would see Clint's red truck the moment he pulled in. He had called an hour ago and said he was on the way home. He'd had to stay until his mom was registered and checked in as an indigent patient.

Tired of looking out the window, she pulled out her phone and scrolled through her messages. At the sound of tires crunching over the gravel, she looked up and saw Clint roll his truck to a stop next to her vehicle. She raced from the study and through the front door. He was already at the steps. Without a word, they embraced and held the hug for a few moments.

He released her and stepped back. "I needed that. It was harder than I thought it would be to leave her there. She looked so small and alone—no more spit and vinegar."

"When can you see her again?"

"Not for a month. They said it will take that long to get her detoxed and going the right direction." He tossed his Stetson onto a chair and took her in his arms again, lifting her up until they were eye to eye. He kissed her. "I'm so glad to see you. It's been a long day."

He set her down, and she grabbed his hand. "Come on inside. We can talk more while I heat up your supper."

He resisted her tug and pulled her toward him. "Before we go in, I want to apologize for all the times I made fun of your faith. I never would have admitted it before, but I was always a bit envious of what you and the others had that I couldn't. Or at least thought I couldn't."

"No need to apologize. I'm just grateful you finally had your eyes opened. This is an answer to my prayers. All our prayers."

"It feels good to not be on the outside of things, especially with you. I need to tell you something. Earlier today, I referred to you as my girlfriend. Are you okay with that?"

A warm feeling washed over her, and she grinned. "In other words, am I okay if we're in an exclusive relationship?"

A small crease formed between his eyes, and then he laughed. "Yes. Those are the words I'm wanting to say."

She wrapped her arms around his waist and looked up at him. "Does this mean I can declare on social media that I'm in a relationship?"

"If you want to."

"Nah. I'm hardly ever on there anymore."

"Good answer." He leaned down and brushed her lips with a tender kiss.

"Hey, you two. We don't allow that kind of stuff around here."

They jumped apart as Jace climbed the steps to the porch.

Lacy laughed. "Hugs and kisses are nice."

"It is unless your wife pulled double duty at the therapeutic center." Jace looked at Clint. "How'd it go with your mom?"

"Surprisingly well. She agreed to be admitted, and they've got her detoxing right now."

Lacy grinned. "Just think, Clint. You've already found your dad, and now you may finally have the mom you always wanted, once she's sober."

He grinned. "Not only that, but when I was at my dad's this morning, I met Nancy, my stepmom and also found out that I have a sister in Oklahoma City, and she and her husband have two children. And I have a brother in Tennessee who's married and has two kids."

Jace laughed. "God is blessing you big-time."

Clint drew Lacy into a side hug. "And a girlfriend that I'm crazy about too." He kissed the top of her head.

Lacy's heart fluttered as she wrapped her arm around his waist and waited for Clint to lean down and kiss her.

Jace crossed his arms in mock displeasure. "And now I've got to put up with all this PDA."

Clint looked at Jace and snorted. "Seems I remember quite a bit of PDA happening that whole rodeo weekend you and Syd got back together."

Jace laughed. "That was different. This is my cousin you're locking lips with. I need to watch out for her." He glanced at Lacy and then Clint. "Seriously, I'm glad to finally see you two together. Hearing both of you lament how much you were wanting to start something but never telling each other was about to drive me crazy."

Lacy laughed. "I never said all that."

"Oh, yes, you did," Jace said. "And what you didn't say was plain on your face."

"Well, transparency is always a good thing, isn't it? I'm about to heat up our leftovers for Clint. Is Syd able to join us later for some ice cream? I think we've got some celebrating to do."

Jace pulled his phone from his pocket. "I'll call her now. I'm sure she'll be home from work by then."

Chapter 27

One Month Later

Lacy glanced at Clint as he drove down the highway toward town, admiring how nice he looked in a new button-down shirt and pressed dark blue jeans. Instead of his ever-present scuffed brown boots, he had on the same shiny black ones he'd worn to Jace and Syd's wedding. His black leather jacket finished off the look. It was finally turning cooler at night, and he'd need it later.

She glanced down at the skirt she'd splurged on that day when she and Syd spent an afternoon shopping. The sales clerk had mentioned that the color was called dusty aqua and the style boho-chic, whatever that meant. She'd fallen in love with the hand-embroidered beading, and when she'd learned it was on sale, she bought it.

Syd wouldn't let her head home without completing the outfit, and by the time they returned to the ranch, Lacy had added a cream jersey blouse with three-quarter sleeves and a scalloped hem and a pair of new slip-on wedge sandals. She had to admit, she hadn't felt this girly since she'd worn her bridesmaid's dress for Sydney and Jace's wedding. And seeing the look on Clint's face when he came to pick her up a short while ago, the outfit was worth every penny spent.

He glanced over and took her hand. "I'm glad you recommended the Ranch over that French place I suggested."

She chuckled. "I may want to learn how to cook those fancy dishes, but that doesn't mean I want you feeling uncomfortable in that kind of place. I love a good meal and a rustic setting like the Ranch's. And I love their farm-to-table concept."

He squeezed her hand, and butterflies erupted in her stomach. The past month, dating Clint had been heaven, but she'd been in similar spots before when her heart and emotions raced faster to the next level than the guy's had … floating on air one day and having nothing but memories the next because the man met someone else. Hopefully, the love she felt for Clint would be reciprocated and she just needed to learn patience.

They arrived at the sprawling building that looked more like a supersized ranch house than a restaurant. Lots of trucks and SUVs along with some expensive rides filled the parking lot. Word was getting around about the Ranch's cuisine and how most of their food was harvested at a farm just outside of town. She'd spent time that afternoon on their website, studying their menu. She only had to decide which entrée to order: the braised pork with roasted vegetables or the pan-seared sea bass.

After Clint gave the hostess his name, another young woman wearing a crisp white shirt and black pants led them into the main dining room. Comfortable booths lined the walls, and tables and chairs filled the middle of the dimly lit room. They stopped in front of a booth at the end of a row and Lacy slid onto the bench that circled around the table, expecting Clint to take a seat across from her. Instead, he nudged her, said, "Slide over," and slipped in beside her. He smiled. "Much cozier than staring at each other across the table, don't you think?"

Who was this romantic man, and what had he done with Clint? With the flickering candle in the middle of the table and the subdued overhead lighting, everything seemed to send a romantic vibe. Maybe this would be the night he'd say those elusive words.

"It is much nicer," she agreed.

He picked up a menu and flicked on the tiny flashlight sitting on the table. "I don't think I've ever eaten at a place where I needed a flashlight to see the offerings."

Lacy laughed. "Full disclosure—I spent time on their website this afternoon and practically have the menu memorized."

"Should have known. So, what does the future chef recommend for our dining pleasure?"

"I'm going to have the seared sea bass. It was a hard choice between that or the braised pork. I'm sure your choices will be between porterhouse and filet."

He slid his arm around her waist. "Why don't I order the braised pork so you can taste both dishes?"

She stared at him. "That's a great idea. I love it. But why no steak?"

"I can eat steak most anytime."

She loved him even more for his wanting her to enjoy herself to the utmost. "It's not even my birthday, but I feel as though it could be with this five-star restaurant, wonderful atmosphere, and handsome guy treating me so well."

He nudged her closer to his side. "It's not your birthday? I thought it was. Now what am I going to do when it is your birthday?"

She elbowed him in the ribs.

"Hey, watch it. That's where I had my injury last year."

She pulled her arm away. "I'm sorry. I didn't realize you were still sore there."

"I'm not. Just ribbing ya, that's all." He laughed. "It's a joke. Get it?"

She snorted. "Very funny, Palmer."

The server returned and took their orders. After she brought their sweet teas and left again, Clint took Lacy's hand and squeezed it. "All kidding aside, I think we're in a really good place right now." He leaned in and kissed her temple.

She faced him and held his gaze. "Much better than being in the friend zone." She plucked a roll out of the basket on the table and ripped it in half.

He took the bread from her and put it on the saucer in front of her, then placed his bent index finger under her chin and gently pulled her head toward him until she faced him. His lips, soft and gentle, brushed against hers, and tingles ran down her neck.

He kissed the tip of her nose, then grabbed a roll. "I'd better eat something before I throw caution to the wind and have the PDA police telling us to take it outside."

She picked up one of the halves of her bread and buttered it. "I agree, totally. Maybe you should sit across from me."

He leaned back and stared at her. "Never. I can behave." He pushed a piece of roll into his mouth.

She laughed and shook her head.

By the time the entrées arrived, they'd both finished their rolls and were working on one they'd split between them.

After the server left, Lacy stared at the perfectly seared sea bass on its bed of roasted carrots and potato puree and then peeked over at Clint's dish. The pork was browned just right, and the roasted root veggies looked yummy.

"Do you want me to say a blessing?"

She started. "Are you comfortable doing that? I've never heard you pray before a meal before."

"First time for everything." He took her hand and prayed a few sentences, but she couldn't have repeated what he'd said. Having him in this new role and holding her hand while he blessed the food, she was on distraction overload.

As they finished their meals, the server asked whether they wanted dessert. Clint looked at his watch and then ordered molten lava cake for two, asking if it could it be brought right away. The server left, and Lacy stared at him. "How did you know that lava cake was what I would have ordered?"

He winced. "Oops. My bad. I know you love chocolate and—"

"No worries. But what's the rush?"

"I'm sorry, babe. Just wasn't thinking,"

He'd never called her *babe* before. This had to be the night he'd say those words.

Their server brought the lava cake along with two forks and placed the dessert between them.

Clint dipped his fork into the dessert and dragged a portion of the cake toward him. Luscious liquid chocolate flowed out onto the plate. He trailed the cake through the sauce and held the utensil near Lacy's mouth. "You first."

She closed her mouth over the fork and gazed into his eyes. Could they capture the moment forever? She let the taste of rich chocolate linger in her mouth for a moment before swallowing. "Oh, that is good. Your turn." She scooped up some cake and sauce and held it up. He took it the same way she had, letting his mouth close over the fork and holding the pose a moment. He swallowed. "That's really good. Do you think you could make this at home?"

"Of course."

They finished off the cake, sharing a kiss the same way they'd eaten the pie on their first official date. Had it already been over a month ago?

Clint pulled his billfold from his pocket and slipped some cash inside the leatherette folder the server had left. "I don't need change. Shall we go?"

Her heart sank. Maybe by next week he'd get the nerve to tell her.

On the way to the ranch, Clint took a turnoff onto the lane that led to the river site where they'd enjoyed so many family gatherings in the past.

"Where are we going?"

"I need to check on something. Should have done it earlier."

"Now, in your dress clothes?"

"We won't get messed up."

"What do you mean *we?*"

"I need your opinion."

The man was a mystery. If he thought she'd be willing to walk along that muddy riverbank in her new shoes, he had another think coming.

They arrived at the river, and he parked. "Wait here a minute. I won't be long." He climbed out of the truck and sauntered off into the inky darkness.

Relieved that he'd obviously changed his mind about needing her opinion, she leaned her head against the headrest and closed her eyes. If the man didn't declare his feelings for her soon, she'd have to one-up him and say those three little words first.

She opened her eyes. He'd been gone longer than the time he'd said it would take. She reached for the door handle.

Suddenly, white lights went on all around her. Little Italian lights and larger ones shaped like little balls hung from the trees, while tiny ones created a pathway to the water.

Unable to suppress a grin, she climbed out, not giving her new shoes a single thought. She spun around, taking in the lights overhead and the ones wrapped around several tree trunks. It had to have taken hours to set all this up. Was she in a Hallmark movie? No man would do this for his girl unless he really loved her.

"Clint? Where are you?"

"Over here." He came up the path carrying a single white rose in his hand. "I thought ending the evening like this would be much better than hanging around that restaurant." He handed her the rose, then offered his elbow.

She tilted her head. "What are you up to, Mr. Palmer?"

"Come with me, and you'll find out."

As they strolled between the lights, her heart felt as though it would explode. She tried to speak, but her words became tangled somewhere in her throat. Was this what she thought it was?

They came to the water's edge, and Clint hunched down and lit a couple of lanterns. He stood and kissed her, then knelt on one knee. "Lacy Roberts, I love you with all my heart." He held out a ring. "Will you marry me?"

She moved her mouth, but nothing came out. "I … I …"

"Honey, if you don't say yes soon, my leg is going to give out."

"Yes. Of course I'll marry you."

He stood and slipped the ring onto her finger, then kissed her again. "I've loved you for a long time, Lacy."

"I love you too. You can't see it, but I'm crying."

Their lips found each other. Finally, her man had declared his love, and he was going to be her husband. She wrapped her arms around his waist and pulled him closer as he deepened the kiss. Goose bumps trailed down her neck and spine, and butterflies erupted in her stomach.

The kiss broke, and Clint leaned back. "It's time to announce our engagement, don't you think?"

"You mean to call people?"

"No need for that." He took a deep breath and shouted, "She said yes!"

Horns honked and firecrackers sounded all around them. One by one, a circle of car lights bathed them in light. A car door slammed and Sydney ran up and hugged her, followed by Jace and Aunt Carolyn, and then Tim and Nancy emerged from the other side.

A tall man stepped out of the shadows and Lacy gasped. "Dad?"

He wrapped her in a hug. "Wouldn't want to miss this exciting event. Your mother is here too. We've missed too many times with you, and I want to correct that."

Mom came around Dad and took Lacy into her arms. "Sweetie, we're both so happy for you and Clint."

She laughed. "So everyone was in on this except me."

Clint chuckled. "It takes an entire family to get engaged. I asked for ideas on how to do it, and Syd suggested this. When I called your parents to ask for your hand and told them how I was going to propose, they insisted on flying out to be a part of it."

She looked at her father. "You said it's okay?"

"Of course I did. Your mother gave me the dickens on our way home the last time we were here. She said she had a feeling you two were sweet on each other and I'd better prepare myself. Clint and I had a long talk the night he called, and I can't be more pleased to see him marry you."

"That goes for me too, honey." Her mom pulled her into another hug and then held up Lacy's hand in the dim light. "I want a good look at that sparkler."

"You'll get a look at it when we all go back to the house for a celebration," Clint said. "We have cake and ice cream."

"Good thing you thought of that, Palmer." Jace laughed. "You know how we McGowans usually celebrate events like this."

"No!" Lacy stepped back from the water's edge. "I'm not going in there with my new outfit on."

Jace pulled her into a side hug. "No worries. We'll dunk you later when you're more appropriately dressed."

Tim stepped over. "Before we move on to dessert, I want to give both of you a congratulatory hug." He wrapped one arm around Clint's shoulders and his other arm around Lacy and pulled them both close. "You did good, son. Lacy, I can't wait for you to be my daughter-in-law."

The lump in Lacy's throat grew until she was afraid she'd not be able to talk. She whispered her thanks.

"Okay, everyone, let's go! Lacy and I will lead the way." Clint took her by the hand and led her up the path to the truck.

Soon, a line of cars trailed up the lane behind them toward the house.

Lacy rested her hand on Clint's knee. "How in the world did you pull this off? It must have taken hours to string the lights."

"Jace, Dad, and Nancy came over today and helped while you were shopping in town with Syd. It was tight, but we finished about ten minutes before you returned."

"I can't believe you ordered the lava cake when you knew we'd be having cake and ice cream later.”

“I didn’t want you suspecting anything, and you know I always order dessert.” He pulled the truck to a stop in front of the house.

She laughed. “I’d have thought you were sick if you declined. Smart move. Please say those words one more time.”

“Will you marry me?”

“No, silly. You know the ones.”

“Oh, *those* words.” He grinned. “Lacy Roberts, I love you, and I will until my dying day. I can’t wait to be your husband and love you each and every day that God gives us.” He kissed her, and she kissed him right back. She loved him too, and that was the truth.

Epilogue

The Following April

Clint stood in front of his bedroom mirror and adjusted his tie, then took the dark brown vest Jace held out and slipped it on. His heart pounded against his chest. "Thanks for being here. I'd have about gone crazy getting ready by myself."

Jace laughed. "Good thing you scheduled this before rodeo season got into full swing."

"Of course I scheduled it this way. I need to be joining you in taking our bulls to rodeos, remember?"

"Would you have guessed a couple of years ago that we'd both be married and business partners—and me with a kid on the way?"

Clint fiddled with his tie. "It's been quite a year with me finding my dad—and my mom going to rehab. I don't know if I'm more nervous about getting married or wondering whether Mom will show up today like she promised. Having a sober mother for the first time in my life would be the best wedding present, birthday present, and Christmas gift combined. Did I tell you Mom was okay with me changing my last name to Steele and using Palmer as my middle name?"

"Oh, about a half dozen times. *Clint Steele* has a nice ring to it. I'm praying your mom will show."

"It's a good thing we're having a small wedding. A large crowd would have freaked her out." Clint checked his watch.

Jace gave him a friendly punch on the arm. "It's only been five minutes since the last time you looked at it. We have fifteen minutes before showtime."

"You have the rings, right?"

Jace patted his vest pocket. "Both of them right here."

They stepped into the apartment's living room, and Jace looked around. "I don't know why you two don't just live here."

"And share it with a bunch of cowboys whenever we hire on extra help? Like

I told you, we want a place of our own away from the action. We're only a few minutes down the road."

Jace chuckled. "Yeah, not very romantic. I get it. And if the owner ever decides to sell that little piece of land, it will be perfect for the two of you."

"That's our dream." He started to look at his watch but held back. "I still can't believe Lacy wants to marry me."

"She loves you like crazy and has for a long time. Did you ever think that we'd be cousins-in-law?"

Clint grinned. "Finally, a member of the family for real."

"As if you weren't before." Jace picked up a black Stetson from where it rested on the couch and set it on Clint's head. "Come on. It's time to go. Remember, we're to head around from the back and wait behind the barn until we get the high sign."

Lacy grinned at her image in the floor-length mirror, loving the simple, cream, A-line lace dress. She lifted the skirt and grinned at her new boots. She'd made sure the dress's hem lifted when she walked, to display them. She glanced over her shoulder at her matron of honor. Syd looked adorable in her dress—its color was labeled "seafoam"—that flared out slightly below the bustline. The hint of a baby bump caused by the little girl she was carrying made Lacy smile even more.

Sydney gathered Lacy into an embrace. "I'm so stinkin' happy for you—and even happier that you'll be living just down the road and not far away."

Lacy laughed. "Yeah, a built-in babysitter for little Annie when she appears."

"Hey, I bet it won't be long before I'll be able to return the favor."

Lacy rolled her eyes. "I hope we can get used to married life before that happens." She glanced at where her clock radio sat until that morning when it was moved to her new home. She and Clint had taken possession of the rental a month ago and worked on the small ranch house almost daily, painting and decorating. But neither would sleep there for the first time until tonight. They were postponing the honeymoon until later. Clint had promised to surprise her with a special vacation, and all she knew was that it would be somewhere warm and beachy.

"Okay, soon-to-be-Mrs.-Steele, it's time," Syd announced.

They walked to the front door of the ranch house and met up with Aunt Carolyn. She looked smashing in the wig she'd been wearing the last six months. Instead of choosing one that looked similar to her own hair color, she'd chosen an auburn bob, saying she'd always wanted to be a redhead and now was her chance. Her chemo had ended a couple of months ago, but she was waiting until her hair had grown in enough to style it before she stopped wearing the wig.

The threesome walked together to where the ceremony would take place—in front of the same barn where Jace and Syd had been married. Today, the weather was in the seventies and sunny, but if it had rained, they'd have moved the ceremony inside the barn.

When they reached the copse of trees a short distance from the ceremony space, they stopped, and Jace walked up and grinned. "Clint is going to flip out when he sees you, cuz." He kissed his wife, then held out his elbow to his mom. They waited while he escorted her down the aisle between the white folding chairs.

Dad approached, looking a bit out of place in the Western-style attire the men were wearing. A year ago he would have balked at the long-sleeved white shirt and suspenders with no jacket, but yesterday when he tried on the clothing, he joked that it was about time he looked like he belonged on the ranch when he visited. His eyes twinkled. "Where is the little girl I used to push in her stroller down the sidewalk to show her off? You are a beautiful bride, Lacy."

Her eyes misted over. Ever since she and Clint became engaged, she'd had multiple conversations with her dad. He'd tried to convince them to marry in their church in San Diego, but they'd wanted it simple and on the ranch. He finally warmed to the idea, not once rescinding the offer to pay for the wedding as he would have in the past.

A moment later, Betty Jones, the church's wedding coordinator, came up to Lacy. "The groom is about to take his place. You need to stay right here so no one sees you when Sydney starts down the aisle."

The string quartet playing in the background switched to a new melody, which was their cue. Syd glanced at Lacy. "You ready?"

Lacy bobbed her head several times. "Absolutely."

Sydney walked across the grass and down the aisle. Lacy leaned over to peek, but before she could catch sight of Clint, the wedding coordinator blocked her view and then stepped aside. "Okay, Lacy, it's time."

Dad guided her to the spot that had been marked out on the grass with tape, and the quartet switched to Pachelbel's *Canon*. Lacy had always wanted it at her wedding. She'd second-guessed her decision not to go with a more country-like band, but she so wanted the Pachelbel piece, and to have it sound like she imagined, the quartet was the way to go rather than the band.

Everyone stood and turned toward Lacy. At the end of the aisle, Clint beamed at her. Their gazes locked, and she and Dad began their short walk.

Tim and Nancy Steele smiled from the front row. Behind Tim, an attractive woman Lacy didn't recognize caught her eye, and then she nearly gasped. Clint's mom had made it. In modest makeup, with her highlighted hair styled in a fashionable spiky cut, she appeared much younger than Lacy remembered—she'd met her the first time Clint was allowed to visit Diane in rehab.

Lacy's eyes misted over, and she offered her new mother-in-law a smile before focusing again on her groom. All handsome in his brown vest, black jeans, and black Stetson, Clint grinned and blinked at the moisture in his eyes. She and Dad arrived next to him, and he whispered, "You are beautiful."

"You're not so bad yourself."

Her father placed her hand in Clint's, then kissed her on the cheek and stepped back. Clint squeezed her hand, and together they took a step toward the pastor. God had made it all come together in His time, and she was one happy bride.